PEACE TRAIN

A Love Story

Renée Mollan-Masters

© Reality Productions 2017

Copyright © 2017 by Renée Mollan-Masters

PEACE TRAIN

All rights reserved. No part of this publication may be reproduced, distributed, or transmitted in any form or by any means, including photocopying, recording, or other electronic or mechanical methods, without the prior written permission of the publisher, except in the case of brief quotations embodied in critical reviews and certain other noncommercial uses permitted by copyright law. For permission requests, write to the publisher, addressed "Attention: Permissions Coordinator," at info@beyondpublishing.net

Quantity sales special discounts are available on quantity purchases by corporations, associations, and others. For details, contact the publisher at the address above.

Orders by U.S. trade bookstores and wholesalers.
Email info@BeyondPublishing.net

The Beyond Publishing Speakers Bureau can bring authors to your live event. For more information or to book an event contact the Beyond Publishing Speakers Bureau speak@BeyondPublishing.net

The Author can be reached directly @ BeyondPublishing.net/Author RenéeMollan-Masters

Manufactured and printed in the United States of America distributed globally by BeyondPublishing.net

New York | Los Angeles | London | Sydney

Library of Congress Control Number: 2018933441

10 9 8 7 6 5 4 3 2 1   978-1-947256-20-0

Out beyond ideas of wrongdoing and rightdoing there is a field. I'll meet you there.

~Rumi

Prologue

The setting sun cast shadows across the cobbled streets of Jerusalem. Sara Salinger cuddled her baby close to her chest; the smell of her sister-in-law Amani's home-cooked meal still clung to little Farah's black curly hair. Nothing in the world could measure the love she felt for her baby girl and how she had opened so many hearts, most especially hers and Shacker's.

"You smell so good I could eat you," she cooed to her daughter as she made her way through the crowds. Delicious odors of eateries crafted by experienced hands wafted from street cafés and the city block bustled with shoppers and merchants. The sounds of commerce were familiar to Sara. Jerusalem was her home.

"Ooh, Farah, do you smell that, sweetheart? Fresh rolls. Let's hurry to get some challah to surprise your daddy before he comes home." Farah squirmed slightly as she gurgled in response.

A welcoming jingle greeted Sara as she opened the door of her favorite café. She smiled at the sight of tables displaying brightly-colored tablecloths and fresh flowers in appreciation of their regulars, but also intriguing to new passersby. The rich smell of black coffee filled her senses and the smell of freshly baked chocolate babka and sufganiyots, along with other treats, made Sara's stomach hungry again.

"What will it be for you and the pretty baby?" The man behind the counter smiled warmly, his hair as dark and curly as Farah's.

Sara pointed to the fresh challah.

"Of course," he smiled.

Pleased, Sara moved Farah to her left hip, then reached into her purse with her right hand for a few shekels.

Without warning, an explosion of mass energy overpowered Sara's right side like a Mac truck supplied with hot white, liquid shock, while the front windows of the shop shattered into a million sparkling diamonds, razor sharp enough to tear one's heart into just as many pieces. The sound split her ears open to a place in the universe where sound no longer registered, while the floor ripped from underneath her like the merciless riptides of the beaches of her childhood. Her hands flung out from her sides, thrusting open her fingers like a rag doll, no longer commanding her own body. Shekels floated and twisted in the air before her eyes, sparkling oddly outside of time as she floated down, down, down. Another blow to her left temple and cheekbone followed; a violent riptide, a force had pulled her to the cement floor in response to the hot, white, liquid shock wave. Without stopping for her to catch up and register what just happened, time and thought disappeared into black infinity. All went dark.

~~~

Acrid odors of hot smoke, chemicals, burned dust and dreams filled Sara's nostrils bringing her back to semi-consciousness. What was once a bakery was now a blown-out building of shattered glass and wooden fragments. Searing pain in Sara's forehead mingled its way rudely into the crude, putrid smells. Sirens teased her pounding head as earthquakes tease lava, jostling it from calm to chaos and confusion. Panic erupted from her shattering maternal heart, *Farah!* Sara fumbled around the floor, feebly attempting to plant her feet on some steady ground. As she put down a hand to steady herself, she saw the pool of blood she'd been laying in; blackness took over once again as she succumbed helplessly to the lower abyss.

~~~

PART ONE

Chapter 1

10 Years Earlier…

Sara swayed back and forth with the motion of the old school bus as it squeaked and rumbled down the rough-grated road, drowning out all other sounds that echoed among the vast forest spaces of the brisk summer day. The heavy rain from that morning had ended its ceremonious cleansing dance, opening the sky for a new day of Pacific Northwest colors. Glimmering shades of forest green, sky blue, and a hopeful gold rippled majestically by them through the anxious fingerprints on their windows. It was as if the elements of the forest were bowing happily at their arrival. "Welcome," the forest seemed to whisper as the bus of teens who held their bags filled with generations of burdens floated under the dancing tree branches above.

Sara glanced around at the other teens, sixteen in all, each occupying their own seat, not daring anything else, including a whisper, at least yet. Eight boys and eight girls, all from the other side of the world—Palestine and Israel— sensing their strangeness to one another along with the familiar masking of their common hopes, dreams and fears.

The bus and the trees listened to the voices of inner turmoil inside the minds of the youthful passengers like whispers, always present on the first fateful ride through the parted trees on the road to camp. The arguments and pressures from the voices of their homelands and their peoples ever present in their heads, none more than those of their parents, closest relatives and friends.

Be careful. Dana's grandmother had cautioned softly with a weight of seriousness included. *Your parents' death is in the past. Don't let the stories you hear awaken something that is best left there.* Her warning sang out like a trance-like song from synagogue as Dana was packing a photo of her grandparents into her suitcase before zipping it closed. The words teased her, stirring questions long left in slumber before now. *Awaken what?* She had thought at that moment. Dana was leaning against her window on the bus, sitting in the second seat on the right-hand side as she remembered her grandmother's words. Her parents were killed when she was a baby. She hardly knew them. Even with her curiosity about who they were, and how she was like them, and even though family was everything next to God in her religion, it was still as if the violence had happened to someone else. How could she be afraid to look at the death of people she had never known? She liked the idea of the camp, but mostly she wanted a chance to come to the U.S. She was fascinated by how a country so large could function without a common religion when her own country was so divided by having more than one. As she pondered all this, her dark blond ponytail bounced along with the movements of the bus.

Dana was sitting in the fourth seat behind Sara in a blue shirt, a mirrored reflection of the sky, as though bringing tangible pieces of the light blue into the dusty surroundings of the rickety old bus. Her thoughts wandered lucidly back to the week she had brought the flyer about the camp home from school. *Go.* Her grandmother pleaded. *See things you won't see here,* as though this camp was Dana's only hope to know something other than the anger and hatred in which she had grown up. *Then tell us everything.* Dana was curious about her grandparents' obsession for peace in an interested way, though they didn't always see the solution the same as she did. Dana always felt anything was possible, but that was harder for her grandparents who dwelled in the stories of her family's past. They had seen their parents anger and pain as a bitter acid that had carved out the very crevices of their faces and solidified into stone when they landed in Jerusalem where they had been promised a better life after the death camps. But, instead, they lived out the rest of their lives in a constant haunting reminder of what should have been left behind. All the elements of the death camps lurked in the shadows of the streets, as a stealth predator occasionally announcing its dark presence via abusive words, bullets ricocheting, or bombs carelessly killing anonymous, innocent children. One of them was Dana's best friend when she was seven, and her own parent's when she was a baby. Why did Dana feel so hopeful? She wondered. Was her fate going to be all that different? Was this camp a part of it?

As her thoughts meandered in synch with the bus, Tarif, a Palestinian boy from Jerusalem, slouching in the furthest seat to the back on the left, brooded under the weight of his confusion. He was usually masked in a costume of anger he'd borrowed from his father from time to time. The trees and beings of the forest had become quite familiar with his kind of burdens during these first few days, as well as how they changed over the weeks until the campers left. They carried with them new ideas and anxieties on how they were going to incorporate what they learned back home into their ordinary lives.

In their patient compassion, the grandmother tree branches whispered a hushed lullaby of comfort, lulling Tarif's grieved heart as his mind drifted into the memory of his mother telling him the story that convinced him to come, a decision that was a great disappointment to his father, whom he'd idolized. She told him that she could not hate the Jews as his father did and would never raise a hand or share a word to harm them. His mother went on to explain that when she was little, she had the terrifying experience of being surrounded by a gang of Jewish boys when she took a wrong turn from market one day, leading her down an alley in a Palestinian ghetto. The boys had worked themselves up through the courage of their numbers to abuse and attack her. The hatred in their eyes was unlike anything she had ever seen, a total separation from love or God so far removed from their natural childlike innocence, and it terrified her in a way that she could never forget. There was something so dark behind their eyes, beyond the individual hearts driving them, that not even those boys could stop themselves from the forces that drove them, even if they had wanted to. She knew their eyes revealed the hatred of centuries of persecution and abuse. She believed that very day she would be the sacrificial lamb they would slaughter to avenge generations of pain, and the day of her final breath. She spoke to Tarif about what flashed through her mind back then: her parents and how her life would be taken from everyone she loved over one simple mistake, a wrong turn, and how Tarif might never have been born.

She went on to tell that just as the beating began, and she had given up any hope that her prayers could be answered, an old man discovered the gang of children and her quivering body hunched over sideways in a fetal position on the wet street. He waved his cane with great authority and hollered with the fierceness of Allah himself, she claimed. When she looked up into his eyes expecting a merciful angel, she saw in them a fierce sparkle of loving light, not darkness, as she recognized that he was merely a kind, gentle Jewish elder who, at his age, had risked his life to stand up to the gang and save hers.

Was it her shaking with tears strolling down her face as she told the story, or was it the story itself that convinced Tarif to say yes to her and come to this camp? He couldn't say. He was unsettled. Sitting on this stupid, plastic covered seat in a smelly American bus, all he could think about was how could he face his father when he got home?

Don't touch them! Don't ever let them touch you! His father had belted furiously at him when he tried to play with a Jewish girl across the street at age three. His father's convictions were sharpened by all of the fear of God in his eyes and a finger pointing right at the center of Tarif's heart, where now a scar neatly covers his most tender parts so exquisitely that Tarif had forgotten he'd had any, much like his father. A solution came to him as he drifted off into sleep. He may have promised his mom he would come, but he could honor his father by not making any friends.

Others on the bus were also lost deep in the recesses of their memories. The friends who had teased them for wanting to come to camp with the *other*. The grandparents who spit and shamed their parents for allowing their child to go. The brother who pretended to only care about the possibility of pretty girls at camp, but actually worried about what this would mean to his friends, and how it could upset the family if his sibling went.

Wind from one of the open bus windows whipped Sara's jet black, shoulder length hair around her face. She pushed it out of her eyes and adjusted her backpack once again to counterbalance the sways of the bus. All the kids had bags of some kind on their laps, filled with supplies for the future and a few meager connections to what they'd left behind, at least for the next few weeks.

Sara sat thoughtfully in her seat in the middle of the left side row behind a good-looking boy she promised herself she would find as much as possible about without seeming obvious. After glancing around the bus, sizing up her fellow campers, she secretly smiled to herself and wondered, *what was this camp that promised their parents something better? Maybe a place of uncommon stories or adventure*, she daydreamed. Her own mother was supportive of her interests to come to America, the country where her parents had been born. Sara was five when they left and hadn't been back to see her grandmother since. She was eager to get to know this land and her people they had left behind here. Camp intrigued her but she wasn't without her doubts.

Stay open. Her mom had said as if reading her mind while Sara read the flyer her mom had handed her from the school where her mother had taught. Sara was skeptical at first as she thought of her father's failed attempts to bring about peace, as well as her own. Sara had once tried to create a day of play between kids from Palestine and Israel, but the administrators in charge of the center kept bringing up concerns until summer finally passed into autumn and everyone had lost interest. Her mom had been a major source of support then, and Sara's heart had broken for her mom in memory of her father as much as it did for the dream once again smothered by old stories and fear that never seemed to end.

If only everyone could see the possibility.

But they didn't, and already she decided she didn't have what it took to be a leader of peace or take over her father's dream. She was determined to get on with being an ordinary girl instead and indulge more in her interest in boys like her friends, much to their delight. This summer was going to be completely different she had decided, until the flyer had come.

As the bus glided and rocked, Sara glanced at their driver for a few moments as he steered the bus nonchalantly through curves. He seemed bored, or at least uninterested, much like some of the elders she had known at the center. She wondered how many times he'd done this before. He seemed completely unaware of the cargo of hope and possibility he carried, as if Palestine and Israel coming to peace was an obvious and natural every day experience. His straw-colored hair lay plastered to his scalp underneath the plastic mesh of his cap, and his neon orange t-shirt had seen better days. Yet he didn't seem to notice, which was beyond Sara, at sixteen, who couldn't imagine leaving the house without at least three mirror checks just in case a cute boy might be within a thousand feet of her or her friends. As she assessed the driver, her thoughts lightened humorously. She prayed she'd never be so bored with her life that she would enter a day not caring what she wore or how her hair looked.

Another bump landed her uncomfortably once again on her green, fake leather seat, which seemed to be rapidly changing from a soft, thin cushion to a hard slate of rock beneath her. *How far out in the forest are were now? How much farther?* She wondered, feeling herself getting impatient. To avoid thinking about the growing ache in her tailbone, her mind wandered again to her friends she'd left behind at home. Would she have any stories to tell them that would help them to understand and be supportive?

This again? One had said. *Why not just drop it and be with us this summer?* And then there was her best friend Anya, *but you'll be gone so long,* she said. Anya had been her best friend since they had come to Jerusalem, but she had never understood Sara's family wanting to bring the Palestinians and Jews together. *It's ridiculous,* she would complain, wanting Sara to be more like her. *I probably won't get chosen anyway,* Sara had said to soothe her, really believing it.

But Dr. Meg, the camp counselor in America was fascinated by Sara's attempt to create a day of play, even more so that it fell through in the end, much to Sara's surprise.

Sara wasn't completely without understanding of her friends. Secretly she hoped for more than just what the camp brochure talked about. She had ideas beyond all that the camp offered, including daydreams about the possibility of romances or long kisses. She only dared to hope to at least have that. She laughed to herself at her fantasies of how one romantic kiss could lead to world peace, and then she cringed at what her father might say at her silliness.

Before her thoughts could once again melt deliciously into more daydreams, the dusty yellow bus lurched to a halt. Sara quickly looked out the window at a sea of redwoods mixed with the trail of dust behind them, briefly catching the eye of another girl on the bus doing the same.

The driver motioned them with a wave of his right hand in a way that said this was it, time to get off. Relieved to finally stand up, the campers grabbed their various items quickly and silently made their way out of the bus one by one, greeted by the smell of evergreen firs and redwoods mixed with the odor of burnt oil from the hot bus engine.

"Welcome to Peace Camp. Or should I say Shalom Lekha and Salam?" A tall woman wearing a green camp shirt and tan Columbia shorts confidently spoke as she stood in on a spot between them and a trail that Sara hoped would lead to some semblance of civilization.

"I'm Dr. Meg," she smiled, taking each face in and sizing up her task for the next few weeks ahead.

Sara thought she looked to be in her forties, though she seemed to have more energy than any of the disoriented teens standing dazed at her disposal, many of whom awkwardly shifted from one foot to the other shifting their packs. Dr. Meg seemed to know their anxieties as she gave them time to take in their surroundings, then she spoke.

"Thousands of kids have come to this very spot with a lot of questions and not knowing a single soul when they got here," she started thoughtfully. "These guardian pines know their stories well." She looked up at two towering trees that seemed like they'd been there since the forest began. "Trust me," she smiled kindly, "You are not alone." Sara wondered what she meant by that, but didn't have much more time to consider it.

"Let's head toward your new homes for the next three weeks, shall we?" Dr. Meg chirped enthusiastically in a way that might have been annoying on an ordinary day, but soothed a concerned and tender Sara after her long, silent trip alone in her thoughts. She was used to having Anya or her mom to talk to. But Anya had abandoned her before she left to follow her family's beliefs of hatred and separation, claiming Sara was crazy and unstable. She sucked in her breath as she let in the thought that she would be facing the weeks ahead alone without any support from her former best friend.

The sixteen campers slung their packs on their backs and stumbled awkwardly forward in silence as they gazed around at the towering "guardians" Dr. Meg had pointed to. Sara noted how they softened the light of the bright sky above them. Now in the crisper air of the lakeside forest Sara zipped up her favorite sweatshirt as she became aware of the foreign dogwoods and mountain ash, which reminded her how far she was from home. Her eyes were not accustomed to all of these shapes, smells and sights. She thought about her mother at home, no doubt sleeping now, and felt a pang in her chest. What did Dr. Meg mean the trees knew the camper's stories well? How well? What happens to their stories here?

She smiled to herself in a sudden change of thought, back to something much lighter. *Did any of these stories involve romance?* Before her thought had a chance to evolve into anything more interesting, her toe caught a tree root that was fingering its way into the well-worn path beneath her. It lurched her awkwardly forward, narrowly missing the unhappy boy hunched over in front of her, whom she remembered from the back of the bus. Turning a light shade of red at her near miss, and the irony of her stumbling at the mere question of romantic stories, she thought to herself, *focus, Sarah,* as she surveyed the silence of the group. *None of us are even talking to each other yet.* Her eyes caught more craggy roots firmly planted in the heavily-trodden path ahead, as thoughts wandered into her head, *Tread thoughtfully, more obstacles lay ahead.*

From the front of the pack, Dr. Meg's experienced voice interrupted Sara's thoughts as she slowed the group and turned toward them. "The boys' lodging is down this path." She pointed to an opening to the left of the tired group. "Just follow it straight that way and your counselor, Rob, will be in the Eagle Cabin waiting for you."

The first boy looked ahead, and then hesitantly at his crew behind him, perhaps at the thought of leading these weary boys without an American to keep them safe from long held traditions of abuse to the other. But hesitance seemed to surrender into something stronger and simpler, a kind of good humor at this unexpected role, as though he understood these moments were part of the bargain for getting so much time away from home, parent free. The eight boys, each with their own reasons for hesitation, silently filed toward the path ahead, perhaps with similar surrendered understanding. They slowly disappeared into the mysterious branches before them as the girls continued on behind

Dr. Meg in equal silence. The knotted path of critter holes and tree roots, slightly softened by burnt red pine needles, soon opened into a vista of deep blue water surrounded by even more trees in a full radius around them. The delicious odor of the needles and moist rich dirt seemed to renew Sara's body with each breath, a welcomed salve to her sinuses and lungs from the burning oil and chalky dust after the hour-long bus ride. Ahead, the sun danced on the water without hesitation, leaving glittering diamonds and prancing fairies that appeared to a sleepy Sara to offer promises of untold magic in the days to come.

Dr. Meg stopped in front of an old log cabin that suddenly came into view just around the left of the path without warning or fanfare. With similar confidence, but slightly distracted by her glance to the other buildings further down the shore, Dr. Meg announced, "All right, girls. This is your home for the next three weeks. We call it Bear Cabin. Your counselor, Tandy, is waiting inside."

Not wanting to leave the confident Dr. Meg just yet, the only person Sara had actually met so far on this strangely mixed journey, and the only real voice she had heard after the bus ride started, she at first reluctantly followed the other girls to the stairs of the cabin, wondering what was in store now. She quickly adjusted to the next pieces of her American adventure, beginning abruptly with the rushed greeting of musty air, causing several of the girls to cough as she stepped inside the door.

Tandy, a blond headed young woman, about 5' 5" foot five with freckles and a pony tail, laughed as she briskly pushed open cabin windows. "Sorry about that. I just got in here from the counselor cabin," she grunted as she athletically punched at one swollen window frame that had obviously absorbed moisture during the rain that morning. Grunting again, she finished her sentence, "These windows were closed over the weekend from the previous camp session. Trust me, it's better than letting the rain take over the place and dealing with mildewed mattresses." The window finally freed and she puffed her bangs back with her breath while she brushed her hands, as though she'd done this a hundred times. She spoke with the authority of experience and the humility of a good friend. Sara immediately relaxed. She felt this could be someone she might confide in, her number one criteria for a new friend.

Tandy continued in a friendly authority, "Go ahead and find a bunk anywhere and get settled. You'll want to have everything ready for bed. We still have a long day ahead and it'll be dark when we get back after fire council."

Sara looked around quickly, wishing she had someone to advise her, as they all looked about the same. A pretty girl with dark curly hair sat on the first lower bunk to the left. Her smooth dark features framed her golden-brown face, while the sparkling metal medallion on her bracelet gave her away. *Definitely a Palestinian*, Sara, an Israeli, concluded. She smiled to herself. *Perfect,* she thought to herself. She took the top bunk above the Palestinian and began arranging her sleeping bag for the night. Thinking about boys on the bus made these first few hours lighter and therefore bearable, but her true reason for being here was her father. Ever since he died, Sara felt different. By the time she was ten, her heart longed to be a part of the magic of peace, a dream he'd had that he would never get to see realized. Her thoughts flashed to her mom who raised her alone since she was five. She couldn't wait to write her about her new bunkmate.

As Sara looked around at the other girls, she noticed the knots in her stomach begin to loosen. She quietly sighed with relief. They all seemed to be just like any other girls. From her bunk, she stuck her head out the window, breathing in the scented air and taking in the gorgeous view of the lake. *Wow, it is beautiful here,* she realized, delighted. She had lived her whole life in the city. There was nothing like this at home in Israel.

After each girl had laid out her sleeping bag and the most important personal items, like a photo from home, or a trinket that had a special meaning only known to its owner, Tandy stood in the center of the room. "Okay, girls. This is the time when we introduce ourselves." She smiled infectiously with a twinkle. "We definitely want to get a head start with each other before we meet up with the boys." You can talk from your bunks but just be loud enough, so we can all hear you. To start off, I'll go first.

"I'm a student at the University of Washington. I also coach basketball for inner city kids during the school year. Ever since I was in third grade and had a crush on a Sudanese refugee, I've had a passion for peace and friendship among diverse groups of people. I think bringing kids together from different backgrounds is one of the most important things we can do for peace. She then looked over at Sara. "Let's start here and then go around."

Sara secretly winced inside. She glanced around at all of the girls. *What do I tell them? That I'm typical of my nationality, from my dark hair to the shape of my nose? That I'm tall like my dad was? And slim like my mother is?* She felt her chest tighten as she cleared her throat. "Shalom, I'm Sara. I was born here in the United States and my family moved to Israel when I was three." She noticed a couple of girls' eyes widen. She guessed this was their first time in America. "I live in Jerusalem with my mother. She's a teacher. My father died in a car accident when I was five, and, uh, I'm sixteen and I play some of the sports." Sara quickly evaluated what she shared about her dad. *Too much too soon*? But she quickly decided she wouldn't be the only one in the circle who had lost someone close.

The next girl to share was Sara's bunkmate. Sara was relieved that her turn was over, and at the same time eager to find out more about her new bunk companion. She said a little prayer that this girl was as nice as she looked.

"Salam. My name is Amani. As you can guess," referring to her greeting, different from the Israeli Shalom, "I'm Palestinian and I also live in Jerusalem with my mother and sometimes with my older brother, Shacker. He's also here at camp." A couple of girls gave her a sympathetic look and groan. Amani returned an appreciative smile that also said she was fine with it. "My father and mother divorced two years ago, so my brother sometimes lives with my dad."

Tandy added, "As you may have noticed, here in America we are preoccupied with what people do for a living." Sara laughed and nodded with the other girls. In Israel, people's first questions were about family and their day. Sometimes you might know someone for weeks without knowing their career. It seemed strange to have career be a more important question, but she made a point to remember to ask while here. "So, my curious American mind wants to know," Tandy followed, "What do your parents do Amani?"

"Oh!" She exclaimed realizing that's what Tandy was leading up to. "Well, my dad is a doctor at a Palestinian hospital," two Palestinian girls gasped knowing the horrors there, "and my mother is a nurse at a clinic." She responded obediently wondering why it was important to know.

One by one, Sara learned about the other girls she would share the cabin with for the next three weeks. There was Rebecca, a small girl with red hair from Haifa, whose father was a rabbi; athletic Dana, with beautiful long black hair, from Bethlehem whose parents were killed when she was a baby; Brenna from Tel Aviv with beautiful auburn hair and freckles who loves fashion design and looks it; Reehm from Ashdod whose father was very progressive and was immediately intrigued by the focus of the camp; timid Adeela from Hebron whose parents were both artists and are known as free thinkers among her friends, which made everybody laugh appreciatively; and Bahr from Hebron whose father was opposed to her coming but she and her mother won out.

As the last two girls finished, the camp bell rang out. Tandy walked toward the door. "Lunch! We're just in time!" She pointed to a pile of green shirts at the end of her bed. "These are the camp t-shirts. You'll want them for later, so you can just put them on your bunks for now. "

Trying to keep their eagerness in check, the girls politely pushed off their bunks and began sorting through the pile of shirts to find their size. Sara found one that looked right and threw it onto her bunk. She would look at it later.

The path to the dining hall was covered in tree shavings put there by staff earlier that summer. It felt soft underfoot. Sara felt a hundred pounds lighter after being introduced to her new bunkmates as she walked directly behind Tandy.

As the line of girls neared the dining hall, the guys came filing out of a path to the left. Sara smiled to herself. At the front of the line was the boy who already had caught her eye on the bus. Suddenly anxious not to trip again, she quickly glanced at the ground below her feet. *No tree roots there*, she smiled. Remembering the strange thoughts, she'd had earlier, *perhaps there would be no obstacles either.*

The dining hall was filled with unfamiliar smells of American camp food. Sara wondered if it was anything like the food in the American movies she had seen. She didn't remember much of her life before Jerusalem. Her eyes moved throughout the long wooden tables and benches that had fed hungry campers for decades. The echo of each step on the wooden floors bounced to the vaulted ceilings, magnifying everything. The dining hall was majestically surrounded by three walls of windows, providing a stunning panoramic view of the lake. Sara gasped to herself. She loved water from her childhood days at the beach with her father, and this was a spectacular example of it. Even though it was summer, a large fire was already blazing in the stone-covered hearth to stave off the cool air from the morning summer rain, keeping them warm in the large, hollow building.

Dr. Meg stood at the front of the room next to the fireplace with a young man Sara hadn't seen yet. "A warm American welcome to all of you." The youthful looking man with short black hair and long dark lashes called out in a chipper voice. "My name is Rob. For the half of you that haven't met me yet, I am the guys' cabin counselor, and I'm here to help all of you survive the wild out here with a lot of fun and activities that will make it easy for all of you to get to know each other. However, we also have a few things that some of us consider not as fun from time to time, and a few rules to follow."

Sara wondered how long Rob had been a counselor at this camp and if he had come here as a camper. What did he know about Palestinians and Israelis? Did it matter? As if to answer her, he began, "Before I get started, I came to this camp for the first time when I was 14. I'm Palestinian, but I grew up in America, and I have a half-brother whose mother is Jewish." Campers' eyebrows raised and there were a few hushed gasps as mouths opened. "As you can imagine it was a little confusing for all of us at times, even for my father who loved us both. We had family back in Palestine, and this made it very difficult for me and my brother. This camp was a miracle, because we felt the tension even this far away. We learned it was okay to love each other no matter what anyone else thought. Okay, so enough about me for now." Sara caught herself with her mouth gaping open. She couldn't believe his story. It was a rare story at home that happened every once in a while, but usually with grave consequences to the families. She had so many questions rolling around in her head.

"We'll continue to get to know each other over the next few weeks." Rob continued, "But for now, let's talk about the rules and what you can expect. This afternoon we'll have a swimming test to see who'll be able to swim in the lake. Cabin groups will also be assigned activities such as art, acting, nature walks, bird watching, softball, soccer and volleyball. Each morning we will sound the wake-up bell at 7:00 am."

A collective groan filled the air. Dr. Meg, who had been silently supportive next to Rob, grinned and nodded knowingly, as though this was the same reaction shared at every camp session from the beginning of time.

Rob laughed and rolled his eyes. "I know, I felt the same way when I was a camper, but you'll thank me when you're the first one to get to the showers, because we don't always have enough hot water for everyone. It's on a first-come first-serve basis." This seemed to impress the campers because several immediately sat up straighter as though their lives depended on listening better. "Flag raising is at 8:00. Lights out at 11 pm—no exceptions. In addition to your regular activities, we host fire circles around the campfire each night. This is not optional. What happens at these circles helps bring the entire experience of camp together. It's where a lot of cool things can happen. However, you should know that it's what you bring to the fire circle that creates the magic. We are often surprised by what unfolds there," he added as he looked at a smiling and nodding Tandy, then Dr. Meg, who nodded in agreement with both of them in return.

Rob seemed to soften his tone to get ready to say something more serious, when suddenly the campers could hear a shriek through the kitchen door where faint noises of clanging had been heard earlier.

"Get out of here you crazy mutt!" An older woman's voice called out. "Don't you know this is a kitchen?! My food is for people, not dogs!" The door at the back of the room leading to the kitchen flew open and a short haired blond woman burst out chasing after a small wirehaired dog waving a large metal spoon in the air. "Now, go on! Where's Kurt who's supposed to be feeding you?" Just then, the bus driver comes barging through the front door, animated.

"Sparky!" he shouted, his deep voice booming through the dining hall like an oversized bowling ball that had missed all the pins bouncing off the back wall. The little dog with curly hair stopped short as soon as he saw Kurt.

"There you are!" he shouted. Sparky wasn't ready to lose his freedom just yet, or the prospects of a tasty meal. He looked back at the cook with the spoon, then darted into the crowd of tables, benches and campers, weaving through their legs as they tried to help by attempting to grasp him, or at least to slow him down. Camper after camper bent down to try to catch him between their legs, but he was too little and too fast. He seemed to know exactly how to keep everyone moving. Finally, a few campers jumped up to help corral him as he darted out from underneath the last table toward the kitchen door. Sparky caught on and scurried back under the tables where he expertly stirred up more chaos. The scene of back and forth, and here and there, became so ridiculous that shouts and groans easily rolled into bursts of laughter and cheers. Just as campers were throwing up their hands and holding their sides from laughing so hard, Sparky ran toward Tandy and sat as if nothing just happened, with a look of *what's all the excitement about*. More laughter burst out just as two girls headed toward him to grab his collar; he changed his mind and darted back underneath the tables in the direction of the kitchen, starting the whole charade all over again. Finally, two boys and one of the girls corralled Sparky by the fireplace. Everyone cheered and rushed over to join them forming a tight circle to close any gaps between their legs. Everyone, that is, except the one boy Sara noticed, who sat several feet away from the crowd with a grimace on his face like he was repulsed. It was the same boy Sara saw sitting in the back of the bus that first day with a cloud over his head.

Just then Kurt made his way into the group, hovering over the dog as they took turns petting it, all the while laughing and shaking their heads. After a few minutes of standing there, the group parted to let Kurt snap on the leash as he gratefully announced, "Thanks. I couldn't have done it without you." As he walked out with Sparky gingerly trotting at his side, Sara thought she saw Dr. Meg wink at the cook and the cook return with a wink of her own as she headed toward the kitchen.

"That's Yolanda, our cook." Dr. Meg said loudly as she waved her hand in Yolanda's direction. "I highly suggest you be nice to her as the most important part of our camp experience is entirely in her hands," she joked as Yolanda waved her spoon in the air combining a mock threat and wave to everyone as she exited.

As she headed out the door, Rob smiled and said, "So now you've met Sparky, our latest addition to the family. We haven't decided who is training who yet, but anyone who isn't up in time for flag raising risks being awoken by intense and violent licking from Sparky. I don't know what's worse to tell you the truth, a sponge bath from Sparky, or the camp showers," he added as he and Tandy laughed aloud together. The laughter was infectious, and the campers continued with their excitement. They couldn't believe how they'd each ended up on the floor at one time or another as the dog darted in one direction and then abruptly changed, slipping out from underneath their grasps. One boy marveled at how fast Sparky could switch directions before they could anticipate his next move. And another couldn't believe how, even after he'd thought he'd caught him, Sparky managed to wiggle right out of his hands as if he had been covered in oil. The campers were all so busy either catching the dog, or laughing and retelling the story, that many had forgotten the rules at home, including not to touch others. Dr. Meg looked down at an invisible piece of dirt on the floor and brushed it with her feet, cheeks glowing while sporting an all-knowing smile.

While the campers began to find their seats again at the tables, Rob and Tandy helped Yolanda roll out the dinner carts with trays of food. Still laughing, the campers eyed their dinner of hamburger and French fries. Some had never had a hamburger before, though the lightened mood had an air of mischief and adventure, and they were excited to try new things. One kid asked what the red stuff was for and another stated, 'for your fries' and demonstrated.

Tandy added, "It's ketchup." While the two, who happened to be Palestinian and Israeli, helped each other with this new cuisine.

Soon the campers were laughing and joking about the dog again. "He was fast!" Albert, a smaller boy with glasses shouted.

"Faster than any of us!" Added Brenna.

"They should call him bullet train," Aharon, a tall, light-haired and well-built boy laughed.

"Too bad he can't play dodge ball," Rob joked.

"What's that?" Dana asked.

"Whatever the game, I want that dog on my team!" Shacker, the cute boy Sara had noticed earlier, declared as he broke into a winning smile. A familiar buzz of laughter, jokes and tales about dogs spread like a warm fire into the room. Something had shifted in a magical alchemical process over a simple dog. They entered the dining room quietly, their stories intact. At the end of the meal, they left the lodge like regular teenagers: noisy, cracking cheesy jokes and bantering as if they had been like this all day. One dog overshadowed their burdens and made the world a little more ordinary again. Dr. Meg, smiled. *it's only the beginning.*

Chapter 2

That evening at dinner, Dr. Meg finished the announcements which had been interrupted serendipitously by Sparky at lunch. One of them included KP, or kitchen patrol assignments for the different campers that week. Sara was assigned her first KP duty the following morning after breakfast, along with Amani, Rebecca, Aharon and, much to her delight, Shacker. What would be a disgusting job of scraping food into bins and washing endless utensils turned into one of the most enjoyable duties at camp.

"Gross," Amani said making a face while scraping someone's leftover scrambled eggs and pancakes covered in ketchup into a trash bin beside her. She and Sara, along with Shacker, Aharon, and Rebecca, wore aprons and long, yellow rubber gloves as they cleaned up after the morning meal. All the other campers were enjoying some morning free time reading, taking a morning hike, or throwing a Frisbee around on the grassy field. Amani brushed her long dark ponytail from her shoulder with her forearm.

"Just like home! Right?" Shacker joked playfully at Amani remembering all the times at home when he and Amani had fought over who was going to wash and who was going to dry dishes. She walked over and gave her brother a big wet rubber-gloved slap on the back.

"Even better!" she grinned enjoying her new tool to tease him with.

"Hey!" he protested.

Sara grinned as she scraped some hash browns into the trash. She wondered how things would be different if she'd had a brother to grow up with. She shrugged off the thought. She loved what she had with her mom. They may not have joked around like this when they were doing dishes together, but that's where they often had their best talks. There were five or six members on each KP team who stayed behind and cleared the dirty dishes, so they could put them into tubs. The tubs were then loaded onto a cart to be taken to the sprayer station where the dishes were rinsed before being loaded into a commercial-sized dishwasher. It was the sprayer part of dishwashing where all the fun was discovered—it was difficult to control and had a tendency to come into a life of its own the for the first few times while the campers learned how to and where to hold it properly. True to form, suddenly Amani and Sara heard a shriek come from the sink area.

"I can't turn it off! It's going everywhere!" Rebecca cried out. She volunteered to be the sprayer this morning. They looked up to see Rebecca's unforgettably shocked and horrified face as she wrestled with the nozzle that was spraying in all directions and creating a water park of soggy food, suds, soaked clothes and puddles. Shacker and Aharon had been collecting the last of the plates from the tables, putting them on a rolling cart to bring in to Sara and Amani who were, by now, at Rebecca's side getting soaked without making any progress. They came running in as soon as they heard the shriek, where all the fun was happening. Shacker jumped in with his usual style, Amani thought, all masculine bravado and no plan.

"Whatever you're doing, it isn't helping!" Amani yelled.

"Better than you!" He bragged humorously as he got a face full of water in surprise.

"Why don't we just turn it off?" Rebecca yelled.

"Brilliant." Aharon called out. "Where?" Since this was their first KP duty, nobody really knew the kitchen except Rebecca, who was totally consumed and blinded by the water covering her glasses. Sara's eye happened to catch a glimpse of the faucet valve to the right but was overcome with fits of laughter mixed with covering her face by the flashes of the chaotic comedy before her. It was just too much, and she couldn't get the words out to tell Aharon that she could see it, and Shacker and Rebecca were in the way, so no one could reach it without a feat of self-sacrifice and being completely drenched.

"Oh seriously!" Amani laughed as she bravely lunged for it after her eye had caught it in the chaos of Rebecca and Shacker's dance. She looked at Aharon, teasing his manhood, "You really know how to impress a girl Aharon! You couldn't even find the faucet!" she joked.

Aharon laughed. "Hey, I'm as good in the kitchen as Shacker."

Amani teased again, "Like I said." She knew darn well Shacker was cheerful when it was his turn to help in the kitchen with a meal, especially since having to step up at their dad's home with his long work hours.

They were all laughing hysterically while Rebecca kept trying to apologize for getting them all wet. By now, all five of them were dripping with water and overcome with laughter until their sides were cramping. After finally taking a few deep breaths, and surveying the disaster before them, Rebecca whined, "I'm so, so sorry," with a hint of guilt, and then started giggling again despite herself. "I don't think I should do spray duty next time." Rebecca pushed her wet hair out of her face. She definitely was the most soaked of the group. "I think I better go get dry."

Aharon was bent over laughing and shaking his head trying to get some words out as Shacker said, "Don't worry about it, Rebecca. Aharon needed a shower anyway—he was starting to stink!"

"Hey! You think that's me? It's you, man!" Aharon shot back pointing at Shacker, then slapping his hand on the counter as if to say stop, he couldn't stand one more joke.

Rebecca ran out the door sloshing before noticing the bathroom and the towel closet to the left of the cook's station. Shacker turned to Sara and Amani who were assessing their own damage. Amani's hair was half out of her pony tail, flattened like a wet matted scarf across her face.

Shacker took pity, "We're good here. Why don't you two go get cleaned up," he added kindly as he pointed to the bathroom around the corner. Amani gave him a grateful look. But to save face, he added, "Well, we couldn't let anyone catch you looking like that." Amani rolled her eyes and snapped the glove she had just taken off at him.

Sara's jeans were soaked through. "You sure?"

Shacker's eyes twinkled and a mischievous grin creased his lips. "Oh yeah, I'm sure."

Amani added, "Don't worry about him. It may seem like a generous sacrifice, but he always finds a way to avoid any suffering."

Sara thought his tone was a little suspicious, but she was eyeing the bathroom that Rebecca missed, eager to find something dry to work with before sloshing down the path to their cabin. Once there, Sara headed straight to the cupboard with the dry towels. She handed one to Amani who took out her ponytail and then started drying off her thick wavy hair. Sara wrung out her straight ponytail and started patting her clothes dry. "Rebecca was hilarious. Did you see her face?"

Amani laughed. "Yes! That was so much fun!"

"I haven't had fun like that in a long time," Sara laughed, patting down her jeans.

Their reminiscing over the sprayer debacle was cut short when they heard a loud *thunk* at the door.

"Shacker!" Amani's eyes narrowed. Sara had no idea what had just happened, but she felt a sense of dread and her eyes grew wider in sync with Amani's growing narrower. "I knew Shacker was up to something when he let us go. I think he just wedged something up against the door!" Amani set the towel down on a nearby sink and quickly made her way over to the door to check. Sure enough, she couldn't make it budge an inch. "Ugh! I should've known!"

Sara didn't like the idea of being trapped in a bathroom until the cook came back to start lunch. Her keen mind surveyed their escape options while her eyes quickly discovered a small ventilation window high above, and to the right of, the sinks. With her long legs, she could step onto the sink and reach up to the small window only to find it was stuck, just like their cabin windows were the day before. This time, however, it looked like the window was coated with layers upon layers of paint, a quick fix for years of winter damage.

"Painted shut," Sara sighed. Sara jumped down and sat beside Amani, who had already given up and was seated on the floor against the wall. "Well, someone is bound to find us sooner or later." Amani looked around the room eager to find something to do. On the counter, stacked next to the sink, she noticed a pile of paper towels. She jumped up off the floor to grab one and then squashed it skillfully until it was a loose ball. Sara gave her an inquisitive look.

"Paper towel football!" Amani responded, delighted. Sara rose in anticipation, eager to do something fun, and to get to know Amani a little better. Just like with the dishes, what could have been a drag turned into something delightful. The girls laughed as they kicked the homemade ball between them. Amani scored a goal between Sara's legs and mocked a triumphant celebratory winner's circle worthy of the World Cup. When she was done she asked, "Do you play football?" their word for soccer.

"Just for my school team."

Amani's face lit up. "Me too!"

Sara's mind flashed to her competitive approach to football. She wondered if Amani was anything like her. "How good are you?"

Amani grinned big. "We won all our matches last year."

"Wow, you are good. We're good, but not that good." Sara laughed.

As the girls continued to talk about sports, Amani reached into her pocket and took out a new stick of ChapStick. "Have you seen these? There's color, but to my mom it's ChapStick."

Sara admired the glossy pink on Amani's perfect lips. She really was pretty. "Can I try?"

"Sure." Amani tossed the ChapStick over to Sara.

"Wow!" She felt the satin gloss as she quickly wiped it across her lips. "This feels great. How do I look?" Sara puckered her lips a bit and posed. half teasing. Both girls laughed again.

Sara tossed the ChapStick back and her face became somber as she crossed her arms and leaned against the counter in all seriousness. "So, tell me, why did you decide to come to this camp?"

A wry grin spread across Amani's face. She looked so much like her brother, Sara thought. "To meet boys."

Sara smiled back. Her heart felt like it was filling. *What if Amani becomes my new best friend?*

Amani brushed back her nearly dry hair and said, "Honestly?" she said as though she was about to confide something. "My mother and I talked about this camp a lot. I really wondered what would happen if I made friends with an Israeli. I was curious, and I'm sick of the anger back home between people. My mom, being a nurse, deals with the problems of the violence all the time. But my father is another story. If I ever came home with an Israeli boyfriend, I know my father would disown me.

Sara sighed and felt a pang of sadness, "My mom hates the killing too." Sara slid down to the floor to be on Amani's level. It felt solid, just like this first step with Amani. She stretched out her legs, crossing them at the ankles as she thought out loud. "You'd think we could find a better way to solve our differences." She shifted her legs and looked over at Amani. "My father died in a car accident when I was five, but I haven't lost anyone in our conflicts, close to me, except for my cousin. I really didn't know him. But I hear adults talk and everyone is so angry. *Maybe they're scared.* She thought, as though the pine trees had whispered it to her. She paused on that for a moment and then said, "My grandmother always makes me feel afraid, like we are never going to be safe. She lives here, in the States. Before my grandfather died, they were very protective of us, always wanting us to move back here, or at least come visit more often."

"That would be amazing, to live here!" Amani moved to sit cross-legged in front of Sara. She still had the ChapStick in her hands and was tossing it from hand to hand slowly. "My mother and father divorced a few years ago. I live with my mother and Shacker mostly lives with my father. My uncle was killed. Most of my family is very angry, but my mother is the reason I'm here. She's different. She's very tolerant, you know? She refuses to hate, so she's the reason I'm here."

As Sara watched Amani fidget with her ChapStick lip balm, her mind started thinking about the first few days of camp. *People have told me all my life we have nothing in common, but here we are. She's a Palestinian-Muslim and I'm Israeli. How could that be true?*

Thinking about the bond they were forming just by being locked in here, Sara asked, "So how do we pay these guys back?" referring to Shacker and Aharon.

"We've got to think of something good. My brother is such a pain."

"Really? He seems so fun to be around." Realizing she might have spoken too truthfully, Sara felt her face redden.

"It's okay with me if you think he's cute; everybody does." Amani said as Sara felt her face redden hotter until she glanced over at Amani's understanding smile. Then they both giggled.

Amani looked down at her watch. "I'm getting cold and I want to change into some dry clothes. Why don't we just try yelling for help?" Both girls stood and started yelling, their voices without an exit outlet, echoed off the tiled floor and walls. After a few minutes, they heard some commotion at the door. It suddenly swung open and they saw Yolanda, the camp cook with a confused look on her face as she looked them up and down. They were still damp enough to see that something significant had happened during dish duty.

Amani raised her hand and said, "Don't ask. My brother can be a real pain."

Yolanda shrugged and laughed knowingly. "I have six brothers. Enough said, honey." Amani gave her an empathetic look, and then she and Sara quickly left to change in the cabin.

As they walked along the path that would soon become as familiar to them as home, Amani quietly said to Sara, "I bet you money that Shacker and Aharon won't say anything to us."

Sara smirked. "We've got to get them back."

"Definitely!"

The afternoon sun was high above them, but the trees helped keep the path cool. Most of the campers were down by the lake or playing on the field. Sara liked the distant sound of their laughter and shouts as they walked, her long arms swinging lazily at her side.

Suddenly, both girls heard a crack, like the sound of a heavy stick smacking against a tree trunk. They stopped to look around. Sara thought it came from just up ahead on the path. Her eyes caught a glimpse of Tarif leaning up against a pine tree about ten yards ahead of them. He had a broken branch in his hand.

"Sara, maybe we should turn around and wait until later. Tarif gives me the creeps." Sara hated the idea of having to sit around in her wet clothes, waiting for someone to come along to escort them. It seemed so ridiculous.

Before Amani responded, Tarif started slowly making his way toward them, turning the limb over in his hands like a baseball bat.

"Hey Jew girl," he sneered. "Aren't you two cute together, like two little chickens out for a little walk."

Just in that moment Shacker and Aharon walked up. Sara, relieved, turned to Amani and under her breath said, "So what's his problem?"

Shacker, overhearing this, surprised the girls by saying, "Oh, don't mind him. The guys will soften him up. Say, what have you girls been up to?"

"We have both been locked in the girl's bathroom for the last hour. You wouldn't know anything about that would you?" asked Amani.

Shacker with a smirk on his face; "NO, we have no idea. We have been cleaning up the kitchen this whole time."

Aharon, "Exactly."

Amani, "Sure."

With that the boys waved and walked on towards their cabin. They yelled back smiling, "See you girls later."

Sara leans into Amani and they begin walking back to their cabin, "Let's get them back." Amani smiles and the two link arms celebrating their new friendship.

Chapter 3

The bonfire blazed and crackled, smoke billowing softly upward into a star-filled night. Sara, full of dinner, basked in the fire's warmth from her spot on the bench. Sitting beside Amani, her bunkmate, and Brenna from Tel Aviv, they sipped hot cocoa and sang campfire songs with the rest of the campers. Sara smiled as she looked at the faces around her. This was only day two of camp, but it already felt like she had known some of the other campers much longer. As they sang, Sara couldn't help but notice Shacker sitting on the opposite side of the fire. As if she could read Sara's mind, Amani leaned in and nudged her. Sara blushed as she wondered if Amani saw her staring at him.

Just then, Dr. Meg stood up to address the group. "Good evening campers. By now you've figured out where the bathrooms are and that we weren't kidding when we said that flag raising is at 8:00," she said with a bit of mischief in her eyes. A mixture of laughs and groans surrounded the fire. "So now that we've gotten the easy stuff handled," more groans and giggles, "It's time to find out more about what we're doing here. But before we do that, I'm here to answer any questions."

Tandy raised her hand. Dr. Meg teased with a look of mocked warning, and then joked, "Yesssssss?" in a long, drawn out tone.

"Dr. Meg, why are *you* here?" Tandy asked with a mischievous twinkle in her eye as though she knew the answer and had rehearsed the question ahead of time.

"Yeah," one boy bravely said, genuinely curious.

Dr. Meg smiled a knowing smile and shook her head at Tandy. "Good question Tandy," she replied. Sara was enjoying their intimate humor. It was refreshing and different from the way teachers treated each other at home. Amani raised her eyebrows and looked at Sara, also amused and curious. No one knew what was going to happen next.

Dr. Meg then looked thoughtfully at her feet and shuffled the dirt with the toe of her shoe. "When I was very young," she started, pausing for a moment, "I came to this camp just like you. I was part of an inner-city project from Los Angeles. This was my first experience of pine trees, fresh water lakes and stars," she said while motioning her hands upward and looking where she was waving.

"Where I went to school, there were a lot of problems between kids of different colors, religions and economic backgrounds. Kids were dying in gangs, or from drugs. It was a different kind of war than what you might know, but it was a powerless feeling for a lot of us. You never knew if your best friend was going to make it to graduation with you, or if you would be hit in a drive-by shooting yourself." She looked up at Tandy and then looked around each kid at the fire.

"Then, when I got to college, I got curious and decided to explore my Jewish roots, the ones my parents had left behind because of what had happened to my grandparents during the war. No one talked about it, they just tried to forget it, and to forget where we came from. As I learned more about the fallout of that war, I realized that what was happening in Israel and Palestine felt familiar somehow, even though we were worlds apart, and I had never seen or heard a bomb. I also believed that there could be something different than what you or I grew up with.

"Since then, I've been passionate about helping people come together in nature like when I was a kid. Without the pressure around us at home, at camp we could forget for a while why we were supposed to hate each other, or be afraid of each other and avoid friendships. And," she shrugged, "we also managed to learn a few new things about ourselves that came in handy when we got back home. I felt more confident somehow, and less afraid when I left.

"Every summer we bring kids together and every summer there's at least a few who don't believe this will work, but somehow it always does. I trust these majestic trees and the pureness of the lake water, along with the magic of simply hanging out together. The rest, well, the rest is just part of the mystery of time spent together when there is no right or wrong, when there is no pressure to hate each other.

Tandy smiled a compassionate smile. Sara wondered if she saw a tear forming on Tandy's face. Tandy looked like she understood Dr. Meg even more than she implied on that first day. Would she learn more about Tandy too?

Dr. Meg smiled and looked around. "A big part of my job here is to listen. I am available anytime you might need an ear. And, each night we will meet like this. It's important to share together. We want to hear what is going on with you.

"When we meet as a group, there are some ground rules. Tandy and the other counselors can help you with remembering these. We don't cross talk here. Does everyone know what that is?"

The thin boy next to Amani's brother that we met earlier with Shacker raised his hand. "Hi. My name is Aharon. I think cross talking means that, uh, that we say what we say, and no one can talk to us about it. We just must listen.

Dr. Meg smiled and nodded her head. "Very nicely stated; it sounds like you've done something like this before." Aharon grinned and then said "I have nine younger brothers and sisters. I know all about cross talk." Everyone laughed.

"It is a very powerful thing for someone to just listen to you without arguing, or trying to fix it, or making it right or wrong." Dr. Meg continued smiling at Aharon. Then she looked out at the circle. "When it is your turn, you can say whatever we want but it's important to be quiet when someone else is talking." She paused thoughtfully for a moment and then said, "I have also found in my own experience here that being honest is a big part of the magic. It contributes to everyone's experience in the end, even if it doesn't feel like it at first, but most importantly it makes a difference for yourself."

Dr. Meg shifted her weight and leaned forward slightly, "So tonight we're going to start off easy. Just for now, I'd like you to share what you're feeling right now, and something you've noticed about yourself since you got here. If you don't want to speak at one of these, that's ok. We allow two passes during the three weeks we are here. But I encourage you to consider making the effort to speak openly even when it feels uncomfortable. Sometimes when we don't want to talk, talking anyway opens us up for the greatest magic to happen." She raised her eyebrows looking at them, and then gently bit her lower lip with a knowing nod.

The fire again popped and crackled. Tandy added two more logs to the blaze, sending a spray of sparks up into the air. Sara focused her attention on the fire as she felt her chest tighten again. Sharing in front of others definitely wasn't her favorite.

She glanced up to see Amani's brother raise his hand. This changed her mood slightly.

"Salam, my name is Shacker. How do I feel? I feel happy. I am very happy to be here, and I have a new friend. It's this guy, Aharon." Shacker nudged him and grinned. "He's Israeli and I'm Palestinian. We've been shooting hoops and it's great. I like that all the stuff we experience at home isn't here. I feel free to just be friendly with everyone. "

Sara unconsciously nodded her head in agreement. It was nice to be friendly with everyone, no matter where they came from or who their father and mother were. She found herself staring dreamily at Shacker again.

Dr. Meg followed up kindly, "And what's the one thing you've noticed about yourself since you've gotten here?"

"Uh," he stopped to think and then flashed a big grin, "I can out eat Aharon three to one." Everyone laughed.

And then Aharon chimed in, "Yeah but we all pay for it in the cabin when we're trying to sleep!" He made a face and a motion with his left hand like he was trying to wave away a strong smell. Everyone laughed harder, including Shacker.

After a few moments, Brenna tentatively raised her hand and Dr. Meg called on her.

"Shalom, my name is Brenna." She briefly looked down at the ground and tucked curly hair behind her ear. She shyly looked back up at the crowd and began again. "I'm feeling a little uncomfortable. I don't like to speak in front of people." She laughed a little, looking at the ground once again while many of the campers smiled or giggled empathetically with her. Surprised and relieved, she became more at ease, and when she continued, her voice was still gentle, but it was also a little louder and more confident. "I've noticed that I'm having a good time too, and that I really want to say it to all of you." Several of the girls smiled appreciatively. Dr. Meg seemed to be holding back a big, all-knowing grin, covering her mouth with a few fingers. Sara wondered what else she knew would evolve from their coming together here in this strange place of wonderful bewitching magic.

Brenna continued, "What I really want to say is I loved playing dodge ball with everyone last night after dinner; I laughed so much my sides hurt." The other campers laughed and nodded joyfully at the memory. One of the boys pointed at Aharon and smirked teasingly as he nodded, referring to how often he was hit with the ball. Brenna's confidence grew with this new group camaraderie. "I wasn't afraid. It felt like we'd all been friends for a lot longer than a few hours. I'm surprised by this. At home this would never happen." Many thoughtful nods, giggles and grins followed this comment, in agreement.

Smiling kindly with a notable spark in her eyes, Dr. Meg poked a long stick into the fire, sending a few sparks into the air as if to applaud in excitement for the bursts of laughter. "Life can be full of wonderful surprises."

Aharon raised his hand. "Shalom. You know that my name is Aharon," he said as he waved his hand dismissively and rolled his eyes playfully. "As you probably already know, I'm *not* shy," glancing kindly at Brenna. Everyone laughed and Shacker gave him a playful shove with his hand as if to agree. Aharon shrugged as he admitted, "I was scared when I got here."

The campers protested lightly in disagreement as if to say *You? No way*! "I was!" Aharon insisted. "Not that I was going to let any of you know about it!" More understanding sounds from other campers and Tandy, who remembered her first days as a camper. "But now I am having a wonderful time. I like all these weird and smelly guys." he said as he shoved Shacker back with a big grin and waved his hand in front of his nose again. "We've been having fun together. Don't tell my mom, but I thought I came because I wanted to see what America was like, but I like being here more than I thought." He added jokingly, "That crazy bell for flag raising is brutal though!"

Everyone groaned in agreement. "The guys had a terrible time this morning. We didn't know if it was a rocket or an alarm or what!" They boys started laughing heartily, making jokes as they remembered the chaos that ensued the morning wake-up bell that morning. "I'm telling you that is the first thing I'm putting on my camp evaluation, to change that. It needs to be later, seriously."

"Much later!" Amani chimed in spacing off into the fire as if she was feeling the fatigue from the early morning wake-up calls.

Peace Train

Dr. Meg smiled and added with a laugh of amusement "Many people have tried to get that changed and no one has succeeded in all the years I've been here." There was a long pause as the fire crackled and campers relaxed into feeling the warmth and glow, more from their joined laughter than the dancing flames.

One boy raised his hand. His skin was darker than most of the other campers and his clothes looked out of place for a summer camp setting. He wore long, dark cotton pants rather than the shorts or jeans the other kids wore. His brow furrowed, almost casting shadows over his eyes in the firelight. Even in the beautiful glow of the campfire, Sara thought, he seemed to have a dark cloud over him.

Dr. Meg nodded to the boy and he began.

"My name is Tarif, and I don't know why you are all playing it so safe, talking like everything is so wonderful. I don't feel like him at all," he said pointing at Aharon. "I'm Palestinian and I feel very uncomfortable here. I have never been around an Israeli before and now I have to sleep with them. It's hard not to touch them in such close quarters. What my father says about them seems true. They are dirty and loud and pushy." He was now hunched over shifting his knees back and forth while rubbing his hands on his cheeks and chin as if unconsciously rubbing off the exposure. Sara's stomach tightened.

"I wonder how I got into this situation." He added, almost to himself since he wasn't connecting to anyone else. Sara thought, *like the rest of us, you volunteered!* But she really didn't know, and she realized she shouldn't judge. Parents can be very demanding. As if to respond to her judgment of him, Tarif added, "I wish I could go home. I hate it here."

Most of the campers shifted uncomfortably. A few threw each other glances, and a couple of them rolled their eyes. One girl looked like she might cry. A few others stared into the ground, as if they prayed to melt into it if they could. In the tension, a few whispers rose into the air as the temperature seemed to rise.

Smiling gently and thoughtfully, as if this was nothing different than the campers who were surprised by their good experiences, Dr. Meg said, "Thank you Tarif." Carefully she continued, "It takes courage to be honest about how you feel, especially when it doesn't seem to match what others are sharing. I know it must be very uncomfortable for some of you," as she looked out across the fire at those who found it hard to look back. "It's not always so easy for everyone at first. But I'd like to invite you to consider something that I have noticed makes all the difference in these situations, whether going to your first day at a new school, or sharing a cabin with someone completely different from you. It takes a willingness to feel differently, she paused dramatically, "And that's what it will take for us to be successful here."

When she announced this last statement, she said it like it was her mission. She held herself in a way that didn't allow the tension that seemed to balance the rising heat with a cool head. Sara appreciated her strength and vowed to be like her one day. Dr. Meg's eyes conveyed a clarity. As she looked around the circle, there was a distinct look in her eyes transmitting a message. It was as if she knew her mission must, in time, become theirs.

"Let's try the idea on of coming to this circle being willing to feel something different the next few days and see what happens." She didn't say this with the knowing grin she'd had earlier, but with an authentic gesture, a hopeful vulnerability, looking out at them. For the first time, Sara realized Dr. Meg's destiny for these next few weeks was tied up in theirs, and she needed them to meet somewhere in a field of greater possibilities than most of the campers had ever known. Sara looked at Tarif and wondered if they were attempting the impossible, but she didn't feel daunted by it. To her surprise, she felt excited. Dr. Meg looked at Tarif and gestured a hand toward him, careful not to touch him, "Know that I am always available to talk," she looked out at the circle as if to say the same to everyone else. Many returned her eye contact thoughtfully and understood. After a moment, the tension seemed to break.

Amani raised her hand next. "Salam, I'm Amani." With her smart sense of humor, she continued, "I had no idea what it would be like to have this experience with my brother, Shacker." She pointed to him with a caring smile and everyone laughed. Aharon put his hand on his heart mockingly as he nodded vigorously in a teasing empathetic response to Amani. "I have never been around Israelis much either." Her beautiful long lashes and dark eyes shined in the firelight. "I am finding them different than I expected. I think they are just like me. I know it's early, but I'm actually kind of excited and I love the girls in my cabin," she smiled as she put her arm around Sara. "It doesn't seem to matter where we come from. So, I agree with my brother. I feel so free just to be me and to enjoy everyone. It's such a relief." She gave out a big breath when she said this and then laughed whole-heartedly. The remaining tension was broken.

But Tarif just seemed frustrated and more alone. Something in the jokes and the laughter and in Tarif's strangeness had an influence on Sara. Her heart started to pound and before she knew it, her hand was in the air. Dr. Meg nodded in her direction. *What was I thinking*? She panicked. Then she thought of Dr. Meg's strength and decided she wanted to practice it here and now. "Shalom, I'm Sara. I'm Israeli and it's funny," she said as she tucked her hair behind her ear with one of her long, feminine fingers. She didn't notice Shacker's back straighten and his eyes solidly on her as she continued, "but, even though I don't know anyone that well yet, I think I feel safer here than anywhere I've ever been. Where I come from doesn't seem to matter, at least in the girls' cabin. We just do what I'd be doing with my friends at school. I was afraid I might want to go home when we first arrived because I didn't know anyone, and I thought it might be too challenging to ever actually be together, but now I can't wait to see what's ahead." She paused thoughtfully and then laughed softly, "I agree with Aharon though, that bell is terrible. I think it would take us a lot further toward world peace to have more sleep in the morning." Everyone clapped and cheered at her powerful finish. Sara's heart swelled as she looked again at the now familiar faces aglow by the firelight. She felt something she had never experienced before: community with the *other*.

The short guy who asked about the ketchup on the first day raised his hand. His messy black hair stuck out in all directions. Sara rolled her eyes inside when she first saw him, as his messy hair reminded her of the bus driver, but now she softened. He adjusted his glasses before he spoke. It seemed like a nervous gesture; Sara guessed he did it often. It was actually sweet.

"Shalom. My name is Albert and I too am Israeli, and I hate my cabin. Tarif makes us all feel like we are poison and I wish I could be in the girl's cabin." She and Amani exchanged a look.

Someone in the group giggled at his comment about the girl's cabin, and Sara heard another boy mumble something under his breath. Dr. Meg gently corrected them with a glance that they now reverently respected. "Albert, please continue."

Albert looked around and then adjusted his glasses again. "As I was saying, I would like to be in the girl's cabin." Shacker lightly hit Aharon and nodded to say, *wouldn't we all, brother!* Amani and a couple of other girls rolled their eyes at his suggestion, amused in a way that said, *of course you would.* "What?" Albert said defensively. "It would feel so much safer. I don't feel safe here like you do, but I did have a good time playing the game last night." He snapped his fingers as if he just realized, "I felt completely safe then." And then as though he was talking to himself in a way that matched his wild hair and glasses, "That was a new experience. I think I feel safe right now." He locked up as if to suddenly complete his speech, which was partly just to himself, and concluded, "Thanks for listening."

A good-looking Palestinian named Amar raised his hand next. He shared that he was from a refugee camp in Jerusalem. Sara's gut dropped at this. She couldn't imagine living there. He went on to share that his family, like Tarif's family, had suffered much over the years. Sara noticed that he didn't seem to be angry like Tarif, but sweet and thoughtful. He reported that earlier in the year he had met an Israeli girl. Sara's eyebrows raised. Amani caught her and nudged her, playfully grinning. Tam cleared his throat and continued, "Our long talks back home put things into perspective for me. Our friendship has encouraged me to want to do something positive with my life. I want to live a life that is good, peaceful, and free. That is why I came to this camp."

Dr. Meg raised her eyebrows and took a deep breath. This was an unexpected helpful turn. She had known about his friendship from Amar's essay, but hadn't expected he'd share it so soon. "Thank you. I like your desires for life. I think they are worth the courageous acts they require, just like coming to this camp."

Rebecca raised her hand. Sara immediately remembered comforting her the night before. She seemed okay afterwards, but Rebecca's shoulders still drooped, and her face looked glum. Sara was disappointed she hadn't made that much of a difference. She vowed to be a better shoulder to lean on.

"Shalom. I'm Rebecca and honestly, I'm very homesick. I've never been away from home before and all of this is so strange. Sara has been wonderful. I am so thankful she is here." Sara smiled a little to herself. "But, if I could, I would really like to go home."

Dr. Meg walked over, and sat next to her. Tandy tended the fire as if they were switching places seamlessly. It felt very safe. Dr. Meg spoke more quietly but loud enough for others to hear. "What you are experiencing is not that unusual. I felt that way the first time I came here." Rebecca looked surprised. Dr. Meg gave her a warm, friendly look. "I'm glad Sara was there for you. Why don't you sit next to me for breakfast tomorrow? And we can talk a bit more afterwards if you need to."

Rebecca nodded her head, and Sara felt relief. She didn't have any more ideas on how to soothe Rebecca. She was happy the experts were on board. Tonight was the first night she'd noticed that Dr. Meg had a comforting and calming way about her, in addition to solid strength.

As sparks continued to fly up into the darkening night sky and the firelight softened, a few more campers shared their feelings and what they had noticed about themselves, while two chose to pass.

True to her promise, Dr. Meg let them pass and gave no indication of judgment or concern. Sara thought she was so smooth. She, on the other hand, was dying to know what the campers thought and felt inside, and why they passed. By the time Dr. Meg wrapped up the circle, the fire had burned down to embers.

"Thank you for your honesty and courage tonight," Dr. Meg chimed as she looked specifically toward Albert, Tarif and Rebecca, and then smiled at Shacker, the joker. The circle was ending for the evening. "You now all have free time until 11 o'clock when lights are out. I will remind you, however, that after dark, boys stay out of the girls' cabins and girls stay out of the boys'." A few of the boys groaned and several girls giggled. "I thank you ahead of time for your cooperation," she declared amusingly. "There are a few promises that make all the difference to the parents who sent you here," she admitted with a big grin. Several campers rolled their eyes and nodded their heads in understanding. "No kidding," one girl whispered, "my father would kill me if I were with a boy after dark."

Shacker caught up to Amani and Sara on their way along the path to the girls' cabin. "Hey, Sis."

"Oh hey, Shacker." She paused as if that was all, and then added as though reading Shacker's mind, "You know Sara."

Shacker smiled coyly at Sara and she felt her heart flip a little as she grinned back and said Shalom. He easily fell into step with his sister. "So how about that gathering tonight?"

"What part?" Sara asked not sure how to respond. Was he talking about the jokes? Tarif? What they'd learned about Dr. Meg? So many things had happened.

"Well I can say I'm sure glad I am not in your cabin. That Tarif guy has an attitude." Amani responded.

He laughed, "Ah, he's ok. He's just scared." And then with a flash of his charismatic grin as he turned onto his path to the boys cabin he said, "We'll, as I said, we'll shape him up."

"That I would like to see." Amani returned honestly. Then she looked at Sara and shook her head as if to say she knew Shacker's methods of mischief. "I don't want to know," she added rolling her eyes and giggling.

The girls' cabin was warm and cozy and a welcome change from the damp, lake air that had been gradually wrapping itself around them at the campfire. The dim lights made Sara feel sleepy in the growing familiarity and comfort of her newfound cabin family, and home. So much happened tonight, things she didn't understand. Her heart longed for more laughter and camaraderie and, yet she couldn't imagine how it would all unfold in the coming days. She sensed that there was a vulnerability to the warmth in the group, despite her own heart opening. Anxiety rose inside her, wondering how she would stand up to being tested in some way without Dr. Meg around to help. She knew that not everyone was ready for the warm feelings, and Dr. Meg's own quiet intensity at the end seemed to verify all that. The possibility of more was still so young, just as they all were.

Sara gazed around the room. She saw several girls whisper and giggle as they dressed in their pajamas and climbed into their bunks. Others, exhausted and thoughtful, quietly got ready while taking the evening in. A definite energy filled the room from their bonfire experience. As she slipped into her sleeping bag above Amani's bunk, Sara focused on the aspect she liked the most. She could feel a spacious light in her heart that she had never noticed before. Hope perhaps.

Tandy seemed to understand what Sara and the other girls were mulling over. While leaning on her elbow tucked into her bunk she asked in a gentle voice, "So what did you all think of the fire circle tonight?" She then changed her voice to imitate Dr. Meg while wagging a finger. "Be sure not to cross talk, now." Several girls giggled. Dana, the girl in the bunk across from her shared reflectively how she thought it was the hardest part of camp so far, and several others agreed. Tandy softly reached her arm out toward her and said, "It gets easier." Sara thought about this and relaxed. She trusted Tandy.

Her mind easily wandered to the flames crackling gently in the night air from the fire circle. Voices from the evening whispered to her while images blurred into the unfettered world of unstoppable dreams, until she fell into a deep asleep.

Chapter 4

The next afternoon, Amani and Sara headed to the sand court by the flag poles to bump the volleyball back and forth. A wonderful sweet smell wafted through the air from the white Alyssum flowers surrounding the court that had been planted by another group of campers the year before.

Sara bumped the ball over the net to Amani. "So do you think we can rally to twenty without dropping the ball?"

Amani puts on her competitive face. "Yes!"

Sara hit a serve. "Do you play this at home?"

"Not as a sport—just for fun."

The girls laughed about some of the boys in the dining hall that morning. Several hadn't bothered to comb their hair or change their shorts. Amani shared that she'd suspected they'd been up past curfew. Amani slammed the ball over the net and Sara missed it by an inch. Amani groaned but then laughed it off. "Well at least we made it to ten. Let's try again." Sara served, and Amani easily hit it back over.

Then, after another hit, Sara decided to change the subject into a more serious tone, "What are your dreams? I mean, what do you want for your life?"

Amani gave her a strange look, but then got thoughtful. "I don't know. I think I would like to be a nurse like my mom. I would also like to have a marriage that is better than what my mother and father had. If it can't be better, I'll just stay single. My parents spent their whole married lives fighting; there's no way I want that for my life." She volleyed the ball back to Sara. "How about you?"

"I want to teach. But I'd also like to have a radio show. I love the talk shows." Sara slammed the ball over the net a little too hard and Amani couldn't connect with it in time.

"Maybe you can do both," Amani suggested as she missed it and then went after the ball. "What about marriage?"

"I don't know. I'm kind of a romantic. I want to marry my best friend. You wanna still try for twenty?" Sara asked.

"Okay, sure, but first, what do you mean, you want to marry your best friend?" Amani brushed aside her ponytail and tossed the ball to Sara to serve.

Sara stood still for a moment holding the volleyball. "Well, you know, best friends. Someone who accepts me as I am, appreciates me, and supports me fully. We would be real partners. We would be together, but we wouldn't cling to one another."

"What about love? You didn't mention love," Amani challenged.

Sara shrugged her shoulders a bit. "All those things are love."

"What about religion?" Amani probed further.

Sara smiled, "I would want to have the same spiritual beliefs, too, but not necessarily religion."

The girls continued to hit the ball back and forth. They lost count several times and had to start over.

Peace Train

"Have you ever thought about, I mean do you have a hero?" Amani asked thoughtfully thinking about the times when she needed someone to look up to other than her parents.

"Don't laugh," Sara said after a moment. Amani had an intrigued but gentle look on her face that made Sara feel she could tell her anything. "You probably don't know her," she paused, "Eunice Kennedy Shriver." Sara lobbed the ball back over the net, not bothering to serve it. "She was an athlete actually, before girls really could be one. She was really good at basketball."

"Basketball? How is that heroic?" Amani asked, admittedly a little disappointed, even as much as she loved sports.

She is my hero because she was able to influence the cultures of over a hundred countries worldwide in ten years, just for starters. And she did it by focusing on what she loved—sports. She never talked about how poorly people were treating others with intellectual problems. And believe me, most places were **not** treating that segment of their population very well. She just went in and began training these individuals in sports. The athletes began to feel better and thus, their communities began to see that they had value and dignity and should be treated as such. I believe that the reason this worked is that she focused on the solution instead of the problem."

"Really? That's kind of cool."

"Yeah, I think so," Sara continued.

"I can get that!" Amani agreed, remembering about her own experience with sports. "She was John F. Kennedy's sister, the American President."

"How do you know all this? I barely know who the prime minister is!" Amani admired.

Sheepishly, Sara replied "I can't stop listening to the talk shows. I'm addicted." She laughed at herself.

Amani popped the ball high in the air light-heartedly and complimented, "You're really smart, aren't you? Just like my brother," she shook her head. Sara had never thought of herself much like that. But maybe it was true. Her dad certainly was.

Just as the girls reached twenty-five points, Shacker sauntered up and Sara noticed the world got a little brighter with his presence. His green camp T-shirt fit him perfectly, which seemed to cause all that intelligence Amani was referring to, to leak out her ears until all she could hear was her pounding heart. *Did volleyball cause that?* She didn't think they were playing that hard.

"Salam, girls! Hey Sis, can I play?"

"We're not really playing, just hitting the ball back and forth and talking."

Shacker looked over at Sara and smiled. "Sounds like fun. So what were you girls talking about—girl stuff?"

"We were talking about friendship and marriage. You know, the stuff that didn't really exist in our home." Amani's shoulders drooped a little when she said the last part.

Sara looked at Shacker and cocked her head. "Don't you think best friends should marry?"

He shrugged, "I don't know. I'm not attracted to my best friend. He's a guy." His eyes sparkled their dreamy, mysterious sparkle. "No seriously, I've never had a girl for a friend. Is that possible?"

They all laughed. "You've had me," Amani insisted.

"Well I'm certainly not going to marry you!" he joked as they all laughed.

"Good." Amani said as she wrapped her arm in his and gave him a girlish hug. Then she suddenly seemed worried. "What time is it, Sara?"

Sara glanced at her watch. "A little after 2:00."

"I was supposed to meet Rebecca at the cabin at 2:00 to exchange T-shirts! Shoot! I'm late," she shouted as she ran toward the path to the cabin.

Just as quickly as Sara's brains had leaked out, Amani, her only buffer to keep the conversation going, was gone. Shacker and Sara looked at each other again, more timidly this time.

Shacker suddenly didn't look like the relaxed, confident guy he always was. His color flushed a little. He looked around, then stared at the ball for a moment until he said, "Hey, you want to take a walk?"

"Sure." *I would go anywhere with you.* Sara thought.

Shacker motioned for her to follow. "I know this place around the lake that's beautiful. It's not too far."

Sara set the volleyball down and started walking. The path was well worn as though many had taken this same walk before them, for the same reasons. They wound their way around the lake following the ghosts of past camp lovers from decades before. The ground felt soft beneath Sara's feet and she could smell the fresh scent of pine from the nearby trees. The silence in the beauty might have been delicious, but Sara thought it was awkward with Shacker. He always seemed to know what to say, until now. "So how did you get the name Shacker?" she started, breaking the silence.

"I was named after my great, great grandfather Shakir, but my sister couldn't say it right when she first started talking so she called me Shack, which eventually evolved into Shacker as she could say more syllables." He spoke with an easy laugh as he talked about Amani. They often teased each other, but it was clear they actually really cared about each other. She sensed that Shacker looked out for Amani and that she was there for him as a feminine presence to help guide his heart in the right direction. Sara liked that about them. "My mom says my grandfather was a very good guy and she wanted me to be like him. How about you?"

"I'm named after my great aunt who lived here in the States."

"You were born here right? How did you end up in Israel?"

Sara stepped over a tree root, more easily than before, she noted. "My parents moved to Israel when I was three."

"Wow, so you're a dual citizen? What do your parents do? It's not easy to just pack up and start over in another country."

"When I was five, my father was killed in a car accident. He was a teacher."

"Oh. I'm sorry. I didn't know. Amani didn't say." Shacker sympathized. He seemed genuinely compassionate in his response. Something new.

"Obviously my grandparents wanted us to move back to the States right away, but Mom had a great job as a teacher by then, so we stayed." Changing the topic, she added. "I'm going to visit my grandmother in New York after camp is over." Shacker didn't say anything. A few steps later, Sara picked up a stick from the path and changed the subject again. "Amani says you're smart. What do you plan to do when you are done with school?"

"She said that? Oh, I'm thinking about being a nurse practitioner. My father is a doctor and my mom is a nurse." He laughed, "I figure I can please them both. I'm really good at being in the middle! I really don't want to be a doctor anyway, the way my dad talks about it. Especially his work in the Palestinian hospital. But I could get into being a nurse practitioner at a clinic somewhere. It's less school." Shacker turned his head to look at Sara. "How about you?"

"I've heard about those hospitals. They're really awful, aren't they?" Shacker shrugged as if to say no big deal, but she detected a sadness flash across his eyes. "I don't know what I want to do,

Peace Train 55

really. I think I'd like to work in radio. I listen to the radio all the time and I started volunteering at a radio station after school. I think it would be fun to have my own talk show."

"What would you talk about?"

"Everything. I love current events and news. But I really love stories that inspire," she smiled joyfully as she thought of the talk show that introduced her to her hero.

The pair walked in silence for a few moments. Sara's fears about Palestinian boys were fading. She had the feeling that their life experiences were much more the same than anyone would guess, just as she had noticed with Amani. "Are you a Christian?"

Shacker ran his hand through his thick, dark hair. "No, my parents are Muslim. I am not sure what I am. How about you?"

"My mom is Jewish, and I really like the rituals, but I am more into spiritual stuff than religious stuff."

"What do you mean by that?" he asked genuinely.

"I am not really into all the rules of religion."

Shacker nodded and smiled. "I don't like rules either."

They had come upon an area nestled by a small ridge on the other end of the lake. They walked over several rocks and down a short path. Sara was surprised to see a small waterfall tucked between a grove of pine trees that circled a crystal pool at the bottom. Ferns were everywhere, and the sound from the water falling was like lightly falling drops of music into a deep pool of aged silence. Just then, a butterfly flew by.

Shacker almost whispered, "Isn't this beautiful?" He seemed to be genuinely enchanted by it. She had never really seen him be still before. He was always laughing or joking.

Sara nodded. "It's magical."

Shacker suddenly shifted from calm and enchanted to nervous, with that familiar mischievous twinkle in his eye. He shuffled his feet a bit and then looked Sara in the eyes. "I know this will sound crazy, but here goes." Sara's eyebrows raised, and her eyes grew big. *What now?* "I have always wondered what it would feel like to kiss an Israeli girl. You know, like an experiment."

Sara's insides did a double flip. Shacker's eyes seemed so deep—as though they held a million different thoughts, and not just of kissing and pranks. She had also wondered what it would be like to kiss a Palestinian, but she never thought she'd be talking about it.

She realized he had just said something that needed a response. "Oh, really?" Her mind was swirling. Her eyes stared at the ground as she quietly thought *I've been wondering that too.*

Clearly catching himself and feeling embarrassed he looked away and said, "Oh forget it! I'm sorry. I'm just talking crazy."

"No wait!" Sara shouted in disbelief, coming out of her trance, realizing what he was saying.

Misunderstanding, Shacker thought she was offended and scrambled to find a way to fix the moment, "I'm so sorry, I – I didn't mean…"

"No. No, I mean," she took a breath and looked directly into his eyes, "I've had the same thought."

"Really? You have?" He grinned with relief.

Thinking about all of the times she had noticed him across from her at fire council or in the dining hall, or the way he laughed covered in water during KP, "Well, yes," she swallowed.

"It's just that I've always heard we were so different, and it made me wonder." He babbled nervously. Shacker's heart pounded with excitement. He shook his head in disbelief. He had wondered about this so many times. *What would it be like? Would it feel different? Are we really that different? Israeli girls are so attractive. At least, she is.* "So, would you like to experiment?" he said with a soft, hopeful look in his eyes.

He's so dreamy, Sara thought as she swallowed, took a breath, and then shrugged. "It scares me a little, but I wonder too." She flashed a grin as she tilted her head in the sunlight, "Let's break the rules."

There was an awkward moment and then he moved closer to her. Her heart was in her throat as he picked up her clammy hand. He smelled so good. As they moved closer, their noses touched, and Sara stepped away laughing nervously.

Ever so gently, Shacker moved in closer again. He picked up her hand gently and touched his lips on Sara's, carefully. Time stopped while a gentle buzz of electricity surged through her. As if the electricity turned a light on inside, an explosion of thoughts and emotions raced through her, some confusing. It wasn't supposed to feel this good, was it? She was interrupted by a voice from beyond the bushes on the trail they had just come from.

"Hey, what are you two doing?" Aharon asked.

Sara jumped back, her face instantly crimson.

Shacker quickly shifted back into his smooth, boyish self. "Aharon, don't be such an old lady! I have never kissed an Israeli girl, and Sara has never kissed a Palestinian boy. We were just curious about how it would feel." Sara was amazed at how quickly he could shift into the old Shacker that she had known better, until now.

Aharon laughed, "Well that's the stupidest thing I've ever heard. How did it feel?" All three turned around to head back toward camp. Aharon walked gingerly in front of them waving a small branch he had picked up from a bush beside him. Sara and Shacker looked at each other silently and smiled.

Shacker leaned down and whispered to Sara, "New rule: Israelis and Palestinians must kiss at least once."

Sara focused on the path in front of her until she noticed Shacker gently take her hand for just a moment. It was strong, yet gentle. She glanced up at him and drank in his tender smile. He released her hand, but he didn't stop smiling.

Chapter 5

As the three trekked along the path toward camp, they began to hear squeals of laughter and mayhem. As they stepped off the trail and onto the main beach, they could see campers chasing each other, tossing water balloons in the outside patio of the arts and crafts building which stood just beyond the volleyball court. It was a playful twist of events that Amani and Brenna had managed to start when they were supposed to be making papier-mâché shapes. But when Brenna went to wash her hands in the outdoor sink provided by the patio, she noticed a plastic package on the counter that said water balloons and it sparked an instinctive reaction in her, as if the package laid itself on the counter to tempt her into using the balloons for the true intended purpose. As soon as the guys saw Shacker coming up the path, they easily drew him into the chaos and fun. This was right up his alley, an activity loaded with spontaneity, pranks and laughter. He didn't waste any time to include Sara when he grabbed her right arm attempting to smash a small one on her back. She squealed as she twisted and writhed trying to get ahold of one herself.

Amani and Brenna were splashing more water on themselves, the counters and anyone nearby that they could get with the balloons. Then they rushed to fill more, which were usually grabbed by other campers before they even had time to tie them off. Sara felt relieved to be running around laughing as she let out all the pent-up energy inside her that had taken her by surprise during the kiss. She wasn't sure what she was feeling, and she didn't want anybody to notice just yet.

Eventually they ran out of water balloons and began to grab any nearby bowls or buckets or anything they could find. One guy was filling his cap with water. Until half of them ended up either jumping in the lake or being pushed in while the rest laughed and cheered from the beach. Between splashes and cheers, Sara noticed Tarif staying at his post as usual, avoiding any possible fun as he watched their squeals and delight in the freedom of their unburdened play.

Right when Shacker came running up to Sara with Aharon to grab her and toss her in, the bell rang, signaling the end of afternoon activities and the time to get ready for dinner. Sara had been saved from the ultimate plunge.

Gradually people trudged out of the lake collecting extra t-shirts, hats, sneakers, hair ties, or broken pieces of water balloon that now littered the ground.

"I wonder what Dr. Meg's gonna say," Aharon whistled surveying the mess as campers hustled to pick up what they could find on their way back to their cabins.

Back at the cabin, Sara put on dry jeans and a white top, then hung her water balloon-soaked clothes to dry on the deck railing outside. Amani walked up to the cabin late, having lingered behind with Brenna to clean up their mess at the sink, her clothes drenched as well.

"Hey Sara. So where were you and Shacker when the balloon fight broke out?" Amani raised her eyebrows and cocked her head a bit, as though she knew the answer to the question, but there was also something else behind her eyes. *Anger?* Sara was taken off guard.

As Sara fiddled with the clothes on the rail, her heart began to race. She had never felt uncomfortable to answer one of Amani's questions before. She had a strange feeling of guilt when what she really wanted was to confide her excitement. "He asked me to go for a walk and we went to this really beautiful place on the other side of the lake. I can take you there tomorrow if you like."

Amani jammed her hands onto her hips. "Really? Is that all?"

Sara continued fidgeting with her clothes, surprised by this sudden change in Amani. She had never seen her act this way before. It was as though something was taking over her new best friend. *Should I tell her the truth?* She contemplated. She tried to be very calm and cool about it, as if it was no big deal even though she felt so many things all at once. "Well, as an experiment, we kissed."

"What?" she looked incredulous. "You kissed my brother?"

Sara quickly turned around to see if anyone else was listening, worried that it would get out and ruin everything. They were all inside. She turned to look her friend in the eye. "Amani, it was just an experiment. It didn't mean anything." Trying to lighten the mood, Sara grinned and said, "Although I must say, it was very nice."

Amani threw up her arms and huffed.

"What?" Sara asked, feeling defensive and scared that she might be about to lose her best friend, and she didn't have a clue why.

"How could you ask that question? How could you…?" She interrupted herself exasperated. "Great. I've just lost my friend."

"What are you talking about?" Sara was sincerely confused. What did one have to do with the other?

"Because, don't you see? You'll be spending all of your time with *him*. It *always* happens," she said raising her arms in a dramatic flair. "All my friends leave me for their boyfriends. I suddenly become the most boring person in the world compared to whomever they suddenly are interested in." She sighed with some sadness in her eyes. "And the worst of it is, I never end up with one myself!"

Shocked, Sara didn't know where to start, so she started with the most obvious thing she could answer. "Amani, he is not my boyfriend. It was an experiment. We don't even know each other very well." *Though it didn't quite feel that way,* she admitted to herself. Sara moved to put her hand on Amani's shoulder, but Amani abruptly turned to leave.

"Well, I'm going to dinner with everyone else," she retorted over her shoulder. By now the rest of the girls had exited the cabin out the other door in the front and headed down to the dining hall.

Sara stood on the deck bewildered. It was too much all in one afternoon. A kiss that felt like it lasted a lifetime, and then losing her newest best friend over, dare she think it? – was she falling in love? Finally, aware that the sun had dipped, and her stomach was growling, she felt her heart pulling in all directions. She'd never felt this mix of emotions before and they didn't feel as good as she expected them to. Amani was the only person she wanted to talk with to sort it all out, but now she was part of the mess of feelings and thoughts. For the first time at camp, she felt unsettled.

But she couldn't deny that she knew what Amani was talking about. Sara's friends had also done this to her from time to time. But her friendship with Amani was different. It was stronger than that. *Wasn't it?* This camp felt so different, more real than anything else in her life somehow, which included her and Amani. There wasn't the narrow-minded, or shallow thinking here that was so prevalent back home, even with all the fun they had, like the water balloon fight. Sara sat on the bench on the front deck trying to sort some of this out before facing her friends at dinner as her stomach panged, nagging for her attention. Things were different here, *weren't they*?

In these woods, life could be lived how it was meant to be, she heard the phrase rise up from the breeze of the trees as though it were absolutely true. She looked out at the lake as if looking for that voice and noticed its placid beauty. For the first time, she knew a peace that she had felt both inside at the council fire, and outside all around her. She knew she had to help Amani understand.

Sara headed inside to grab her sweatshirt for the fire circle that night, then jogged down the path to the dining hall. She was alone with her thoughts until she ran into Shacker.

His face lit up when he saw her. "Hey Sara! Want to walk together?"

Sara's stomach did that flip thing again, but she also had Amani on her mind. *Should I say anything?* She thought, but before she could answer herself, her mouth was already bursting open and vomiting the truth as if someone reached in and grabbed it out of her. Something about Shacker was definitely changing the self-control she was used to. "I think I might have made a mistake, Shacker." She said as though they had been friends all their lives. "I told your sister that we kissed. She is furious with me." She stepped ahead in the path and turned around walking backwards intending to burst out ahead. "Would you please tell her it was just an experiment?"

Shacker let out a big sigh, but he didn't seem surprised. "Oh boy. I'm so sorry. That usually happens to me. When she gets mad, it can take her days to cool down. Yeah. I'll talk to her."

Shacker's smile was kind and reassuring, though not totally convincing. Sara had an uncomfortable feeling that things with Amani might not smooth over so easily.

~~~

When Sara woke up the next day, she hung her head over her bunk to say good morning to Amani, as usual. She didn't want to let yesterday change their fun in the morning. But Amani wasn't there, so Sara grabbed her toiletry bag and headed to the bathroom. Just as she walked in, Amani pushed the door open and headed back to the main cabin. Sara felt doubts creep in as she rushed to get ready to catch up with Amani. As she was tying her shoes she noticed that Amani had left the cabin with some of the other girls. She felt that same pain in her heart she'd had yesterday. *I'm not the one who has left her because of Shacker she left me because of him.* She shook her head, hurt by the strange and unwanted irony of it all. She brushed out her long ponytail, pulled on her sweatshirt and headed to the flag poles by herself for the first time since camp started.

At breakfast, Shacker cut in line next to Sara by the cereal station. He leaned over to her, keeping his voice low. "So I tried talking to my sister at flags. Try getting her alone and talking to her again. I think she'll listen. She always comes to her senses. She just has to see your side."

"And be willing to feel differently," Sara said, her big eyes looking up into his confident ones. "Right?"

Shacker smiled. "Don't we all from time to time," he said with a twinkle in his eye referring to their *rule breaking* kiss. Sara blushed.

After breakfast, Sara followed Amani to the bathrooms where she cornered her, determined to get on the same side again.

"Amani, we have to talk. I don't want to go through the rest of camp this way. Tell me what's going on. You're acting so strange. I've never seen you this way."

Amani's eyes flashed. "Strange? You're the one who's acting strange all lovey dovey with my brother. Everything was fine until then."

Sara's heart sank and her voice softened a bit. "Amani, it was an experiment to see what it would feel like. It had nothing to do with love or feelings or anything. I like your brother, but we're not together." *At least not while you're acting like this!*

Amani let her shoulders sag, then crossed her arms in front of her chest. "I don't see what difference that makes; you were still kissing."

"Amani, how does that change our friendship? I'm not changing it. I wish you wouldn't. Is there any way you might be willing to feel differently?"

This got Amani. Sara was right. The only one changing their friendship was her, but it didn't change the hurt. She uncrossed her arms as her eyes filled with tears. "I have been through this before with my brother. I make a good friend and we have fun together and then my brother starts paying attention to her and she starts ignoring me. She becomes Shacker's girlfriend and then when it doesn't work out between them, it's even worse. My former friend looks at me like it was all my fault for having him as my brother. It really hurts, Sara, because I like my brother, as crude and as obnoxious as he can be at times, and I like my friends. I don't want to be hurt like that again."

Sara moved close to Amani, putting her arm through Amani's arm in an act of unity. "Thank you for telling me. I'm sorry. That can feel pretty bad. But you're the best friend I've ever had. I mean it. I feel so comfortable and free with you, like we can talk about anything. And we have so much fun together! I don't want to mess that up." Sara paused and then straightened as she said, "I will not talk to your brother anymore if it means we can be friends again."

Amani shifted her weight to her other foot but kept staring at the ground.

"Amani, I'm sorry I kissed him. I really am. If I could take it back, I would. You mean so much to me."

"Was it fun? I mean he's always wanted to kiss an Israeli." Sara looked at her surprised. "He told me about the experiment. I'm more like Shacker than you'd think. I agree, some rules should be broken. She smiled shyly and looked at the ground.

"You mean Aharon?" Sara probed gently. Amani couldn't help having a big grin as she blushed, still looking at the floor.

"Just, could you keep it cool while we're at camp at least? Like, not let him take over what we have, leaving me like a piece of dust on a shelf that's just waiting to be cleaned off?" Sara grimaced at the image, but understood she was talking about the past, not their situation now.

"If you do the same with Aharon," she teased, though half serious too. She didn't want to lose Amani to Aharon anymore than Amani wanted to lose her to Shacker.

Amani looked up, her eyes sparkling with their newest bond of sisterhood. Relieved to finally have Amani back, Sara grabbed her and hugged her. Both girls had tears as Amani hugged Sara even tighter.

But the victory of the moment of winning back her best friend was quickly replaced by a pang in her heart as she thought about Shacker. She noticed since yesterday that she thought of him all too often, about every five minutes. Even this surprised Sara who had never felt like this with a boy before. It would be difficult to keep her pact with Amani, yet it made so much sense in more ways than one. After all, there would be no way she and Shacker could continue to *experiment* after camp in their environment at home. This was the first time she thought of life after camp since she had gotten here, which just added to the weight in her heart as she realized that just staying friends with Amani would be difficult enough

Chapter 6

The lake was surrounded by a beautiful white, sandy beach that rippled into the forest of pines guarding it. It was nearing the end of their first week at camp and the weather had continued to improve since their first day, when the cool air had hung over the forest after its morning rain. Near the lodge, a long pier jutted out to where you couldn't see its depth, let alone the seaweed waving lazily in the gentle current below. On the right was the swimming area, which was roped off to keep swimmers in a designated area apart from the boaters. On the left, the kayak racks stood proudly, the boats waiting for their next playful glide in the water. Next to them were three tall buckets filled with oars. At the end of the rack, life jackets hung like orange bumpers with their white straps. Campers were oriented to the rules of the beach and the lake from their first day of camp. One rule they emphasized was that everyone who went out in a boat must wear a life vest.

Aharon stood in front of the rack, pulling a red kayak off the bottom and dragging it to the beach opposite the swimming area. After pulling the nose of the kayak into the water, he loaded two paddles and two life jackets into it.

"Hi Aharon. Are you going out to see the turtles by yourself?" Amani asked him as she helped him with the last paddle. She had been sitting on the beach making friendship bracelets with Albert and Tandy when she saw him, and she decided to come ask what he was up to as an excuse to talk.

"Well everyone else has gone. Do you want to come with me?"

Amani's heart raced, but she had planned to meet up with Sara and Dana in a few minutes to listen to each other's CDs. She hated passing up the opportunity with Aharon and she didn't want him to think she wasn't interested, but her conversation that morning burned in her ears. She couldn't suddenly change her mind about being with Sara to spend the afternoon with Aharon.

"I'm sorry," she apologized. Not hiding her disappointment. "I'm meeting up with a couple of the girls to exchange CDs in a few minutes."

Just as he was taking off his shoes and socks, Aharon looked over to see Tarif walking up to them.

"Oh great, here comes Tarif," Amani said, noticing him too.

"He wants to go with me," Aharon said disappointed. "I told him maybe."

"Don't do it Aharon. You'll just be sorry," Amani urged, remembering all too well her encounter with Tarif on the trail after their KP duty together. "I better go. I can't stand him and I don't want to cause any trouble. I don't think I could feel any differently about him, even if I *was* willing. It would take a miracle," she added sarcastically, though in all honesty.

Just then Tarif approached Aharon. "So, can I go? I said I was a turtle expert." Aharon gave him an unenthusiastic look and then looked up helplessly at Amani. "I will pay." Tarif took a wad of crumpled cash out of his pocket.

Aharon noticed that Tarif's usual cold and stand-offish demeanor was absent. He shook his head in his usual humility that complimented his humor and jokes. Amani melted. She just loved that about him. "Don't worry about it. I don't need your money. Here, put on your life vest and help me get this thing into the water." Amani shook her head and waved her hand as if to say *I give up*, and she turned around to leave for the beach to get her things before meeting Dana and Sara at the cabin.

Tarif put the money back in his pocket, but not before glancing at Aharon with confusion in his eyes. No one had treated him with any kindness here. He took the vest, but instead of putting it on, he threw it into the two-man vessel before they grabbed each end to push it into the lake. Then they each took a paddle as they gingerly climbed in, awkwardly navigating their bodies, the narrow boat and the paddle. After getting situated, Aharon buckled on his life vest and they shoved off. At first, they were as silent as the lake.

The silence didn't bother Aharon. He had fond memories of fishing with his father who was a fisherman by trade. They often sat together quietly admiring the majesty of the water and what mysteries lay underneath its dark, placid surface. Fishing with his father was one of his favorite ways they would spend time together.

Tarif didn't seem as comfortable with the paddle as Aharon. The way he sat high in the boat told Aharon that Tarif probably didn't have that kind of experience with his dad, as he threw the center of gravity to one side and then the other with each paddle. Occasionally their paddles would hit when they got out of rhythm. At first Aharon could awkwardly work around it to keep the boat going in a straight line, but he could sense a rising tension in Tarif. Then, as if a dark cloud appeared over Tarif's head, where open sky would normally be, Aharon felt his stomach sink. He had an uncomfortable feeling the mood in the boat was about to change to what it was typically like at night with Tarif in the cabin when they would all be getting ready for bed.

"Hey idiot-Jew, quit paddling so fast."

Aharon's heart rate increased and he felt his hands start to sweat. Memories of home flashed before his eyes, of other Palestinian boys. After reminding himself he wasn't at home, he felt the heat rise in his neck with anger. "I'm not an idiot," he tried to say in a calm voice not to expose his anxiety or anger.

Tarif glared back at him. "No? What's the matter, Jew? You can't stand the truth?"

Aharon looked ahead as the boat rocked unsteadily. He saw something new in Tarif's eyes. *Was it fear? Fear of what?* Aharon loved being on the water. It was like a natural mother to him when he was on the boat with his dad, a kind of sweet, silky womb of comfort, silence and beauty. Aharon took in a breath through his teeth losing his cool, "What truth? You wouldn't know truth if you drowned in it."

Tarif answered smugly, "That sounds like something an Idiot-Jew would say. You are so stupid you don't even know how much you are hated."

Aharon felt the heat come back into his neck again until he found himself baiting Tarif, which he knew was stupid, just like Tarif said, but he couldn't seem to stop himself. "And all too well all too well you're going to enlighten me," he spit out through clenched teeth.

Tarif's mouth twisted into a malicious sneer. "Well, the Holocaust should give you some idea. Too bad the Germans didn't get the job done. Then you came to our country and took our land from everybody. Common thieves and thugs.

Before Aharon had a chance to think about that, the boat slowed to a stop. All stood still. All had been fine, gliding along the water easily, until they were snagged from something imperceptible underneath the surface. Neither could seem to see what dark trick had managed to capture them from their unique position in the boat.

Unbelievable. Here? Aharon thought, wanting more than anything to be able to move and get out of there. Both boys desperately started moving their bodies back and forth trying to dislodge the boat, but it wouldn't budge. But Tarif wasn't patient enough. Faster than Aharon could tell him not to, Tarif naively stood up to see what the problem was. It was too perfect, a brief image flashed through Aharon's mind that solved all of Aharon's problems at once. Without stopping to think, Aharon shoved his oar against Tarif's side, knocking him into the water on his back, creating a large wake and dangerously swaying the boat. Aharon's eye caught the life vest Tarif had refused earlier in the bottom of the boat. As a final gesture of force, he thrust it over the side at Tarif as if to cast off all the hurtful things he'd ever heard about being a Jew, giving all of his pain to Tarif.

Tarif's head surfaced. He was enraged, sputtering between large gulps of water, "What did -- you do that -- for, you idiot?! Help me – get -- back – in the – boat!" He flailed around in the water reaching for the life vest, his sputters, gasps and splashes creating a cacophony much like what he brought with him everywhere and to everyone at camp. The brief breaks from his voice when he went under were strangely welcomed and blissful to Aharon. Tarif's head bobbed like a lead sinker. Without his weight to hold the boat in place, the narrow kayak began to dislodge from its hidden captor that had stopped them in the first place. *Finally, I'm free.* Aharon thought.

The heat in Aharon's neck moved up to his cheeks. He picked up the paddle with the energy of his anger to get as far away from Tarif as possible. As he did, he noticed how odd Tarif's movements were, at least from the perspective of a fisherman's son. *What was Tarif fighting?* He couldn't seem to stop.

Aharon knew from experience that getting worked up in the water just made everything an enemy when it could be his friend. All that he needed was right there, including the water itself. *Just relax you idiot*, Aharon urged silently, without words. All he had to do was surrender to the large infinite being of the lake by floating on his back. *She,* the water, would easily cradle him as a tender baby, just as she had done for Aharon so often when he needed time to think in the thick silence away from all his brothers and sisters. Tarif was fighting his very refuge. However, Aharon had never stopped to consider what that might ask of Tarif. To be held and cradled by her tenderly, Tarif had to completely open in total trust, exposing the most vulnerable and tender parts of himself toward the vast, welcoming sky, including his heart.

Aharon thought he noticed fear in Tarif's voice as he began to paddle backwards beyond this hell and back to land. Tarif barked, "Hey!" Underneath his tough command was the terror that ultimately turned every one of his environments into the enemy. He spluttered, struggling to find a way to control the life vest bobbing in front of him. "Where are you going?!"

Aharon kept paddling. His anger, mixed with exhilaration from this power over Tarif, filled his veins and pumped his blood. "Away from you!" He couldn't paddle fast enough from this pathetic Palestinian rat, who did everything he could to interrupt any tender threads of peace he'd had these past weeks. Memories of his friendship with Shacker flooded him along with the laughs he'd had with all the campers, including the Palestinians. There was genuine love. And then his mind flashed to all the years of fighting and abuse back in Jerusalem. With the rhetoric of hatred even in his own people. He'd had enough. *No more!*

Tarif was getting tired from splashing and coughing, all the while fighting the weight of his clothes and boots. He would never take them off while sharing a boat with a Jew. "Wait, don't go. Hey, I'm sorry I said that stuff." Desperate, he pleaded, "Please!"

Aharon, lost in his trance of fury and pain didn't stop, despite Tarif's voice getting weaker and higher in pitch. "Too bad, you rat." *Let him drown. The world would be a better place.* By now Aharon was breaking out from underneath the pine canopy toward the open lake and sky. But before he could look up to enjoy it, a warm, gooey liquid landed on his head, *splat!* And then slid down his right temple. He looked up instinctively to see where it came from as he reached up to wipe it off. There hadn't been a cloud in the sky all day. His eyes registered just above him a quiet bird gliding effortlessly above him across the free sky. *Is that a dove?* He thought as he noticed the color and wing span. They had just learned about them here at camp from Rob during a lunch hike the day before. Aharon shook his head in frustration at the potential irony. What if that was a message from God to him? Even he had to laugh quietly to himself. If so, it was a perfect delivery in a highly unexpected package. *What am I doing?*

Aharon looked out toward the splashing and sputtering of Tarif's tiring body, but now through new lenses. *Is that terror? Was that there before? Where was his anger?* He couldn't remember. Aharon felt confused. *Wasn't Tarif just putting on a show for sympathy?* That would be something he would expect of Tarif. *Wouldn't anyone?* Aharon shook his head and felt his pulse quicken as his brow once again furrowed, remembering Tarif's words furiously flying like angry arrows in his mind. He sighed. *Aharon, this is your moment to be willing to feel differently.* He found his own thoughts difficult to swallow. *At least, for now, don't let him drown.*

Aharon quickly turned toward Tarif, who had finally stopped flailing, having found a new hold on the life vest to keep his head and shoulders out of the water. At that synchronistic moment, Tarif gave himself over to his aid, the life vest, just as Aharon gave into the power of his heart, rather than their simultaneous anger.

But it still didn't take away what had happened. "Tarif, what you said to me was about the worst thing I have ever heard. You don't deserve to be in a boat with anyone, especially not with me," accused Aharon. He was referring to being a Jew when he said that.

Tarif pleaded as he shivered, "Fine. Okay. I didn't mean it." Looking away, "I—ah—I still need your help," he said spitting water out of his mouth as he rested his chin closer to the life vest.

Aharon looked intently at him. "But I am an idiot, remember? And I stole your land."

Just then, Tarif gave a hard kick to get a better vantage. The life vest slipped unexpectedly from his grasp floating out into the water several feet away from him. His mouth filled as he sunk down without his savior. Another round of fighting once again as he started to cough and thrash about in his panic, but with little results as *the enemy* took advantage of his exhaustion pulling him down into the liquid abyss, boots and all.

Aharon realized with dread that Tarif wasn't putting on a show now. He thrust the blade of his paddle back into the water with quick, definitive strokes making record time, yet careful not to run him over or surpass him. Reluctant to feel any differently, to give up his hate and pain, the only story he had ever known of Palestinians since birth, he extended his paddle, and embraced both, the pain, and the task of saving the life before him, such as it was. A shift was required in him beyond what camp had already invited. Tested, revenge would have to remain back home with the statistics of countless bombs, guns and dead children, in order to make room for something that mattered even more to Aharon, his humanity.

With great effort, Tarif grabbed the paddle Aharon had finally offered, pulling hard enough that the boat tilted and moved in his direction. Without hesitation, Aharon grabbed Tarif's shirt, thrusting his left arm over his right to grasp his pants, hoisting Tarif the rest of the way in.

Shaking, they stared into each other's eyes, taking in the gravity of what just happened from their different sides. The boat rocked in the wake of the excitement, but all was silent within its narrow cocoon. Committed to keeping his center of gravity low this time, Tarif awkwardly navigated himself into a better position. He was shaking worse than Aharon. *Was it from fear of almost drowning, or from just now being touched by a Jew?* Considering how Tarif had described his father, Aharon figured they could be equal threats.

Aharon shook his head and looked at the back of Tarif's head. "I'm not really sure what to do with you, Tarif." He leaned on his paddle. "You've been so mean to everyone. What did *we* ever do to you?"

Tarif kept a tight grip on the life vest. Both boys returning to their bold and intent gaze, speaking as much through their eyes as their mouths. Tarif was the first to drop his eyes, quietly shifting his focus toward the water. "It's not you personally." He looked back up at Aharon, narrowing his eyes, "It's your people. Like I said, you stole our land and you keep doing it."

Aharon slumped in resignation. He didn't have a good argument for that. It was too complicated. "It doesn't give you the right to say such awful things to me. I have done nothing to you, personally. Look around you, Tarif. No one's doing anything like that here. Here, we have peace."

"Peace!? You pushed me in!" Tarif protested.

Aharon retorted lightly, "And what did *you* do before that? You deserved it!"

"Maybe." He paused and got quiet again. "But I really can't swim."

That was obvious. Aharon whispered as much to himself as to Tarif, "No hatred is worth dying for."

Tarif glanced desperately at Aharon's paddle. His own was lodged hopelessly underneath him, jutting the length of the boat with the other end wedged between Aharon's leg and the side. He didn't dare move again to pull it out from underneath himself, risking more rocking. "Could we get going already? I'm cold, and I would really like to get back."

Aharon noticed what Tarif was looking at, and his current dilemma. He decided he had one last thing to do before giving up his vantage point. "If I take you back, will you stop talking?"

Tarif considered this request, realizing he didn't really have anything else to talk about with a Jew. "No problem. I'll just be quiet." *Figures,* Aharon thought.

Tarif was shivering, but Aharon thought he saw relief in his eyes. He took off the dry life vest he had put on back at the beach and tossed it to Tarif. "Here, put this on. It'll keep you warm. If you can't swim, then you shouldn't be out here without one."

Tarif put the vest on in silence, appreciating what Aharon had to say for the first time, despite himself. Aharon, on the other hand, was still trying to make sense of him. He had looked intently into Tarif's eyes as he pulled him into the boat and had said to himself, *why can't you just see me as a person, like yourself?* Aharon noticed something shift on Tarif's face as the words streamed across his mind. *Did something finally get in?*

Tarif was busy fastening the life vest, still warm from the heat of Aharon's body. He engaged the straps with unusual commitment as Aharon saw a softening. Maybe Tarif somehow heard his thoughts.

But then Tarif's eyes narrowed suspiciously, "What are you thinking?"

Aharon looked at the back of his head, agitated. He paused, then inquired, "I've wanted to ask you a question ever since that night at fire council when you announced to everyone how miserable you were. Why did you even come to this camp?"

"Why did you?" he retorted, having no idea what he was going to say in truth.

"I came to make friends, but you just seem to hate it here, and it's been that way from the very beginning. So, why come at all?"

Tarif shrugged his shoulders and looked down at his oar. "I don't know. I couldn't say no to my mother," then more quietly as if to himself, *"any more than my father could."*

After another few minutes of silence, Tarif asked again, this time with a softer tone, "What are you thinking now?"

Peace Train

Aharon looked out across the lake. Except for the ripples from their paddling, the lake was now completely calm and peaceful. He looked at Tarif to answer. "I'm thinking that I'm thankful I didn't let you drown."

Chapter 7

Sara saw Aharon walking toward the cabin several yards behind Tarif. Tarif was dripping wet and shivering, hugging himself to stay warm. Both had their heads down and seemed quietly lost in their own worlds, unaware of their surroundings except for the path directly underneath their heavy feet. Sara dismissed this as anything but being tired and trotted up to Aharon enthusiastically, "Hey Aharon. How was your time out on the lake today?"

Aharon looked out at the lake thoughtfully, shook his head, then looked back at Tarif. "I don't think I can really talk about it now. I'm tired and just want to lay down for a while." He looked up at her inquisitive, happy smile. *She couldn't possibly understand. I don't even understand.* He didn't want to disappoint her, so he pointed toward the cabin as if to say he needed to get going, then said with a soft smile, "Maybe another time," hoping she'd forget all about it.

Sara shrugged but her eyes narrowed suspiciously. She had never seen him act like this. Something bigger happened out there beyond Tarif just getting soaking wet. She felt concerned as she watched him walk up the path. *Is he okay?* Amani was right, Aharon should have said no.

~~~

Tarif walked toward Dr. Meg's office, which was in the same building as the dining room but with a separate entrance off to the side. Inside the entry door was a hallway, one side lined with glass cabinets, while at the end hung two solid wood doorways towering like sentries proudly protecting the cabinets' treasures. One door led to the kitchen, and the other was the door to Dr. Meg's office. This was the first time Tarif had been on this side of the building. He slowed his steps to take in the new scenery. Stopping in front of one of the glass casings to study its contents, he noticed it was filled with an array of organized clutter, telling stories of various peace camps held over the years. He could see a variety of photos, t-shirts, newspaper clippings and homemade trophies made from everyday ordinary things.

In one display cabinet, a younger Dr. Meg was standing in a photo next to several campers in matching camp shirts, revealing large grins and stained faces. Beneath the photo was a trophy made of an aluminum pie plate that said, *Gold Medal Winners, Pie Eating Contest, 1986*. The cabinet next to it held photos of staff from different years. One photo was of Dr. Meg's profile while standing on the beach at sunset, looking out thoughtfully over the lake. This was the side of Dr. Meg that Tarif was most familiar with from the fire circles. Other photos were part of the newspaper clippings, some black and white and some in color. They all seemed to have one main theme, how the hundreds of lives that came to this forested haven were forever changed.

Tarif's mind flashed to his dad's anger the last time he came home ranting how the Jew's took his home, and how he'd lost yet another job. His mom cried, shaking her head, while Tarif sat at the dining table with his head down, feeling helpless. All three of them then ate their dinner quietly lost in their own worlds of fear, mixed with fantasies of something better. If Tarif changed like the people in the photographs had, it would make his mother happy. But it would leave his father with nothing.

Dr. Meg was reaching for a wooden box on a shelf above a pair of old wooden chairs with leather upholstery when Tarif slowly entered her office. The chairs looked like those his father had made when he was between jobs to make ends meet. He was good at making furniture and Tarif often helped. "Come on in Tarif. I'm getting ready for fire circle tonight," she explained as she set the box down on her desk. The afternoon since the kayaking incident had passed quickly. It was almost dinnertime.

She brushed off her hands and invited him to sit on one of the chairs while she sat slightly poised on the other, as if compassionately inviting him to meet her at a place in the heart. She looked at his dark hair and tired face and gave herself a minute to take it in. "Rob said you were soaking wet when you got out of the kayak with Aharon and that only one of you was wearing a life jacket. Is that true?"

"We got stuck, and then he pushed me into the lake."

Aharon? That didn't sound like him she thought. "Really?" she inquired, trying to mask her disbelief. "What happened?"

"I said some things that made him really mad. We got stuck and he pushed me."

"Good thing you had a life jacket on, then," Dr. Meg laughed gently, trying to keep things light. She found that was the best approach with teens, she realized over the years, at least until they gave her a cue to go deeper. She remembered that Tarif refused to take the swimming test the first day, saying he didn't plan to swim. She had no idea what his swimming level was, but she had suspected he'd really refused because he couldn't swim.

Sheepishly, Tarif looked down more thoughtfully so than upset, "Actually, I wasn't wearing a life vest. Aharon lent me his afterwards to so I could stay warm." Dr. Meg's eyebrows raised, surprised and then her eyes darkened with concern. She took a slow deep breath to stave off the millions of anxious thoughts attempting to hijack her mind about what could have happened to Tarif. She wanted to stay in the present and not get distracted just then. Experience had taught her that these kinds of moments could be a turning point for the most troubled and confused kids like

Tarif, something that could make all the difference, yet the windows of opportunities are often narrow and not so obvious at first. It took concentration and patience to find them.

"I'm miserable Dr. Meg. I want to go home."

"I can imagine based on the reports I've been hearing around camp. It also sounds like you've been sharing some of that misery with the other campers wherever you go, hmm?" She looked up at him gently with a slight smile, suggesting *it's ok, we can be honest friends here*. She changed tactics. "Whatever happened in the lake must've been quite scary for you." Tarif shrugged not giving away what he felt just yet. "I'm curious, what did you say to Aharon that made him so mad?" she gently probed him with her seasoned skill.

"He told me to enlighten him about how much he was hated. So I told him that it was too bad the Germans didn't get the job done." Tarif's eyes had a look of being unfocused, like he was lost in thought. Although her eyebrows raised again, Dr. Meg noted that his demeanor was different, softer and more inward, rather than the typical sullen sourness with a dark cloud over his head that she observed in him so far.

Tarif wasn't the first teen she'd counseled here that wanted to go home because he was still afraid to let go of all that he knew and learned back home. "Anything else?" Tarif shrugged as if to say, *yes, a few other things,* but he didn't speak further.

"Mmm hmm," she assumed understandingly. She was quiet for a moment, letting him stay with his thoughts, then she continued her gentle invitation to confide with a genuine caring in her tone. "I'm not seeing the anger I usually see Tarif. I'm curious what's happening for you now."

Tarif focused on the bookshelf in front of them. Although his eyes were unfocused, he could swear all the books seemed to say something about peace. "A strange thing happened to me when we were on the lake. Now I'm just confused." Dr. Meg swallowed, listening intently for the window of openness. She sensed it was coming. "Before, when I looked at Aharon or any Israeli, all I saw was a *thing*, like a dog, not a person. After he pulled me out of the water, we sat there for a while, not saying anything, and something changed. My eyes changed. He became something new to me."

"What was that?" she invited, curious.

He looked up at her for the first time since he had entered her office. "A person." He thought about his father and how much he loved him. "It surprised me."

Dr. Meg couldn't help but smile to herself, though she dared not show it. If this was all this summer offered him, it would be far greater than all the fire circles put together.

"We were sitting in that stupid boat, and all I could see was that we were both the same. What happened to me Dr. Meg? Are my eyes different?" He softened even further, "I thought I was going to drown. He should have let me." He paused as Dr. Meg took in the power of his humble honesty. "My father will never understand. He told me if I made friends here, he would disown me." He looked up at her again. "How could I do that to my father?"

Dr. Meg's heart felt the weight of his dilemma and dropped into a deeper place of sadness and empathy. It was always humbling to be reminded of the complexities that held Palestinians and Israelis frozen in their hatred.

"That must be really hard for you," she replied. "Because, as you've noticed," referring to the boat, "this place has a way of bringing people together."

Sadness crept into Tarif's eyes. For the first time, Dr. Meg saw what was underneath his venom and armor. Thinking back on some of her own high school years, she could see her own pain in his, though she couldn't tell him so.

"Tarif, I think you've stumbled into a rare healing. We make people inhuman when we are afraid, or when we have had so much loss that it seems unbearable to face it. We turn them into something we can justify hating, like animals or things. If they are less than human, we can do anything to them and not be accountable."

Tarif swallowed as if carefully weighing this. "I love my father, but my father hates Jews."

"That is a dilemma. Fathers are important to us." Dr. Meg said, well aware of the consequences that can unfold in his family tradition for expressing a different opinion than his father.

She continued, "It sounds like you received a powerful medicine for your eyes today, so that now you can see like a human being again." She drew in a deep breath at the weight of his reality. "Tarif, I can't fix what's happening for you at home. But I think I can help you with how to create a different experience here, if you're willing to feel differently."

Anything to get out of being this miserable, he thought.

"I'm not going to ask you to make friends here, as much as I'd like that for you. I'm just going to invite you to try another perspective.

"Like what?"

"Saying mean things and making people angry only makes enemies and I suspect that is one of the true reasons why you are miserable here this summer. It gets harder to face the day when you have created your surroundings that way." Tarif's thoughts briefly flashed to his father and the three jobs he had lost this last year. "Being nice doesn't necessarily mean you have to make friends. It can, however, go a long way to avoid making enemies, saving yourself some misery in the meantime." She paused while he considered this. "Just try being nice. I think you'll have a better time. What do you think?"

Tarif let out the slightest hint of a smile for the first time since he had been at camp.

"What happened between you and Aharon will be talked about by others. It's important to share your side of the story. I'd like you to do that tonight at the fire council."

"What do I say?" Tarif asked.

"The truth," she suggested, pointing to her heart. Tarif understood and was relieved to have an authority tell him to do just that.

Chapter 8

The fire danced handsomely, displaying its many versions of oranges, reds and yellows as it did every night from its inception when it was first lit, to its maturity when the flames transformed into glowing embers. Sara sat between Brenna and Amani, wishing she could be closer to Shacker, who was sitting laughing with Amar next to him. Dr. Meg stood up and began playing with the dirt on the ground with the toe of her hiking boot, as she often did, though looking more thoughtful than usual that night.

Aharon, who was sitting quietly next to Albert instead of joking with Shacker, kept looking at Tarif with an unusual seriousness in his eyes. Shocked, it almost looked to Sara like he seemed thoughtful and serious, not the usual annoyance or sarcasm attitude from Tarif. Every once in a while, Tarif, who was sitting near Dr. Meg, alone as usual, would catch Aharon's eye in return.

While other campers were laughing and joking about their various activities of that day, Aharon remained somber and thoughtful, as did Tarif. Sara nudged Amani to draw her attention to what she was witnessing. Amani looked inquisitively, then shrugged and turned back to Rebecca on her other side to continue their conversation about their dinner that night. They were trying to figure out if they could make the same shepherd's pie at home.

Dr. Meg held up her hand to signal for everyone to simmer down. She waited for the murmurs to settle into a respectful hush around the circle before she spoke. "Coming to this camp is one of the most courageous things many of us will ever do," she began. She included herself and the counselors intentionally. "And bringing what you receive here back home will be one of your greatest challenges, no doubt. I don't pretend otherwise. Most of us here will have to face friends who won't understand, and some," she looked at Tarif and then around the circle, "will have to face parents you love who also don't understand." Amani and Shacker gave each other a meaningful look.

Courage comes in many forms. When someone admits that they have been wrong, I think that takes great courage. Wouldn't you agree?" Murmurs of agreement were heard throughout the campers. Dr. Meg stepped closer to Tarif. "Aharon and Tarif went through something today that takes us to the heart of what we're doing here. I want to hear from them first tonight because they will bring us a lot to consider. But before we do, I just want to say this: everyone who comes here is invited to change the way they feel. Change isn't something we need to face alone. In fact, we are often more successful when we do it together." She looked kindly at Tarif. "Tarif and I talked earlier today, so I've heard his story about what happened. Aharon, I'd like to hear from you first. What can you share with us about what happened out on the lake?"

Aharon looked around the ring at the other campers and stood up slowly to give himself time to think. He wasn't sure what he needed to say so he cleared his throat and just started. "Tarif and I went kayaking on the lake today." There was a palpable tension in the circle with campers considering the idea of spending time alone with Tarif, which no one had dared to do up to this point. "He said some things that made me very angry. We got caught on something in the water that stopped the boat, and Tarif stood up to see what it was. I was so angry, I pushed him overboard into the water." Several campers snickered thinking this was just another funny story, but Dr. Meg held up her hand with a serious look. The campers hushed again sensing that this was different.

"What he said was so mean that I just wanted to get away from him. So I started to paddle away. He didn't have his life vest on, and I didn't know that he didn't know how to swim." Several mouths dropped with the seriousness of what Aharon just shared. Dr. Meg was weighing this new information. She didn't know he had paddled away at first. "I really wanted to leave him. When I finally realized he was telling the truth that he couldn't swim, I almost left him. I could have let him drown."

"But you didn't." Dr. Meg said kindly as if to invite more.

"No."

"What brought you back?" she asked carefully, genuinely curious. Several campers were leaning in, listening intently. Everyone wanted to know what he was going to reveal next.

Aharon blushed. "A bird pooped on my head." At first everyone was still in disbelief waiting for him to give the real answer. It was too ridiculous, and too perfect to be believable.

"Really!" he insisted. "That's what happened." Slowly the snickers came, and then the laughter. Even Dr. Meg covered her mouth with her fingers trying to be subtle, but she couldn't hide the sparkle of amusement in her eyes. She looked at Tandy and then looked up at her beloved trees feeling thankful for the uncanny magic of this forest. Bird shit saved Tarif's life. The ironies were endless.

"What kind of bird?" Shacker asked as a joke, laughing so hard tears were rolling down his eyes. He didn't expect Aharon to answer.

"Honestly? I think it was a dove." Shacker gave an incredulous look to which Aharon responded defensively, "Well It looked like the ones we saw on our hike." Aharon could understand and even appreciate the laughter, but he wasn't quite ready to participate in it himself, just yet. He was still feeling the pangs of the realities he'd faced that afternoon.

"Seriously? No!" Shacker slapped his leg laughing uncontrollably and rolled backwards off of the log. "A bomb from peace!" At this, everyone lost it, including Rob and Tandy. The fire laughed along with them as it spit up sparks in celebration of tension released from all the campers.

Aharon shrugged as if to say. *What can I say? It happened.* Then more quietly and in reverence he jutted, "something happened; that's for sure." He then looked up at Dr. Meg and signaled that he didn't have any more to say just then. Tarif's eyes had widened with Aharon's true confession. He was too busy nearly drowning to notice what had made Aharon turn back to save him. His eyes seemed to be sparkling in amusement too, even though he had a lot on his mind.

Dr. Meg, still covering her mouth with her fingers while making every effort to be a serious adult to keep the integrity of the circle, took a long deep breath to relax, and then signaled for everyone to settle down. "So as I said before, when someone admits that they have been wrong, I think that takes great courage." Murmurs of agreement were heard throughout the campers. Dr. Meg stepped up to Tarif and signaled him to stand. She was so close she could put her arm around him, but respectfully she didn't. "Tarif has come to realize that he hasn't been fair with all of you. And he wants to ask for a favor. Would you please give him your attention now?" As she spoke she looked at him and subtly pointed to her heart as a reminder of her advice earlier in her office.

Tarif stood up and pushed his hands nervously into his pockets as deep as they could go. "I would like to say something to all of you."

Sara's heart sank as she was weary of Tarif's 'honesty' from previous circles. But then she noticed his demeanor had changed. Many of the campers were looking at him with quiet respect. He had almost drowned that day. It was a sobering idea, even when it involved Tarif. *Maybe this is different,* she thought.

Sara could only imagine how hard Tarif's heart was beating. He shifted his weight and ran his hand nervously through his hair.

"I'm sorry for being the way I have been," he paused. "Not just to Aharon, but to everyone. My father said he would disown me if I ever made friends with a Jew. My mother is different. She doesn't want me to hate. So, I have been very confused. I love my father and I don't want to disappoint him." Everyone around the campfire could appreciate this, not just the Palestinians. Amani gave Shacker a soft, empathic look.

Tarif took a long breath looking at the ground thoughtfully, "After today, I see things differently. I don't want to be miserable anymore." There was a break in Tarif's voice as he spoke next. "I don't really want to be mean. I just didn't want to betray my father."

Dr. Meg waited a moment and then looked softly at Tarif with pride and prodded gently, "Is there anything you need from the group?"

"I am going to try to be different – not mean. I need a new start," Tarif said humbly.

Justin, an Israeli, stood. He was one of the youngest campers. His usual bright, round face was scrunched up in thought and seriousness. "Honestly, Tarif, I hear what you're saying but I don't know if I can trust you."

Everyone was quiet. This was an uncomfortable moment. Justin was acknowledging everyone's negative experiences of Tarif that week. He hadn't given anyone any reason to trust. Yet, Sara thought something real happened on the lake that day. Something had changed. Her mind flashed to his sneering remarks to her on the trail that day with Amani, then to her summer project that had failed, and then to her dad whom she hardly knew, and the peace he had dreamed of, and finally to his death. She felt something stirring in her, but she didn't know what it was, at least not yet.

Aharon stood up and everyone's attention fixed on him. Sara wondered what he was going to do. *Can he forgive Tarif, or will he be more like Justin, maybe even refuse his apology?*

Aharon stood tall, like he was in control, but there was also something humble and mature about the way he carried himself. "Tarif, I discovered something today that surprised me. I've also been confused." This caught Sara and several others by surprise. Aharon always seemed so confident. Aharon continued, "I now know that I've judged you just as much as you've judged me. I've thought some awful things about you, too. I'd also like to put all that behind us and start over." Aharon paused for a moment, looking at Tarif who nodded and shyly gave a small smile. Justin sat with his finger against his mouth thinking this over. Some of the campers' mouths gaped partly open, watching every movement unfolding before their eyes, while others were looking at the ground, or shaking their heads not wanting to accept Tarif. Clearly people were feeling and thinking different things, and no one was ready to make it easier. Sara thought they were going to need help to figure this out, but she didn't look to Dr. Meg. Something else happened instead...

At that moment the fire popped, and Sara found herself standing up before she realized what she was doing. Suddenly she knew what she had to say. "We were asked from the very first fire council to do one thing, to simply be willing to feel differently. If we hold on to old feelings, then we're stuck – nothing changes" She looked directly into Tarif's eyes with all of her courage as her knees shook. "I have also judged you, Tarif. I believed that you were a mean person that couldn't change. I don't think that is true. I think something happened today that maybe changed you. I think if I don't give you a second chance, then why did I come to this camp in the first place?"

Her courage continued rising, as a small crack opened through the crust of her heart, exposing a light she hadn't felt since her father had died. She took a deep breath and tried to steady her shaky voice from feeling some of the sadness that had been locked for so long inside of her, for her father's unseen dreams, for her friends sitting around the fire and back home, for Dr. Meg, and even for Tarif. "I'm willing to feel differently about you, Tarif."

Sara sat down shaking, but not from fear. She had shared what she honestly felt. She didn't fear what others would think. She had simply told the truth.

Dr. Meg entered the circle again, speaking thoughtfully and carefully. "We've heard a lot tonight, and we all have a lot to consider. I want each of you to look deeply inside yourself." She paused, "Are you willing to extend Tarif a second chance? In the morning, I would appreciate your answer."

~~~

The campers were slow to rise, deep in thoughts of their own. There *was a lot* to consider. Slowly, one by one, they rose, some throwing a stick or a few needles on the fire as if a gesture of completion for the night. Shacker looked straight at Sara, his deep brown eyes beaming with pride. *She was wonderful,* he thought.

"You were amazing!" Amani squealed as quietly as she could in Sara's ear. She put her arm around Sara as they walked side-by-side out of the fire ring and down the path to their cabin. "I've decided I'm willing to feel differently. About my brother anyway. It's okay, you can date him."

Sara's eyebrows raised, and her stomach dropped. "It was an experiment, Amani," she whispered. "I didn't say I wanted to date him." *But then,* she thought as she considered this idea, *maybe I'm willing to feel differently.* They continued to walk down the path arm and arm as a warm glow filled her body and the night air grew warmer.

~~~

Back at the cabin, the girls were buzzing in loud whispers about what had happened at the campfire meeting that night.

\Having already changed into her flannel pajamas, Tandy motioned the girls to sit with her on the floor. They all grabbed pillows and blankets and situated themselves comfortably in an oval shape between the two rows of bunks. She began "So, as Dr. Meg said, we have a lot to think about, but she also noted, we don't have to do it alone. It can be really helpful to think through things with others and to hear different perspectives." She paused and looked around at their faces, each with a variety of expressions. "What did you think of tonight? About what was said? Does anyone have anything they want to share?" She then added, "Let's just remember to stick with the heart tonight." The girls got very quiet.

Dana raised her hand. "Well, it's hard because my parents were killed by Jew haters like Tarif. Letting go of the past is asking a lot. I mean just think about it. You have to let go of a lot."

Rebecca interjected, "But Tarif didn't kill your parents. He's just been a jerk."

"Yes, but the way he acts makes me think about it." Several girls gave appreciative and understanding nods.

"What about you Amani?" Brenna asked. She could see her lost in thought.

"It's hard to want to feel differently about someone. What if you want to feel differently, but at the moment you don't?"

Tandy looked to see if she wanted to express her thoughts. "I have found that the first step is always to be willing. If you are willing, something always happens to meet that willingness. I'd like to think that anything is possible."

"Really? Do you think that if we thought differently we could stop the guys from pulling pranks on us!" Adeela laughed in the spirit of teasing.

Peace Train

"Well, almost anything!" Tandy laughed tapping Adeela lightly with her pillow. They all giggled and laughed until Rebecca instinctively picked up her pillow and lightly hit Amani.

"Oh! No way!" Amani squealed as she hit Rebecca back. More squeals and laughter rang out as the girls quickly caught on, until Dana shouted, "Pillow fight!"

Sara stepped back and looked around at her American camp family as in a moment out of time. She was seeing all moments in one as she realized that everyone there was already feeling differently. She quietly closed her eyes in the middle of the squeals of delight and mayhem. *I hope I never forget this moment.* As she opened her eyes and looked at her new best friend another thought came in. *And may I always be willing to feel differently.*

Chapter 9

The next morning, the campers gathered in the main hall after breakfast. Everyone was unusually quiet and the tension in the room was heavy.

Dr. Meg stepped into the circle. "Forgiveness comes easily with friendship. Now is the time to see what people are willing to do when it isn't easy and when there isn't that trust to rely on yet." As she declared this she was staring at her toe while moving an invisible piece of dirt again. And then she looked up at the campers awaiting her thoughts. "When we judge, when we are angry, when we are afraid, when we feel we are better than others, and *even* when we walk away and do nothing, we disconnect from our hearts." She paused. "Consider that the best of you comes from your heart." Dr. Meg looked around the room and made eye contact with every camper as she brushed back her curly hair and continued, "Last night, I asked you to go deep inside and ask yourselves if you could give Tarif a second chance. Who wants to go first?"

Amani raised her hand. "I've noticed a change in Tarif since his kayak trip with Aharon yesterday. There is something different about him. I believe he wants to change." Amani turned her head to look at Tarif. "So yes, Tarif, I am definitely willing to give you a second chance."

Relief washed over Tarif's face. "Salam." He slowly stood up and addressed the group as Sara noticed that he had more energy in his body, spoke with a lighter tone and even offered some eye contact. "I think I understand why I have acted so mean. As I said yesterday, I've never been around Jews before. I've just heard my father talk about how selfish and ruthless they are, and" – He looked down at his feet and almost mumbled-- "and I began to see them as less than human." Sara swallowed and looked over at Amani. "Sometimes I think it's my father's voice coming out of my mouth and not mine." There was a hushed understanding as so many of them had experienced the same thing. "I think I have been seeing the world through his eyes." He paused and then sat down. The room was silent.

Aharon raised his hand. "Dr. Meg," Aharon looked haunted like he desperately needed to speak. Dr. Meg nodded at him. "The other day when Tarif and I were in the kayak, and I started to paddle away, I was so mad. I mean I was so mad; I could've let him die. And I was the one who pushed him in. I could have killed him. I never expected to feel like that, or do something that awful. It bothers me that I have that in me."

Dr. Meg walked toward Aharon and put her hand on his shoulder speaking his name softly "Oh, Aharon," with empathic understanding. "Does anyone want to give Aharon a different perspective?"

"That could have been any one of us, Aharon," Amani spoke softly from the heart.

"I don't know what I would have done if it was me in that boat," Justin piped in honestly.

"I think you've helped me to understand a lot," added Shacker.

Turning to Aharon, Dr. Meg added, "I think you are missing something here. Every one of us in our lifetime will get into situations that challenge us greatly. The question is, what do we do when we are challenged? Do we lose our head and do something stupid which we regret later, or do we do what is right? The point I'm trying to make is that you thought about leaving Tarif, but you didn't. You stopped, turned back and helped him. He didn't deserve to be helped but you did it anyway. To me that showed your maturity and your character."

Aharon smiled, taking a breath of relief for the first time since he was in the boat with Tarif. There was a pause in the room.

Albert raised his hand. Dr. Meg acknowledged him as he adjusted his glasses. "Shalom," he said in a hoarse voice. "I've been awake most of the night." Some of the girls shifted as Sara remembered Rebecca saying it would be harder for the boys. Sara had slept deeply, though she did dream a lot. The hardest part for them that night at the cabin was cleaning up after the pillow fight. Albert continued. "Early this morning, I remembered my grandmother and a last-minute gift my mother made me pack."

He held up his backpack but didn't reveal the contents inside quite yet. "It was in honor of my grandmother who used to tell us a story. She said that in Greek mythology, Poseidon claimed possession of Athens by thrusting his trident into the Acropolis, where a wall of seawater gushed out, spilling over everyone and the land. He felt triumphant by his claim. But even though his water had taken everything, the court awarded Athena the land because she claimed it by planting an olive tree beside the well as a symbol of peace. As he said this, he pulled out a simple olive branch. He nervously pushed up his glasses on his nose again and went on, "Athena was given the land of Athens because she had given the better gift.

"I know I haven't gotten to know all of you, but I've been really happy here. Last night as I laid awake, I wondered why I've been happy. It's because I feel free and peaceful here. There's been many olive trees planted." The hoarseness had crept back in and he cleared his throat again. "I'm scared a lot at home. But here, I'm already sad that these three weeks will end." Albert adjusted his glasses again and then looked out at some of the campers. "I really don't want to go home. I just want to stay here, and I think the reason I feel this way is because I finally understand the meaning of the story my grandmother told me. At home, I keep sticking my trident into the ground everywhere I go, judging people, being afraid that someone is going to bomb me, and continuing to repeat the stories everyone says. And all I've gotten from that in return is fear.

"I'm afraid at the border crossings. I'm afraid as I walk home from school. I'm afraid when I go to the store that someone will blow me up, but here, I smile and say shalom to everyone and the fear has vanished." He held the branch up a little higher to illustrate his point. "At home we would never meet, let alone get into a water balloon fight together," he grinned. "Here, I've been planting olive trees." They all sat in a reverent silence as they considered what he proclaimed. His words moved through them like a powerful river rushing to fill barren lands with its cooling nourishment. But then what he did next surprised them.

Albert walked over to Tarif and handed him the olive branch. "Tarif, I want to give you this branch that my mother gave to me. Hating you is easy because the trident is so familiar, but I want to give you a second chance because it's a better gift, and it'll bring me peace for sure and maybe even a new friend."

Rebecca's mouth fell open in amazement.

Tarif took the branch and nodded a Salam. It was the first time Sara had seen Tarif touch anyone.

One of the boys, Amar, was noticeably upset as he rubbed his hand through his dark, curly hair. An air of fear and concern surrounded him. "Hey man what are you doing? A do-over really? And the olive branch – really? What about retribution? I have been really nice here because I haven't wanted to make waves, especially because I knew I was outnumbered. Tarif, how can you just let it all go? How can you ask us to let it all go? We have been so wronged. We have been treated so badly. What about being right?" Amar sat down quietly. His pain was evident and the dark circles under his eyes told the story of his long stormy night.

Dr. Meg responded carefully, "Being right can create a really powerful feeling."

"For a while," Tandy added. Dr. Meg smiled at her and nodded in silence.

Sara saw Aharon raise his hand again and hope rose in her. The discussion had suddenly gotten uncomfortable, but she was sure Aharon would have something wise to say. She realized that she had started to look at him as a leader, and she was grateful. Dr. Meg nodded at him.

Aharon stood up. "I woke up before anyone else and haven't been able to stop thinking about it. What dawned on me this morning, after my experience with Tarif on the lake, is that it hasn't been easy for any of us on either side. We took their land and then they bombed us. We've been hurting each other in the name of being right for a very long time. We've all treated each other badly. Who's right? Who's wrong? We both are. So, the question is, is being right more important to you than being peaceful?

Dr. Meg smiled at this. She couldn't have said it better herself. Then she asked, "Amar you are asking Tarif to give up being right. Why?"

Amar answered quickly and pointedly, "If we let go of being right, we lose everything."

Dr. Meg raised her eyebrows. "Are you sure about that?"

There was a long silence. Dr. Meg waited for each camper to consider her question. Shacker raised his hand to speak.

"If we are playing a game, sure. Then it's important to win, to be right. But I think something else is going on here. I've been wondering why Aharon and I became friends so quickly. What I

Peace Train

realized is that we had so much in common, that we forgot to talk about our stories. I'm not sure why it was so easy to let them go; it just happened." Shacker glanced over at Aharon and they gave each other a friendly smile. "At home, I wouldn't have given Aharon a moment to see if we had anything in common. When we let go of the story, then we don't have to be right or wrong about anything. Sometimes, I think we have an even greater opportunity than winning." He put his arm around Aharon in demonstration and grinned. "Friendship."

Sara was turning everything over in her mind when she saw Shacker wink at her. *He's enjoying this.* She blushed.

Dr. Meg cleared her throat and smiled at Shacker as she said proudly. "Thank you."

Then Tarif raised his hand. "I just realized something. When I asked everyone for a new beginning, I was actually asking myself for a new beginning. I was asking myself to let go of the past and to start over, no more story. My father doesn't want me to let go of his story. He has chosen to be right and he is miserable. He never smiles. If I come home and don't see it his way, I don't know what will happen. But I want to try something new here and see what happens." He looked over at Amar. "I don't think anybody is asking us to change the world. We are talking about right now here at camp. Let's just see what happens. There's nobody around to judge us."

Dr. Meg responded. "So, let's just simplify this for a minute and look at the original question. What matters more to you? Friendship? Love? The possibility of peace? Or, being right?" She looked around at everyone in the great hall they were gathered in. The air echoed with deafening thoughts, though not a single word was spoken.

Amar shook his head. "Boy, it's hard to give up being right. When I know I'm right, everything is great."

Dr. Meg slowly asked again, "What matters more to you? Friendship? Love? The possibility of peace? Or, being right?"

Shacker piped in, "Amar, remember the first day when we played dodge ball? I don't know about you, but I just forgot everything and had a wonderful time with everyone. Didn't you? Wasn't that better than being right?"

The shadow that had hung perilously over Amar's face was replaced by a lightbulb that became visible in his head and a smile spread across his face for the first time since the conversation had started. *He got it,* Sara thought.

"Something else was going on there. We were just kids playing a wild and wonderful game together and nothing else mattered. We were just teammates having a great old time. It blows your mind when you think about it," Shacker grinned.

Tarif stood up quietly and began to break off pieces of the olive branch. Sara sucked in her breath as she thought maybe he was angry again and had changed his mind. But his movements were slow, thoughtful, even reverent. Amani gave Sara an inquisitive look. *What's he doing?*

"I am planting an olive tree with each of us. I may not be able to be your friend right now, but I can be nicer, and then who knows what might happen." He walked around the circle stopping to hand a piece of the branch to each person. When he got to Amar, he reached out his hand. To Tarif's surprise, Amar grabbed it and pulled himself up from the ground, wrapping Tarif in a big bear hug before he could react. He stood frozen, then softened and closed his eyes.

When Tarif got to the end of the circle, there were three pieces of the branch left. He gave one to Dr. Meg who stood looking at him with flushed cheeks and moist eyes. Then Tarif looked at the last two pieces and said, "This one is for me" as he held one piece up. "And this one I will save for my father."

Sara took her piece and turned it over and over in her hands. It was smooth. She wanted it to last forever.

Dr. Meg took a deep breath as a tear spilled over, then swallowed. "You are all very courageous. Being right is a very powerful feeling. It can be like a drug. When you realize you don't need the drug anymore, you get to discover something that feels much better – "

"Yahhhhh," Shacker interrupted.

Dr. Meg looked down at her shoe and went into a vulnerable intensity again like the first night. "May what has happened here stay with each of you forever." She took another deep breath, looked up at them all, beaming and placing her hands together as if to say *that's it, you're free to go*.

One by one the campers stood, turning to one another and hugging each other. Words were difficult. A new energy was in the air, but what it meant here forward, they didn't know.

Outside, Sara caught up with Aharon and put her hand on his back. "Last night when Dr. Meg said something had happened between you and Tarif in the kayak, I judged you for going with him. I thought it was the stupidest thing to do."

Amani had caught up to them and added "Yeah, I was really afraid for you, too."

Sara finished by revealing, "But now I think it was the bravest. I'm so glad you did."

Aharon nodded. He was somber, but lighter and happier in his spirit from the night before. "It was really terrible at first, and I felt really badly afterwards. Last night was rough. But in the end, I think Tarif might really be a good guy."

"At least we now can see he's human." Amani chimed in. They all laughed at the irony of how both sides saw it so differently just the day before.

Sara gave Aharon a friendly side hug. "This may change his whole life."

Aharon laughed nodded in agreement. "Forget Tarif! It's changed mine!"

"I think it's changed everybody's," Amani said cheerfully as she remembered all the faces and what was said that morning.

Chapter 10

That evening after dinner, the girls walked back to their cabin together. They had all noticed the boys had been late to dinner and wondered what was up. As the girls walked down the path, they tried to walk arm-in-arm and sing as they went, but trees and stumps and things kept hindering their progress and throwing them into fits of laughter. Suddenly, one of the girls ran ahead. She opened the door of the cabin and when she looked inside she froze. The girls saw what was happening, they too froze and then made a mad dash for the cabin. They could not believe their eyes. Their entire cabin had been filled with toilet paper.

Tandy, "Oh my gosh!"

It was impossible to walk through the door without being completely engulfed in TP. The girls groaned.

Sara was annoyed, "How long will it take us to clean this mess up? It's going to take us all night!"

Tandy ran up the step and addressed the girls, "Let's see how quickly we can clean this up. We can brag to the guys and then we can plan our counterattack."

The girls responded with a new sense of purpose. Tandy started her stopwatch, which she always wore around her neck. "Okay girls, ready set go!" The race was on. Each girl sprang into action. They each went to their bunks first and started wadding up the TP there. The wadded TP was thrown into a pile on the floor in the middle of the room. Amani had looked at it not two minutes before and it had been flat and now it was over one foot high. The girls worked like little bees. They pulled down all the streamers that were hanging in the rafters. They unwound their beds that had been neatly packaged. They unwrapped their pillows and some found their sleeping bags full. The pile on the floor grew minute by minute. In ten minutes the job was done.

Tandy reached for her watch and announced, "The winning time is ten minutes and 30 seconds. And our pile is about four feet high."

Sara wondered where they got that much toilet paper. She hoped that they would have enough for the rest of camp. The girls then carried the pile of toilet paper and put it on the guy's front steps and walked away.

That evening, the girls were all in their bunks ready for bed, but no one was sleepy.

Rebecca, who had been snuggled in her sleeping bag, sat up. "We've got to think of something good. They've gotten us practically every day this week." They all laughed, rolled their eyes and groaned. It was both funny and annoying.

"Ugh, you're not kidding. Loosening the lids to the salt shakers was so gross. My eggs were ruined." Adeela complained.

"It wasn't even funny." Amani complained. "At least they could come up with something original."

Rebecca added, "I wish we could! I'm beginning to feel really stupid. And they're not even that smart!" she said teasingly. Several of the girls giggled.

"Tandy, what did you do when you went to camp here? Were the boys this bad then?" Sara asked.

Tandy smiled and rolled her eyes, but didn't answer. "Not that I would ever stoop to such childish pranks at my age, but--" she said suspiciously with a large grin as she reached under her bunk into her duffle bag and pulled out an air horn. "This puppy is a lot more alarming from a foot outside your window than that camp bell is."

The girls all squealed in delight.

Brenna grinned, "Well, you know how the boys *love* their beauty sleep."

Everyone was excited by the possibility.

"That will definitely catch them off guard!" Rebecca exclaimed as they all laughed in delight.

As Tandy set the air horn down, her look of intrigue vanished as well. "I also have another idea for the boys that I think will catch them off guard even better. I want you all to consider it. It's a different kind of revenge, one that they will probably remember much longer than the air horn. Everyone perked up with juicy anticipation expecting the most spectacular prank ever done at summer camp but were surprised by what she revealed. "What if we wrote them letters of acknowledgement—you know, letters that tell them how we admire them. We can keep them all anonymous and just put them in a pile on their doorstep."

"What?" Rebecca asked incredulously.

"No way!" Dana cried disbelievingly.

"How is that revenge?" Rebecca added.

Tandy patiently went on, in a way that Sara suspected came from a deeper knowing. "I know the pranks have even been kind of mean at times."

"Like the salt. I hardly had any breakfast that day." Adeela complained.

Tandy gave Adeela a sympathetic pat. "But have you ever heard the American phrase, 'Kill 'em with kindness'?" The girls were confused and intrigued. "What if we did just that? We shock them with something kind when they're totally not expecting it and they'll feel terrible about the way they've been treating us. It usually stops them in their tracks."

Amani still wasn't sure she was convinced. "So, they pull a bunch of tricks on us, including locking us in the bathroom and toothpaste everywhere, but we just write them sweet notes to get back at them?"

Tandy fluffed her pillow and put her head on her hand, leaning on her elbows. "Sometimes the easiest way to make a bully feel bad is by being nice." She smiled. The girls started to catch on to the brilliance of an idea that was completely new to them. Big grins grew slowly on their faces replacing furrowed brows of confusion as they looked around at each other, eyes shining with delight in silent connection through their planned revenge. Tandy rolled onto her back and folded her hands under her head. "It's not such a bad thing to encourage each other every once in a while, either, you know. You never know what good might come back to you, sometimes when you're least expecting it."

Sara looked down at her friend in the bunk beneath her. Sara had hung out with Amani enough to know that 'kill 'em with kindness' wasn't Amani's style, at least with her brother.

Tandy threw her pillow at Amani playfully. "Oh, come on, Amani! You'll see; I bet it makes them feel ten times worse than any nasty thing we could think of to do to them. But don't forget, we still have this." She picked up the air horn again. "On the last day of camp, we will use this to wake the boys super early. It would be a great ending. Essentially, we would have the last word."

The girls were silent for a few moments. Amani dramatically slumped back on her bed and blew out a breath. Sara had butterflies in her stomach. If the letters were going to be anonymous, she could write Shacker a note. She'd had very little time to be around him since the kiss.

"Shall we do this?" asked Tandy. Most of the girls nodded their heads *yes* and Amani even agreed to do it once she realized she could write a note to Aharon.

Tandy passed out pens and paper to each of them, so they could write their own letter to another boy camper. Amani chose to write to Aharon, and Sara of course chose Shacker. Tandy also passed out envelopes. Once each girl was done with her letter, she folded it up, sealed it inside an envelope and dropped it in the basket at the foot of Tandy's bed. The plan was for Tandy to go out after lights out and deliver the letters in front of the boys' cabin door that night.

It was close to an hour past lights out, and each girl had turned on her flashlight. There was a quiet sleepy buzz of excitement in the cabin as the girls shushed each other between giggles and whispers.

"Shhhhh," warned Tandy as she left with the basket of letters.

Sara kept checking her watch. It seemed to take so long before the girls finally heard Tandy's steps on the wooden deck outside signaling her return. As she came through the door she loudly whispered "I placed the basket on the bottom step. As far as I could tell, no one saw me or heard a thing."

"I can't wait for them to find it in the morning!" Rebecca giggled, a little too loudly.

Sara's heart swelled. In just a few hours, Shacker would be reading her note. *What will he think?* Almost every girl was thinking the same thing.

In the morning, the guys discover the letters on the way to the bathroom. They are stunned and excited. Shacker had read his over and over about five times already.

Dear Shacker,

I am so happy that I get to write you this letter of acknowledgment. You must know that the first moment people meet you, they are taken by your good looks. And then when you open your mouth, you always have something funny to say But I also think you are loving and supportive when you want to be. I don't know how you are able to be so positive. You have a kindness about you that is unusual for guys your age. You seem curious, funny, and fun to be around. I am so glad you're here. You make this experience so much more enjoyable. Good luck. I know that you will always be a success.

Your Friend

P.S. The kiss was amazing!

Chapter 11

The rising sun dusted the morning sky over the lake until dawn was clearly streaming out over the deep, restful night. A mist hovered over the water like the comfort of a soft, willowing cotton. A hazy sleepiness was replaced with the scurrying of the forest creatures when, without warning the clamoring morning bell rudely took over the little comfort left before the dawn. A groan of unified complaint was heard throughout the girl's cabin. The end of the second week was near, equal to the first, though distinct differences were beginning to show. Friendship was fast making its reach out of the fairy dusted sparkling water into the whispering pines, dispersing like delicate spores throughout the open air where they were breathing it all easily and gently into their hearts.

Sara leaned over her bunk and peered down. "Salam, Amani, are you awake?"

Amani stretched her arms out over her head and yawned. "You mean good morning. We're in America, remember?"

"Yah. Right. Good morning. How'd you sleep?"

Amani finally opened her eyes. A sleepy smile spread across her face. "I was having this wonderful dream. I was in the arms of a very cute guy and he was about to kiss me, then his lips suddenly turned into a giant alarm bell!"

"No!" Sara squealed in delight.

Tandy reached under Amani's bunk to grab a stray sock. "That guy sounds like a keeper." she joked as she tossed it on Amani's forehead.

"Gross!" Amani protested.

"Come on, girls—let's get a move on," was Tandy's only response. "Or you're going to be late."

Brenna moaned, squirming down further into her sleeping bag, "Let the boys beat us for a change." She said with a muffled voice. "They're always teasing us about how much time we take to do our hair. Let them be right for a change."

Suddenly awake and motivated, Adeela forced herself out of bed revealing hair that told of a night of wild dreams. As she sat up she exclaimed, "No way! We will never let them be right about us!" They all laughed at her sarcasm given some of the deeper conversations that week. At that, all the girls rallied into high gear, happily moving toward flags to keep their fun intact.

At flag-raising, the girls saw that most of the guys were carrying their letters and reading them with smiles on their faces. Even Tarif was holding his letter rubbing his fingers across it, looking around nervously.

From across the circle, Sara caught Shacker's eye. He smiled to her and mouthed the words, "Thank you." Her face went instantly red as she smiled down at her feet.

The flag poles were situated on a grassy slope beside the lake, which was shimmering in the morning sun. As the flags were being raised, the campers just stood quietly and watched. It was always the same, first the U.S. flag, followed by the Palestinian, then the Israeli. No one ever mentioned why, but Sara appreciated that they had all three.

Peace Train

Suddenly, someone slowly started clapping at the raising of the first flag. Sara grinned. As the second flag began, others joined in until she couldn't stand there and observe anymore, she found herself swept up into it. By the time all the flags were ruffling ceremoniously in the crisp morning breeze, everyone was clapping and cheering.

There was a moment of silence and then someone yelled, "last one to the lodge doesn't get breakfast!"

A horde of campers made a quick dash toward the dining hall door, valiant one moment, and then reduced to a herd of cattle rushing to the feeding troughs the next.

Dr. Meg chuckled in amusement and shook her head. Tandy came up beside her and patted her on the back, "Nothing like the promise of pancakes to remind us not to take ourselves too seriously. They're teenagers first, and stomachs second." She laughed.

~~~

After breakfast, Sara overheard Rob, the boys' counselor, say to Tandy, as he walked up to her in the dining hall. "Nice. Trying the old kill 'em with kindness routine, huh?"

Tandy shrugged her shoulders with a glitter in her eyes, feigning ignorance. "I don't know what you mean."

Rob laughed. "Well, you should know that the guys were very impressed. One guy said he had never read such nice things about himself. Most of my boys were pretty quiet about it all, but I know it meant a great deal to them.

Tandy smiled without saying a word and shrugged in her own confident response. She walked out the dining hall door, eager to get back to her cabin to tell the girls.

~~~

All the girls had planned to meet back at the cabin after breakfast to talk about the boys' reactions. They were all there when Tandy burst through the cabin door.

"It worked! They were surprised and pleased. Good job girls. I'm proud of you. So, now what should we do?"

They all shouted, "The air horn!"

~~~

It was the last night at camp. The girls were in their cabin, already dressed in their pajamas. Sara sat on Amani's lower bunk with her long legs crossed at the ankles. She looked over at Amani and sighed. "What's it going to be like back home? I can't imagine it will be the same after our time here. I'm so different now. I don't want to go back to be the same Sara I was before I came here."

Amani chewed on some licorice. She had already brushed her teeth, but Amani didn't care about things like that. She broke off another piece and put it in her mouth. "I know what you mean. I think I'm even going to miss Tarif. He has added some excitement and it turns out that I really like him."

Amani nodded in agreement and then both girls were quiet for a few moments. Finally, Sara revealed, "Amani, I'm going to miss you so much."

Amani quickly put her hand up to stop Sara from saying anything else. "No, Sara, if you say anything else, I'm probably going to cry."

Sara saw tears pool in Amani's dark eyes. "Amani, I think you're already starting to cry."

Sara wiped at her own tears that had begun to stream down her face. "It's just, I've never had a friend like you before." Sara leaned over to hug Amani and inhaled her familiar vanilla fragrance. *I think you're my new best friend,* Sara thought as she held Amani. She concentrated on all she had learned here. She couldn't imagine ever hating Amani just because she was a Palestinian... It wasn't fair that they would have to face that expectation at home. At least they would have each other and wouldn't have to face it alone.

Sara pulled away from the hug and looked into her eyes. "You know, we don't live all that far from each other. Let's promise to get together at least once a month. This friendship is too important to me, Amani. I want us to be friends for life."

"It's a deal!" Amani's smile spread across her tear-streaked face.

As Sara was about to climb up into her bunk, a beautiful sound wafted in through the windows, at first sounding like whispers from the pines. It was the boys singing, and sometimes whistling, the most beautiful song alongside Rob playing guitar. The girls stopped everything and just listened. They were transfixed.

They heard the song: Michael Row the Boat Ashore.

As the singing rose and fell in its humble emotion, Brenna finally got out of bed and opened the door to the cabin.

"Shhhh," one of the girls commanded when giggling erupted.

Nearly every girl covered her mouth in shock at the beautiful sight. Under a cloudless full moon night, every boy camper was standing in a line, arm-in-arm, as they sang. The light of the moon acted as a spotlight, illuminating their faces, and the forest floor was their stage.

Soon all the girls were humming along as the boys sang.

After all that they had gone through. It was a beautiful ending, one that would stay with everyone for their whole lives. It came to Sara that it was just what she needed as she faced leaving camp and this experience. She wondered to herself in her teen sort of way, *can love really change everything?* She found herself staring at Shacker's handsome face for most of the song. The light of the moon reflected off his shiny dark hair.

As the boys sang the last stanza of the song, they bowed to the girl campers and turned around to walk back to their cabin continuing to hum the tune.

Once the boys' voices were almost out of earshot, Tandy said, "Enchanting. That's one way to say thank you for the letters." A few of the girls giggled.

Rebecca sniffled and wiped a tear from her cheek. "Oh Tandy, how can we wake them with the air horn early in the morning now? Tonight they were so kind, like true gentlemen, to sing us that beautiful song. Are we really going to play a prank on them now?"

A few other sniffles were heard amongst the group. Adeela pulled out a small pack of tissues from her bathrobe and handed them out.

Amani chuckled and said, "Of course we prank them in the morning. They'll love the attention, even if it comes by way of a loud annoying air horn! It will be our way of thanking them!"

All the girls laughed. Tandy put her arm around Amani's shoulders and squeezed her. "I think you're right, Amani. Come on girls, let's get to bed. We'll need to wake up even earlier tomorrow" They groaned and giggled.

Once all the girls were tucked in, Tandy softly hummed the song. Some of the other girls joined in. Sara didn't know how long they kept up the tune. As she drifted off to sleep, her heart was full and ready for the future.

Chapter 12

Tandy's alarm went off at 5:30 am. Sara rolled over and groaned until she remembered why they were getting up ... *to prank the boys!* Instantly, excitement flooded her body and she popped up and leaned down over her bunk's edge to check on Amani.

"Amani, wake up! We've got to go sound the air horn with the others."

All the girls quickly got on their sweatshirts or bathrobes and slip on shoes. Tandy gave Dana the air horn and, within minutes, they were walking down the path towards the boys' cabin. The moon was still high, but the sky was starting to lighten ever so slightly. The girls remained quiet as they walked. They kept their footsteps as silent as possible as they dodged the dried leaves and stepped instead on the dark earth. It didn't seem right disturbing the forest at such an early hour.

Rebecca and Dana crept up the porch steps to the cabin door. Dana suddenly got scared "I can't do it," she whispered.

"Oh here!" Rebecca whispered back, refreshingly even surprising herself.

Rebecca held the air horn as Amani silently turned the knob. The door pushed open easily without a sound. Sara and some of the other girls plugged their ears in preparation. Rebecca extended her arm into the cabin with the air horn and pushed the button. It was so loud that it sounded like a thousand-ton cargo ship had just announced, without minding any manners at all, that it would be docking inside their cabin for the day. It was far louder than any of the girls expected. Terrified, shocked and excited, adrenaline took over Amani's arm as she slammed the cabin door shut chasing each girl sprinting down the path back to their cabin.

~~~

On the way to the last flag-raising, many of the girls walked arm-in-arm down the path. Some skipped, some sang camp songs, and some giggled as they recalled the morning's prank. They met the boys coming out of their cabin, who ran to give them hugs and hi-fives, highly impressed that they had pulled something so stealthily off, especially on the last day.

"Now that one I'll remember!" Shacker laughed slapping Aharon on the back in front of Amani and Sara.

Dr. Meg had a special morning prepared before the campers went their separate ways that afternoon on buses, and then planes, to return to their families. She had the campers gather at the campfire for one final meeting.

Dr. Meg stood before the group; the steam from her hot cocoa wafted into the crisp morning air. "Good morning, everyone. It's hard to believe this is our last meeting together."

Sara sat next to Amani. She put her arm around her friend and squeezed her tightly. Then she looked around at the other campers. A lump formed in her throat.

Dr. Meg took a sip of her coffee and smiled at the group. "I hear that you girls were treated to a wonderful serenade last night. And I hear you guys were treated to quite a different kind of serenade this morning." Everybody laughed at this. "But seriously, campers, I have to say that I'm so proud of you. Here we are on our last morning together, and what started out as a group of strangers now feels like a group of people who truly honor and respect each other." Dr. Meg picked up a pinecone and held it out for the group to see. "What I would like you to do over the next several minutes is to find yourself a pinecone. It shouldn't be too hard to do on this forest floor. Then we will all gather around the fire. I'd then like every camper to share what this time at camp has meant personally. To symbolize our experience, we will throw our pinecones into the fire."

Sara liked the idea of ending with a meaningful activity. She got up and made her way over to a nearby tree. All the campers were quietly hunting for their chosen pinecone. Sara saw a large one sitting at the base of a tall oak tree. The perfectly-shaped pinecone was deep brown in color. She grabbed it and made her way back to the bench to sit next to Amani, who had a smaller pinecone cradled in her hands.

The fire crackled. It wasn't a huge bonfire that morning, but it was warm. Sara could feel its heat on her face and chest. She looked around at the group slowly reassembling around the campfire. Each camper had a pinecone nestled in his or her hands. *Every face I see is the face of a friend. How is that possible? At first, we were so full of fear. And now look at us! We are like a family.*

Dr. Meg stood before the group with a pinecone in her hand. "Campers, this morning we celebrate what you have discovered during the last three weeks. Celebrations put exclamations on experiences, and what we are about to do now will carry this experience on to the next parts of your journeys. So right now, take a moment to think about what you have discovered and received here at camp. As you put that thought into your pinecone, it will become the symbol of these things. When it is your turn, share that thought with us, and then throw your pinecone into the fire. As it burns, those gifts will be released into the world."

Amani and Sara stood together, arm-in-arm. Sara spoke first. "When I was a little girl, I was told that Israeli people and Palestinian people didn't have anything in common. So, I have a question. Why is it that Amani and I talk about everything all day long? I am Israeli, and she is Palestinian. She is my very best friend. So, you ask, what am I most happy about? It is discovering that Palestinians and Israelis do have a lot in common, and I'm so glad to have discovered this. I'm also very glad to have a best friend like Amani."

Sara threw her pinecone into the fire. It crackled and popped in celebration of the gift's release.

Then Amani spoke. "I remember when I was a little girl my father told me to never touch an Israeli. He never really said why, but I believed him. The first day here, as Sara and I were getting settled in our bunks, I wondered what would happen to me if I touched her. What I've discovered over the past three weeks is that she is just like me." Amani turned to Sara with tears in her eyes and said, "I'm going to miss all of your hugs, Sara." She looked back at the group and said, "I've touched so many Israelis here and it has been a wonderful experience. I can hardly wait to tell my father. So I'm thankful for the friendships I've made here. This has been a wonderful journey that I will never forget."

Amani threw her pine cone into the fire and then turned to hug Sara.

Amar spoke next. "When I arrived here, I completely believed that the Israelis needed to leave our land and find a homeland somewhere else. But something has changed for me, and I really don't know how that change happened. I would be sad if the Israelis left. And of course, they deserve to have their own land, just as we do. How could I have missed this so completely? When we sang that song to the girls last night, I felt such brotherhood with the guys. I have never felt that before. So, as I throw this pinecone into the fire, I want to say thank you to everyone here."

The fire crackled as the pinecone was consumed. The sun was rising higher in the sky and soon its heat would be intense, but a couple of hours remained before the morning chill was burned off completely.

Shacker stood with his pinecone. He ran his hand through his thick, dark hair. He smiled his big friendly smile, but then his face took on a thoughtful expression. "Like Amani, I remember being told by my father never to touch an Israeli. I too believed him for a while. The first day here, I met Aharon and we hit if off immediately. I think we've played basketball every day over the past three weeks. Oh, by the way, Aharon is Israeli. We learned the song together that we sang to the girls last night. I too felt brotherhood with the guys as we sang. I can hardly wait to tell my father about my new friends and about all I have experienced here. And Aharon and I have decided to continue playing basketball with each other back home. So, what am I thankful for? Everything! This has been a wonderful adventure."

He threw his pinecone into the fire. The remaining campers took their turns sharing and throwing their pinecones. Some talked about the peace they felt. Others talked about the oneness. But what everyone was really talking about was friendship, love, courage, acceptance, and hope. After a few moments, Dr. Meg stood and asked the boys if they would like to sing the song again.

The boys stood eagerly, as if they had rehearsed it, and began to sing. The sound echoed off the trees; it was almost mystical. Sara closed her eyes and let the sound fill her. She grabbed Amani's hand and squeezed it. Rebecca, who was on Sara's other side, grabbed Sara's hand. Soon, everyone was linked together. The girls started to sing with the boys.

When the song was complete, the teens sat quietly listening to the crackling of the fire, which was beginning to die down, and Dr. Meg spoke her final words to them.

This summer, each of you has found a place inside here," her voice faltered slightly as she tapped her heart. "We have all grown. You helped me to remember why I came here and why I come back year after year. When we are open to possibility, we're able to feel differently, and we learn that people are not mad at others for the reasons they think. People are angry because they bring forward a story from the past.

We have found at our camps that, if two enemies are doing something fun together – like playing a game or catching a loose dog," The campers laughed. "-- these enemies forget their story and discover a connection beyond it. Sometimes friendship blooms, but always the anger softens. We hope you will carry what you have learned here home and remember these faces, and that you are never alone." Referring to the staff she added, "Think of us from time to time. You are wonderful. Please don't forget that."

Dr. Meg looked at each of them in the eyes as she spoke, and when she finished, she fell into a silence. The fire crackled and what remained of the logs fell into the coal embers underneath. She smiled, and with a nod, dismissed the group. It was time to finish packing, to say final goodbyes, and to head onto the buses. Everybody slowly started to get up, but Sara and Amani remained seated on the bench with their arms linked together.

Amani swiped at a tear on her cheek. "Sara, you know it's a strange feeling. When I arrived three weeks ago, I felt sad. I missed my home. And now this morning, I feel sad again because I'm going to miss being with you every day. I'm so glad we're going to stay friends."

Sara squeezed Amani's arm a little tighter. "Yes, let's stick to our plan to meet monthly. I won't be home for a week because I'll be with my grandmother, but I'll call you as soon as I'm back. I know my mother will want to meet you. She is going to love you."

The girls hugged with tears in their eyes. Then they were engulfed by two huge arms. It was Shacker.

"What about me? Can I be your friend, too?"

Amani laughed at her brother. "Of course, silly, but Sara and I are best friends first, so don't butt in."

The three friends hugged each other a little longer, not wanting to let go.

PART TWO

Chapter 13

When Sara was a little girl, her father had pulled her around in a red wagon. He would tell a story about a princess who had the power to change the world.

"Sara," he would say, "the princess possessed this power because she believed it was real." He would tell the story as they journeyed through their old neighborhood, full of old oak trees and flowering shrubs. The smooth sidewalks providing the perfect track for the old red wagon. Often, he would pick a blooming flower on a dirt patch just beside the sidewalk.

"See this, Sara? This flower has so much courage and strength. It pushed through the hard dirt to show the world its beauty." He then gazed into Sara's big eyes. "You can bloom like this flower. Don't ever let the dirt of the world stop you from showing your true beauty." Sara's heart would swell as she looked at the flower and then into her father's smiling face.

When he died, Sara's world got a little less bright. She no longer had someone to remind her to be like the brave, strong flower. But as she left camp, she remembered his lesson.

Maybe I am like that flower after all.

The airport in Tel Aviv bustled with travelers and was carefully guarded by fully-armed soldiers. Sara scanned the terminal and spotted the Baggage Claim sign. She adjusted her backpack, tried to smooth her hair after the long flight, and, after a big sigh, headed toward the carousel to retrieve her bags.

After a full week of visiting with her grandmother, Sara was happy to be back in her country. Even though she missed the serenity of the woods at camp and the peacefulness she felt at her grandmother's farm, she was eager to hug her mother. Her bags were among the first to make their way down the chute and onto the carousel. Sara heaved them off and walked out to the agreed-upon meeting spot to reunite with her mom.

The hot air caused her brow to instantly bead with sweat. Sara wished she had her water bottle handy, but it was empty and packed away in her backpack. She shielded her eyes from the intense sun and scanned the area. It didn't take long for her to spot her mother. But then her heart skipped as she spotted another familiar face.

Amani?! Sara dropped her bags and ran up to Amani, who was wearing a cute sun dress. Her thick, bouncy black hair hung over her shoulders. *She obviously didn't just come off a plane, so what is she doing here?*

Amani hugged Sara tightly. "You're finally here!"

Tears pooled in Sara's eyes; memories of camp rushed through her mind. "But Amani, why are you here? I mean, I didn't expect to see you."

Amani giggled. "You told me when you were flying in, remember? I wrote down your flight number and made plans to be here when you arrived."

In all the excitement, Sara had almost forgotten about her mother. "Mom!" She practically engulfed her mom's petite frame; now the tears were streaming down her face. "Mom, meet Amani, my best friend."

Sara's mom smiled widely. "So, this is the special friend I've been hearing so much about. It truly is wonderful to meet you."

After the introductions, Sara realized that another woman was standing close by—Amani's mother. And then behind her was a tall boy.

"Shacker!" Sara let out a squeal and ran over to him, giving him an even bigger hug than she had given her mom.

He laughed and spoke in her ear. "Hey you. You are finally here." His sincere voice and tight embrace flooded her with warmth.

More tears streamed down Sara's cheeks. *It's that feeling again—the same kind of precious feeling I had so often at camp. It's a feeling of belonging and being known. It feels like camp has come home with me, and I hope it stays forever.*

Amani's and Shacker's mom, Mrs. Rahim, was dressed in her nursing outfit. She laughed and said, "Okay, Shacker, no need to smother the poor girl."

Sara's mother, Ms. Salinger, laughed along. "It would be nice for us all to become a little more acquainted. How about we find a coffee shop and chat for a while?"

Soon the five of them were sitting at a round wooden table with iced coffees.

Ms. Salinger took a sip of her coffee before tucking a strand of her curly hair behind her ear. "So, Amani, you are about the only part of camp I've heard from Sara. During our phone conversations while she was at her grandmother's house, I must have heard your name a dozen times."

Sara blushed as she looked at her best friend. "Yeah, I guess you could say I've missed you a whole bunch since we left camp. I've missed both of you." She glanced at Shacker and blushed a little more as she took a sip of her drink.

Mrs. Rahim and Ms. Salinger began talking to one another about their professions, which gave the three friends an opportunity to catch up on their week apart.

"So, how's it been being back at home this week? I have to admit, I've felt a little nervous about coming back, myself."

Amani and Shacker both nodded their heads and Shacker shrugged his shoulders. "Well, we are definitely not at camp anymore. It's been a little rough trying to relate to people at school, but I'm keeping it light. Maybe my fun attitude will help change things."

After their drinks were finished, Amani and Sara headed to the bathroom. They were holding onto each other like long lost friends. When they opened the door, they began to laugh because it looked just like the camp's bathrooms: small with tiled walls that cause an echo with every sound.

Sara marched up to the sink to wash her hands. "Amani, I still can't believe you met me at the airport. I was so surprised to see you! By the way, I love your mom."

Amani grabbed a paper towel to dry off her hands. "Your mom seems nice, too. I think they're both happy that we're friends. They seem to like each other."

Sara let out a contented sigh. "It feels so good to be home. I loved being with my grandmother but, after camp, it was a little much."

"What do you mean?"

Sara shrugged her shoulders as she dried off her hands. "Well, didn't you need some time to process what happened at camp once you left? I spent hours walking around my grandmother's garden just trying to make sense of what happened to me."

"Yes. I didn't go back to school the first week." Amani tossed her paper towel successfully into the trash can like she was shooting a basketball.

The girls headed back to their table, where the two mothers and Shacker were laughing. "Then it is settled," Mrs. Rahim said. She looked up at Amani and Sara. "Girls, we've decided that we all like each other a bit too much. What do you say we make this a regular gathering? Ms. Salinger, Shacker, and I have decided to meet weekly on Wednesday afternoons. This coming week we can meet at our house. How does that sound?"

Both girls squealed with delight.

Chapter 14

Sara and her mom stepped out of their car and stretched. Sara could feel butterflies in her stomach.

"Sweetie, I think that is the Rahim family house just up ahead—the white one with the grey door." Ms. Salinger smoothed her sundress. Sara checked her white tank top and flowing knee-length skirt.

Amani's and Shacker's house looked very modern. When Sara knocked on the door, Shacker greeted them with his usual flair. "It's great to see you two. Come on in." Shacker motioned Sara and her mom into the spacious living room.

Amani and her mother were sitting on a chocolate brown leather sectional that encircled a glass and metal table. Amani immediately jumped up when she saw Sara, greeting her with a big hug.

Mrs. Rahim was again dressed in her nursing uniform. She had just arrived home from work. "Have a seat, both of you. Amani arranged these refreshments for us while I was at work. Please, enjoy a roll and some tea." Indicating a platter of treats, Mrs. Rahim motioned for her guests to indulge.

Shacker sat down next to his mom. He grabbed a roll and poured himself a mug of tea. "So, Aharon and I have been keeping in touch, and I was thinking that he could join us on these days, too. How does that sound to everyone?"

Mrs. Rahim's face instantly brightened. "Oh, that would be delightful. I met him the other week. He is a charming boy."

Sara swallowed her bite. "Oh, I'd love to see Aharon. I've missed everyone from camp so much; it would be wonderful if we could all stay friends."

After the plans for the following week's get together were set, the girls and Shacker headed to Amani's room to talk while the mothers had another mug of tea together.

Amani's room was decorated in reds and blues with the same glass-and-metal style furniture as the living room. A blue overstuffed chair sat in one corner near the one window, which opened over the street. Shacker sat on the chair while Sara made herself comfortable on the bed.

Amani pulled out the chair to her desk and sat down. She smoothed out her dress and tucked her hair behind her ears. "So, Sara, how is school?"

Sara answered immediately, "Pretty awful." She shifted uncomfortably in her seat as she remembered her week.

Amani nodded in understanding. Sara continued, "All my friends are giving me a hard time. I even got called a Palestinian lover the other day. Someone yelled it across the lunch room. I almost died of embarrassment." Amani shook her head, trying to dismiss the thought from her mind. "I tried to talk to my closest friends about camp, but they just looked at me like I was crazy."

Sara grabbed one of the bed pillows and hugged it, her fingers fidgeting with the edges. *I have sure felt like a fish out of water since returning home.*

"Things haven't been easy for me, either," Amani lamented. "My Facebook page has been filled with nasty comments. I won't even show you them."

Sara winced and then looked up at Shacker. "How about for you, Shacker?"

"Well, the other day, Aharon and I were shooting hoops after school and some of my friends came up. I asked them if they wanted to play. They all looked Aharon up and down and then said some ugly things and said, 'Not with him.' I was disappointed but not really surprised."

Sara nodded. "I know. It sure feels good to talk to you guys."

"I feel so alone at school," revealed Amani, her shoulders slumping.

"I do too. I have never felt that way at school before. I wish we were back at camp."

Amani's brown eyes brightened at the thought. "Wouldn't that be great?"

Shacker leaned forward, resting his arms on his legs. "I'm going to continue to shoot hoops with Aharon. I plan to just ignore my old friends. I know what is important and, of course, I will keep it fun and light."

Sara's mood brightened at Shacker's courage. "That's great, Shacker. I'm going to try to talk to my friends again about what I experienced at camp. I just can't believe they are all so closed-minded."

"Don't get your hopes up," Amani huffed.

Shacker glanced over at his sister with sad eyes. "Sis, we've got to stay positive."

Suddenly they heard a loud knock at the door. The three listened as Mrs. Rahim answered the door. They could hear that Dr. Rahim had entered the home.

"Where are my children?" Dr. Rahim exclaimed, pushing his way past his former wife. He stopped and froze when he saw Sara's mom.

The three kids heard the commotion and quickly reentered the living room. Shacker immediately went over to his father and greeted him.

Dr. Rahim looked intently at Shacker and Amani. "Kids, I want to talk to you. As a matter of fact, I want to talk to all of you. I heard about this meeting. It's wrong. It was fine at camp, but these meetings have got to stop. It is not right for Palestinians and Israelis to be together."

Mrs. Rahim was noticeably disturbed by what Dr. Rahim said. "Dawood, you have no right to say what you are saying. This is my house and I will do whatever I want to do."

Dr. Rahim turned, addressing her pointedly. "Last I checked, my name was on the deed to this house. I may not live here anymore, but it's still mine."

Shacker walked over to his father and gently took his arm and turned him. "Father, we hear you, but I think it is time for you to leave." Shacker kindly but forcibly ushered him out of the room.

Dr. Rahim turned back with a warning. "You mark my words, this is wrong, and I am going to stop it!"

For a long moment, everyone froze, unable to process what had just occurred. Finally, Mrs. Rahim moved back to where she had been sitting. "He is just an arrogant pig. I say we just ignore him and continue. What can he do? Shoot us? He's too chicken."

Mrs. Salinger, hoping to change the mood, asked, "So kids, what were you talking about before we were interrupted?"

Sara began to speak. The tone in her voice betrayed her sadness. "Just how everything is so different at school now. Camp was so great, and everyone cared about each other. At school this week when I tried to explain how we all got along, the kids didn't believe me, and others called me names."

Ms. Salinger reached over and gave her daughter a hug. "Sara, even though it's not perfect, the United States is different. But in our country, there are too many hurt feelings from the past and no one seems able to let them go. You are very lucky you experienced what you did. Maybe the three of you can come up with a plan to help change things."

Mrs. Rahim nodded in agreement. "You kids experienced something important. It only takes a small number to make a difference. Don't be discouraged. Things may change at school. And as for your father, just ignore him and carry on."

Chapter 15

As the weeks went by, the group of six continued to meet regularly. Neither Shacker nor Amani saw much of their father. One week they decided to invite all the members of their extended families to their gathering. They warned everyone that there would be Israelis and Palestinians present, asking anyone having a problem with that to stay home. Amazingly, everyone came, even Dr. Rahim.

Shacker walked up to Sara and whispered in her ear. "It's obvious that many people here are uncomfortable, but at least everyone is getting along."

"I know," Sara said, somewhat in disbelief. "They've been eating together, playing games, and now even dancing together. This has gone way better than I imagined. Your father is definitely not happy, though." Sara casually nodded in Dr. Rahim's direction. "Look, even now he is scowling."

Shacker looked over at his father and then back at Sara. They both started to giggle.

~~~

Sara blew up yet another balloon. Her cheeks were starting to hurt as she tossed the finished balloon over to the side, where a festive pile was forming in her living room. "I don't know, Amani, do you think this whole party idea is such a good idea? I guess I'm starting to get worried that my friends are going to be nasty to your friends. I will be so embarrassed if they're rude."

Amani shrugged and rolled her eyes. "I know, Sara, I'm hoping that doesn't happen. They can be so nasty; it's ridiculous."

Well, at least we can say we tried, right? We can't control how other people behave, so let's just hope for the best. I mean, how can you not have fun when there's a whole heap of balloons and enough sweets to feed an army, plus good music?"

The girls laughed, some of their nervous tension dissolving. Soon the house was filled with a dozen teenage girls. They made baklava together and, before long, the kitchen was a sticky mess. Still, they were working together and laughing with each other. Sara felt that feeling of unity again. *This reminds me of camp!*

~~~

After the last guest left, Sara closed the door and turned to Amani with a heavy sigh. "Well, it mostly went well, but when I asked my friends if they wanted to do this again, they all said no. I just don't understand, Amani."

Amani crossed her arms in front of her chest and shook her head. "My friends said the same thing, Sara. I could tell they had fun, especially when we all made baklava, but it is like they refuse to see the world differently."

Sara furrowed her brow. "Well, we can't give up. We've got to keep trying."

Over the next six months, the girls continued trying to get their friends to connect, but every attempt was met with failure. After a while, Amani just didn't seem to care anymore. Soon even Sara gave up on the whole idea. In fact, Sara realized that the whole feeling of camp was starting to become a distant memory.

Chapter 16

Time flew by. After Amani and Sara graduated from high school, they started seeing less and less of each other. Eventually Amani graduated college with a degree in nursing and Sara chased after her dream of having her own radio show. Sara had moments when she thought about those precious days at camp that one summer, but her memories faded into the hustle of life.

~~~

Sara walked up to the white house and knocked on the familiar grey door. *It all still looks the same. It has been ages since I've been here—years, in fact.* She ran her fingers through her long, thick hair as butterflies chased around in her stomach. As she adjusted her sundress, the door opened.

Amani's eyes widened, and her smile beamed. "Sara!"

The girls wrapped each other in a hug. Sara noticed Amani smelled the way she always did, like fresh vanilla, but now there was a hint of lavender as well.

Amani pulled out of the hug and stared into Sara's eyes. "You look so beautiful, Sara." Then Amani leaned in to whisper in her ear. "Just wait till Shacker sees you! He's gonna have a heart attack." Sara instantly blushed.

"Oh, and Sara, happy belated birthday! Can you believe we are 23 already? Weren't we just 16 yesterday, riding on a bus to some crazy camp?" The girls laughed, then Amani gestured for Sara to enter. "Come on in. Mom already has dinner ready. Father showed up, too—I'm not sure why, but he's here. Once I told Mom you were coming, she decided to make an evening out of it, so we all get to have dinner together. Everyone is eager to see you."

They're all expecting me? Even Shacker? Sara's heart raced as she passed through the foyer into the living room. Dr. and Mrs. Rahim were sitting on the couch some distance apart. Mrs. Rahim stood as Sara entered.

And then she saw him.

Shacker stood up and wiped his palms on his pants.

He seems nervous. Sara tucked a stray strand of hair behind her ear.

Mrs. Rahim immediately opened her arms and walked over to Sara. The warm embrace made Sara feel loved and accepted, but she noticed that Dr. Rahim had sat back down on the couch. He didn't even meet her eyes.

"Okay, okay, it's my turn, Mom," Shacker said. He jokingly grabbed Sara in an exaggerated hug.

Sara instantly relaxed in the presence of Shacker's familiar, lighthearted personality, but then she felt him hug her in a way she had never felt a man hug her before. Instead of making Sara nervous, it made her feel at home.

Shacker's goofiness was suddenly replaced by sincerity. He offered to take her purse, setting it aside. "Sara, you look beautiful. It's really wonderful to see you again after so many years. Here," he gestured towards the brown leather couch, "have a seat. I'll get you a mug of Mom's famous tea."

Despite Dr. Rahim's tense demeanor, the evening was light and fun. Sara felt completely accepted and appreciated by Amani, Shacker, and Mrs. Rahim, Dr. Rahim's behavior hurt her deeply. *Does my presence bother him simply because I am an Israeli?*

After dinner, Dr. Rahim stood up and spoke directly to his former wife. "I'm going to leave you now to your guest. I have some work to finish at the hospital." He said goodnight to his son and daughter. He didn't even acknowledge Sara.

Seated next to Sara, Amani's body went tense with a mixture of embarrassment, disappointment and indignation. She leaned over to Sara and whispered, "Please excuse my father. He just doesn't think like the rest of us yet."

Sara glanced across the table at Shacker. Her heart sank with the awareness that his father's refusal to accept her could shatter her dreams.

~~~

From her seat on the couch, Sara could see out the window into the moonlit sky. Mrs. Rahim had already gone up to bed, but the three young adults stayed up, reliving old memories and talking about old camp friends. Sara set her mug down on the coffee table, glanced out the window again and sighed. "Even though I don't want to go, it is late, and I better head home. I have to be at the radio station early tomorrow morning."

Amani stood up to give her a hug. "Well, Sara, this was too much fun. I have missed you, even more than I realized. Let's get together next week. I will give you a call."

"That sounds wonderful, Amani. Thank you again for inviting me over tonight." Sara turned to say goodbye to Shacker.

He quickly stood and picked up her purse. "Here, let me walk you out to your car."

Sara felt the heat rise in her face. Amani gave her a knowing look and winked, then whispered in her ear, "Actually, I think I will be seeing a lot more of you."

The street was aglow with lights from house porches. The entire street was silent; the only sound was their footsteps on the pavement. When they reached her car, Shacker handed Sara her purse. He looked into her eyes for a few moments before speaking. Then a mischievous grin crossed his face.

"Would you like to experiment with a kiss?"

Sara's heart skipped. Shacker's eyes shone with warmth and gentleness, and she also saw desire in them. Her answer caught in her throat as he took a step closer, bending his face down to meet hers. His lips brushed her cheek. He pulled a bit away to look into her eyes.

"I know how my father feels. But still, Sara, I feel like I have loved you since that summer at camp. We were so young then. I didn't know what to make of my feelings. Now, seeing you after so much time has passed, I know I love you."

Sara's mind swirled as she gazed into Shacker's face. She had dreamed of him saying these exact words, probably a million times. *Is this really happening?*

As if he could read her thoughts, Shacker answered her by softly touching his lips to hers.

Chapter 17

When Shacker wasn't on a date with Sara, he spent most of his time studying to be a nurse practitioner. As they kept their love a secret from his father, the deception gnawed at them both.

One pleasant summer evening, the two lovers sat in their favorite coffee shop. Both of their laptops were open, Sara worked on her radio show script and Shacker was studying. Suddenly, Shacker closed his computer screen and rested his arms on the coffee table. "Sara, I can't keep this a secret any longer. Besides, my father is bound to find out sooner or later. I think he already suspects that something is going on between us. I need to tell him we are dating."

Sara smiled in relief. She had spent many nights lying awake, wondering when Shacker would speak to his father. She respected the Rahim family and knew it was better to be honest even though it would be difficult, especially for Shacker.

She reached across the table and took his hand. "I will stand by you, whatever happens. Maybe it won't be so bad after all. I mean, who wouldn't be happy to have their son date me?" They both giggled, then Shacker leaned in for a kiss.

~~~

The next morning, a stranger dressed in a suit walked up to Sara as she was about to enter the radio station.

"Ms. Salinger?"

Sara smiled at the man. "Yes, I am Ms. Salinger. Can I help you with something?"

He handed her a sealed envelope and then walked away. Sara opened it and took out a letter. Her heart sank as she read.

Dear Ms. Salinger,

It has come to my attention that you and my son have been dating. I must let you know that this is not right. Ducks do not date eagles. Each must stay with their own kind. I have nothing against you except that you are an Israeli. Israelis should not mix with Palestinians, so please keep your hands off my son.

Dr. Dawood Rahim

Sara wadded up the letter as tears began to stream down her face. Instead of throwing it in the trash, she put the crumpled-up paper in her purse so Shacker could read it later.

That night after work, Sara went to the Rahim house. Mrs. Rahim poured her a hot mug of tea. But instead of handing it to Sara, she set it on the coffee table and then wrapped Sara in a warm hug. "Don't you worry, Sara. My ex is just a sour old man. He will come around. My son loves you and that makes you family to me. I don't care about your nationality. To me, you are Sara, the woman my son loves."

Tears pooled in Sara's eyes as she squeezed Mrs. Rahim tighter. "If only Dr. Rahim felt the same way." She blinked as the tears started to stream down her cheeks.

Chapter 18

Five Years Later

Sara picked up Shacker's tie from his dresser and turned to hand it to him. He was dressed in a new dark suit. "I am so proud of you! We all are. It will be fun to celebrate your graduation with everyone ..." She looked into his eyes and slightly raised her eyebrow. "Even with your father." They both smiled as he took the tie and placed it around his neck.

"Hey, don't forget, Sara. You need to be all packed and ready to go after the party."

Sara pouted her lips. "But if you don't tell me where we are going, then how am I supposed to know what to pack?"

"All you get to know is that it is going to be somewhere warm and tropical. I'm not going to tell you anything else, so you can wipe that sexy, pouty look from your face and come and give me a kiss."

~~~

The graduation party went well. Even Shacker's father was smiling and happy for his son's successful completion of the nurse practitioner course. After the party, Shacker drove Sara to a small private airport just outside the city.

Sara gazed out the window and up at the stars. *Where is he taking me ... and by plane?*

He parked, grabbed their bags out of the trunk, and held Sara's hand, leading her towards a private jet.

Sara's eyes grew wide with excitement. "Shacker, whose plane is this?"

His face widened into a smile. "It belongs to my friend's family. The plane is going to take us to Cypress and we will spend the weekend in a beach house along the Mediterranean Sea."

Sara cupped her hand to her mouth and let out a squeal as the two walked hand in hand, suitcases wheeling behind them. They stopped at the bottom of the movable staircase that led into the aircraft, and a flight attendant came down the stairs, gesturing for the suitcases.

"I will take those for you. We intend to depart in fifteen minutes. It's a gorgeous night and I will meet you inside when you are ready." He took the suitcases up the stairs and disappeared into the plane, leaving the two lovers alone.

The night was unusually quiet with no other planes on the tarmac. Even the breeze blew softly. Shacker, acting on impulse, reached into his pocket and pulled out a small box. "Sara, I planned to do this on a beautiful beach, maybe as the sun was setting, but I just can't wait any longer."

He got down on one knee and opened the box, revealing a diamond ring. The warm night air kissed Sara's bare legs, her skirt hitting just above the knee. She peered down at Shacker, knowing what his next words would be, and she felt in that moment that life couldn't possibly be sweeter.

"Sara, will you make me the happiest man on the planet and marry me?"

"Yes, Shacker, forever yes!"

Happy tears ran down both their faces.

Chapter 19

Shacker sat at a table in the lunch room during the fourth day on his new job at the downtown clinic. As he munched his sandwich, he pulled out his phone and began flipping through pictures of himself and Sara on their engagement trip the weekend before in Cypress. His heart swelled. *I get to marry this woman.* He had known for a long time that where a person is from doesn't matter. *A Palestinian can marry an Israeli.* He only wished his father agreed. As if on cue, Shacker looked up and saw Dr. Rahim walking into the lunch room, being led by one of the clinic's receptionists.

"Father?" Smiling but surprised, Shacker stood up and gave his father a warm hug. "Please, have a seat."

"Thank you, Son." Dr. Rahim pulled the chair out and sat down. "So, how is the new job treating you?"

Shacker shared a few stories about some patients he had treated and then some details about his coworkers. "All in all, it's been a great first week. I feel very fortunate to have this job."

"That is great to hear, Son." Dr. Rahim's brow furrowed as his demeanor turned serious. He cleared his throat and got straight to his point. "Shacker, for heaven's sake, what were you thinking by proposing to that Israeli girl? It's one thing to be dating an Israeli, but to ask her to marry you? Oh, Son, come on; you can do better.

Your children will be half-breeds; they will be half Israeli. I can't accept this. I will pay you not to do this. You will ruin your life if you marry that girl."

Anger rose inside of Shacker, but he remained calm. *After all, he is just showing his ignorance.* "Father, I love her."

Dr. Rahim hit the table with his fist. "I don't care if she is the queen. You can't marry her. I forbid it. It is wrong—completely wrong. I have a huge sum of money that I have been saving up for you. It is yours if you call off this wedding."

Shacker's head swam. *My father is trying to buy me out of loving Sara?* Then an idea came to him. "Father, let's call Mom and see what she says."

Dr. Rahim shook his head. "She doesn't know anything. Her head is as screwy as yours."

"Father, she deserves to be heard. I'm going to call her." Shacker grabbed his phone, and a few moments later he said, "Hi Mom. I'm sitting here with Father and he wants me to call off our wedding, but I want to hear what you have to say."

Shacker heard his mother's frustrated sigh. "I think your father should stick to his own business. Let me talk to him."

Shacker handed his father the phone. Dr. Rahim listened without saying anything. Finally, he hung up and looked at Shacker. "I'm not going to say this again. I forbid you to marry that girl, and if you call off the wedding this week, you will receive a large sum of money. It is your decision." Dr. Rahim stood up and walked out of the lunch room.

Shacker sat in bewilderment, wondering what his mom must have said. Then he wrapped up the last of his sandwich and made his way out of the lunch room, trying to refocus on his patients.

On Friday morning, Shacker mailed a letter that he had written. It was addressed to his father, but he sent copies to Sara, Amani, his mother, and Sara's mother.

Dear Father,

This letter is to let you know that I reject your offer.

I am a lucky man. I love and I am loved by a terrific lady. Yes, she is an Israeli, but so what? It has nothing to do with her heart. When we were teenagers, we discovered at camp that there is something more important than heritage, and that something is friendship. Father, I am sorry, but I am marrying my best friend. Yes, our children will be "half-breeds" as you call them. But they will be conceived out of love. Sara and I will teach them that they are loved—not because of their blood but because of their souls. I am sorry you feel the way you do. It separates you from me and my new family. I love you, Father, but I don't agree with you. You are mistaken, and I must do what I know is right and marry my very best friend, Sara.

Love,

Shacker

Chapter 20

"Thankfully, my mom has always been very supportive. In fact, she and I recently opened a preschool for both Israeli and Palestinian children. Well, it is actually open to anyone!"

Sara and Amani looked at each other, their eyes wide with delight. Sara said, "Wow, Brenna! Tell us more."

"It was my mother's idea, actually. I have a degree in early childhood education, but I have never wanted to work in traditional schools, so we created an alternative one. Families come to us because they want their children to be educated from a broader perspective."

"Do you have problems with the children regarding race?" asked Amani.

"Oh no, Amani. You see, these children are under the age of five with very open parents. They have not been taught to hate one another."

"That sounds like the experience Rebecca is having with her children."

"What is the name of your school?" Sara asked.

"The Peace House."

Sara grinned. "That's the perfect name. We are both so happy for you, Brenna."

"Well, I'm so glad you are doing this radio show. I felt so alone when I got home. I think your show can help us reconnect and support one another."

Sara glanced at the blinking lights of the other calls waiting to be answered. "That is my hope too, Brenna. This radio show was founded to bring more peace and support to our area. Amani and I felt lost after camp also. We knew that we had had a really important experience but no one else could relate to it. They just turned away and laughed. We hope that our shared experiences will help us move forward."

"Brenna, please keep in touch. You now know how to reach us. We must go because we have more callers."

"Thanks, girls. This has given me hope. And Sara, special congratulations to you. You got yourself such a hunk."

The friends laughed, and Amani pushed the button for the next caller. "Salam, this is Amani. With whom am I speaking?"

"Shalom, ladies. It's Albert. Remember me?"

Sara's eyes brightened, hearing Albert's voice. She could picture him adjusting his glasses as he spoke. Memories of the olive branch rushed into her mind. "Of course we remember you, Albert! What are you up to these days?"

"I'm doing well. In fact, when I got home from camp, I realized I may have had a better experience than most of the other campers." I didn't care about how people reacted to me, I just kept being nice. The fear that had left me at camp stayed away. My mother couldn't believe it, and so she began doing what I was doing and her fear left too."

"That is wonderful, Albert," Sara said. "I must say, I notice bravery and strength coming through your voice. It is wonderful to hear."

Amani asked, "So Albert, what are you doing now?"

"I am about to leave for the U.S. to enter graduate school in international law. I'm going to Harvard Law School."

Amani let out a low whistle. "We all knew you were smart! Good for you. What do you plan to do when you graduate?"

"I really don't know. I have a chance to stay in the United States, and I may do that. I hate abandoning what you girls are doing here, but I'm really done with all the violence. I want to experience some peace. I hope to find it in the United States."

Amani nodded her head. "We hope you do too, Albert. Send some peace this way when you get there, and please keep in touch. Thank you for your courage."

Another commercial aired before Sara took the last caller of the show. "Shalom, this is Sara. And who is this?"

"Shalom, Sara and Amani. It's Aharon.

Amani's face instantly glowed. "Salam, Aharon."

"I wanted to call today because I recently had an experience with Tarif. Do you remember him from camp?"

"Of course," replied Sara. "How could we ever forget him? For those of you who are listening, Tarif was a very angry camper when he first arrived at camp. He made his hatred for Israelis clear to us all. But then we saw an emotional shift in him, specifically after he spent a day with Aharon out on the lake. So Aharon, tell us about your recent meeting with Tarif."

"Well, unfortunately, life has been rough for him. He told me that when he went home after camp, his father really gave him a hard time. He laughed at him and called him a Jew lover. He never let up. So Tarif moved out. When I saw him the other day, he was very down. I think he is depressed and conflicted."

Amani jumped in. "So the conflict in Tarif, from what we know about him previously having spent a summer with him at camp, is simply this: He loves his father and wants to be liked by him, but he knows his father's beliefs are wrong and he is caught in the middle psychologically."

"That sounds like a correct assessment of his situation, Amani. I'm going to try and stay in touch with him. He really looked bad. It seems as though his anger has turned into a hopelessness that has led him into a depressed state. It was definitely difficult to be around him."

"So Aharon, can you let our audience know what you are up to these days?" asked Sara.

"I'm still going to school and majoring in psychology. I had the same experience you girls had when I got home. I forgot about camp and just went on with my life. I tried to contact Tarif several years ago, but at that time, he avoided me. I think now he might be desperate for a friend, so I am definitely going to be a safe person for him to connect with."

Sara watched as Amani's respect for Aharon seemed to grow. *I'm so glad they are together. When I think about it, he has always been the perfect man for her.* She declared, "Thanks for calling, Aharon. Our time is about over now, but feel free to call in again and let the listeners know how things progress with Tarif." As the girls closed the show, they thanked everyone for listening. Once they removed their headsets, their boss popped in to give them a thumbs up. "Great show, girls. There are a lot of conversations running on Facebook and other social media sites about it. You guys really connected well with the listeners."

Sara hardly heard her boss' praise. Her mind was already on the next task at hand. She grabbed her shopping bag. "Amani, I have to run. I still need to do things for the ceremony tomorrow!"

The girls hugged and Sara left in a hurry, as she had errands to complete before catching a flight to Cypress that evening at seven.

Chapter 21

The wedding day finally arrived. Sara stood on the deck of the house that belonged to Shacker's friend, looking out over the vineyard. The sunsets in Cypress were always magical, which is why she and Shacker had planned to have their ceremony in the evening. *How did I get so lucky?* A slight breeze tickled her face and blew the light and airy fabric of her wedding gown gently around her body. *I'm marrying my best friend and the man of my dreams.*

Sara glanced over at the chairs and the canopy that had been set up to honor her Israeli heritage. She brought to mind the vows that she and Shacker had written to honor the Muslim tradition. Even though they chose not to have a religious ceremony, they wanted it to be a spiritual one of inclusion and peace. Only their immediate family and special friends would be attending. *Intimate, meaningful, and a perfect reflection of our love.* Her heart was full and content. She further reflected on how spiritually compatible she and Shacker were. *I'm so glad we've both been able to let go of our early training to find a place that is peaceful for both of us.*

Sara glanced down at her snow-white dress. It trailed to floor and had bell-shaped sleeves that reached to her elbows. The vintage-style dress was V-neck with an overlay of white lace. It was the same dress her mom had worn when she married Sara's father. *I wish you could be here today, Father, but I know you are always with me in spirit.* Sara thought about her mother, who would stand in her father's stead and walk her down the aisle. A part of her heart ached, wishing Shacker's father could fill the fatherly void in her life, but Sara had resigned herself to the fact that Dr. Rahim would never be a father to her. His protests to their marriage had been loud and clear.

Sara heard footsteps behind her and turned to see Amani walking towards her. Her dress was light blue and also covered in lace, but cut short to show off Amani's figure. Amani smiled widely. "I thought I would find you out here. I just saw some cars pull up, so the guests are starting to arrive. We better get you inside before someone sees you."

Sara chuckled. "Amani, you know I don't care about such traditions, but I will do as you say and go hide out before walking down the aisle." The girls giggled and then Sara became somber. "Amani, I know today you officially become my sister, but ever since that summer we met at camp, your love and friendship have made me feel like we've always been family."

The girls hugged and then Amani smiled. "Sara, we can't get all emotional now. Our makeup will smear! Let's get you inside. Maybe we'll even sneak a drink to calm our nerves. This is a vineyard, after all!"

~~~

The guests were seated in their chairs as the sun set over the Mediterranean Sea in the background. Sara would always remember the sight before her: Shacker waiting for her under the canopy. Their eyes met and she felt a rush of emotion wash over her like nothing she had felt before. The few clouds in the sky were awash with a bright red color, and all the 20 plus guests had smiles on their faces.

Her mom led her down the aisle to Shacker. They joined hands, and the minister began. After sharing some words, he turned to Shacker and invited him to say his vows.

"Sara, I've loved you since we met at camp. You are my very best friend. I will give you the space that you need. I'll listen when you are sad or upset. I'll hold your heart when you are broken. I want to walk my life with you. I want us to celebrate life together and I want you as my partner. I vow that I will love you forever."

The minister then prompted Sara to say her vows.

"Shacker, I got my wish. As you know, I always wanted to marry my very best friend and here you are. For me, our love is a symbol of freedom and of kindness and compassion. I cherish the idea of walking this life with you, no matter what it brings. My hand is in your hand, and I give you my heart completely. I vow that I will love you forever."

Shacker's eyes watered. He squeezed Sara's hands and then they exchanged rings—simple matching gold bands.

The minister looked at Shacker and nodded. "You may kiss your bride." Shacker leaned in and their lips met. They were instantly transported to a place of oneness. When they separated and looked into each other's eyes, it took them a few moments to realize the crowd was cheering and clapping. They turned and smiled to their guests as the new Mr. and Mrs. Rahim.

Chapter 22

For their honeymoon Shacker had reserved a place right on the beach in Cypress. Every morning the two lovebirds got up early and just walked and ran in the small waves. They felt free and so much in love. They couldn't get enough of one another. One day they noticed a middle-aged couple out on the beach with them. They, too, were having such a nice time running in the waves. Shacker remarked to Sara, "I hope we are like that when we are their age."

Sara smiled and relayed, "Why don't we talk to them?"

Shacker surprised her with, "Why?" Sara had already started to walk over to the couple. She smiled at them, and everyone greeted each other with Shaloms.

Gerald and Renee were in their 60's and were both from the United States. They were celebrating their 30th wedding anniversary.

Shacker immediately said, "We are on our honeymoon." Renee spontaneously grabbed Sara and hugged her and then Gerald did the same to Shacker. Then Gerald added, "Let's go over to those rocks and talk."

The group went across to the rocks and after getting to know each other more, Sara asks, "How have you been able to keep your relationship so alive all these years?"

Renee and Gerald smiled and looked at each other and together they said, "We celebrate!"

Shacker confused, thought, *what do they mean, celebrate?*

Gerald saw the confusion and began to speak, "We celebrate at least once a week. We do something different. Sometimes we go out, or I bring flowers or Renee cooks something special. Whatever it may be, it is always a celebration."

Renee adds, "We combine with this, a time when we listen to each other. I mean really listen. We don't debate. We just listen and receive one another."

Gerald steps in, "We believe that families get disconnected with their busy schedules. And during this one night or day, we reconnect. We reconnect primarily by listening and receiving one another."

Sara asks, "Do you talk about things that are bothering you?"

Gerald jumps in, "Of course. But this is not about discussing. It's about really receiving the other person's concern Hearing it and letting it affect you."

Renee adds, "We also talk about the good stuff in the same way. It is very important to hear one another. It's the most important thing we can do."

The four continued to talk for hours. They spent the whole day together. Gerald and Renee departed for home the next day. But Sara and Shacker vowed to do what they had suggested. They were excited. Neither had witnessed a good marriage growing up, so it was nice to have this support. The rest of the week they practiced receiving one another. And when they left for home, they were full and deeply in love.

Their first year of marriage was blissful. They did everything the couple had suggested. As a result, they discovered a depth in their relationship rarely experienced by two people. At times, it even seemed that they were impervious to life's woes, but of course, none of us are.

~~~

Sara fastened the bracelet around her slender wrist. She glanced at her reflection in the mirror and wondered if she should have bought the other dress instead of this one. "Babe, I can't help but wish we were just going out to a fun dinner with Amani and Aharon. Why are your parents having us all over for dinner again? Usually your father does everything possible to avoid me."

Shacker finished buttoning up his shirt and then walked over to Sara and wrapped his arms around her. "Mom really wanted to celebrate the fact that we've been married for a year now. And don't worry, I'm sure my father will be his same stubborn self, so at least there won't be any surprises." Shacker grinned, knowing he was teasing Sara. She relaxed in his arms and gave him a long kiss.

Shacker and Sara walked up to the familiar gray door of Mrs. Rahim's house and let themselves in. The warm but comfortable evening was the perfect opportunity for many of the guests to eat and drink in the backyard. Shacker and Sara found seats next to Aharon and Amani at one of the outside round tables Mrs. Rahim had set out.

"So, Brother, Sara tells me you guys are trying for a baby," Amani said, raising her eyebrows and snickering. "You—a father? I don't know … "

Shacker laughed. "Oh come on, Sis, you know I'll be a great father. It's just taking longer to conceive than we thought it would." Shacker glanced over at Sara and then grabbed her hand. He knew it was a bit of a sore subject for Sara. They had already been trying for a few months, and Sara was beginning to be concerned that something could be wrong. Shacker's face brightened. "I'm sure it will happen when the time is right."

Unfortunately, Dr. Rahim was nearby and overheard their conversation. He raised his voice. "The reason, Son, that you can't conceive is because Israelis and Palestinians should not mate. That is what I have been trying to tell you for years now."

Sara couldn't control her tears. She excused herself and raced off to the bathroom. Shacker held his peace and gathered Sara's purse, then turned to Amani. "Hey Sis, I'm gonna take Sara home. Aharon, maybe you and Amani can come over to our place later this week for dinner."

Aharon stood up to give Shacker a hug. "You bet, Shacker. We would love to." Aharon dropped his voice a bit so only Shacker could hear. "And Shacker, what are you going to do about your father? What he said was out of line."

Shacker nodded his head, then headed out to find his wife.

~~~

To Sara's sheer delight, Dr. Rahim's belief that Palestinians and Israelis couldn't conceive was quickly proven wrong; ten months later, Sara gave birth to a baby girl, Farah.

Farah took after the Rahim family in appearance, having dark curly hair like her father and big brown eyes like her Aunt Amani, but her personality was definitely just like her mother's: full of joy and what seemed like an endless supply of love to give the whole world.

"Ok, little Miss Farah," Sara cooed, "we have to go to Aunt Amani's house so she and Mommy can plan next week's radio show."

Farah playfully kicked her legs and moved her arms around, making it difficult for Sara to get her dressed and ready for their outing. Eventually, after lots of smiles, coos, and determination, Sara succeeded in fastening on Farah's baby clothes. *Six months old already! Where has the time gone? Besides marrying Shacker, Farah is the best thing that has ever happened to me.*

Amani's apartment was near the center of town, about a half block from one of the main streets. Along with the radio show, Amani also helped Shacker at his clinic a few times a week. The apartment was close to both workplaces. As Sara carried Farah through Amani's front door, she looked around the apartment and realized how alike Amani was to her mother in taste and style. Just like Mrs. Rahim's home, Amani's place was decorated with modern décor, including metal and bling everywhere. "It's pure Amani," Sara said to Farah.

Amani met the two in the kitchen. "Here Sara, let me take Miss Farah while you get yourself settled on the couch. I've got a home-cooked meal and tea all set out on the coffee table for us."

Amani danced around with her niece, eliciting all sorts of coos and giggles from Farah. Then she turned to Sara. "Before we get down to radio show business, open that bag there and see what's inside." She pointed to a pink gift bag resting on the floor beside the couch.

Sara picked it up and peeked inside. "Oh Amani, you spoil our little girl!" Sara took out the contents of the bag and squealed: a pink and white frilly dress with a matching frilly diaper cover and pink patent leather shoes. Before starting on their work, they dressed up Farah and took some pictures. Suddenly, the women heard a familiar rap at the door. Shacker stuck his head inside and smiled widely. "Hey, Sis. Salam, babe." He walked in and Farah cooed in delight at her father's voice. "Hey, my little love." He picked up Farah and gave Sara a kiss. "I'm on my lunch break, so I thought I'd pop by and see how my three favorite girls are doing."

Amani huffed. "I was doing great until you barged in, taking away my niece's attention." She laughed and then gave her brother a quick hug.

"Okay, okay," Shacker agreed and handed Farah back to her auntie. "I just had to get my fix. I will leave you now to enjoy your visit together." He walked over, kissed his wife and daughter goodbye, then quickly disappeared out the front door.

Amani laughed. "He's like the wind when he does that!"

Between snacking and playing with Farah, Amani and Sara managed to accomplish a great deal of work. Two hours later, Sara began packing up.

"Amani, thank you again for Farah's adorable outfit. So, you think you and Aharon can come over for dinner later this week?"

Amani carried the plates into the kitchen. "Yes, we'll make it happen. Aharon's been wanting to spend time with Shacker, so he will be happy with the plan."

After hugs and goodbyes, Sara carried Farah on her hip and walked out into the cobblestone street. They passed a corner café, and the smell of fresh challah ticked Sara's nose.

"Ooh, Farah, do you smell that, sweetheart? Fresh rolls. Let's hurry to get some challah to surprise your daddy before he comes home." Farah squirmed slightly as she gurgled in response.

A welcoming jingle greeted Sara as she opened the door of her favorite café. She smiled at the sight of tables displaying brightly-colored tablecloths and fresh flowers in appreciation of their regulars, but also intriguing to new passersby. The rich smell of black coffee filled her senses and the smell of freshly baked chocolate babka and sufganiyots, along with other treats, made Sara's stomach hungry again.

"What will it be for you and the pretty baby?" The man behind the counter smiled warmly, his hair as dark and curly as Farah's.

Sara pointed to the fresh challah.

"Of course," he smiled.

Pleased, Sara moved Farah to her left hip, then reached into her purse with her right hand for a few shekels.

Without warning, an explosion of mass energy overpowered Sara's right side like a Mac truck supplied with hot white, liquid shock, while the front windows of the shop shattered into a million sparkling diamonds, razor sharp enough to tear one's heart into just as many pieces. The sound split her ears open to a place in the universe where sound no longer registered, while the floor ripped from underneath her like the merciless riptides of the beaches of her childhood. Her hands flung out from her sides, thrusting open her fingers as though a rag doll, no longer commanding her own body. Shekels floated and twisted in the air before her eyes, sparkling oddly outside of time as she floated down, down, down. Another blow to her left temple and cheekbone followed; like a violent riptide a force had pulled her to the cement floor as if a response to the hot, white, liquid shock wave. Without stopping for her to catch up and register what just happened, time and thought disappeared into black infinity. All went dark.

~~~

Acrid odors of hot smoke, chemicals, burned dust and dreams filled Sara's nostrils bringing her back to semi-consciousness. What was once a bakery, was now a blown-out building of shattered glass and wood fragments. Searing pain in Sara's forehead forced its way rudely into the crude, putrid smells. Sirens teased her pounding head as earthquakes tease lava, jostling it from calm to chaos and confusion. Panic erupted from her shattering maternal heart, *Farah!* Sara fumbled around the floor, feebly attempting to plant her feet to some steady ground. As she put down a hand to steady herself, she saw the pool of blood she'd been laying in; blackness took over once again as she succumbed helplessly to the lower abyss.

~~~

Finding consciousness again, Sara found herself crying out, "Farah!" Coughing, with her head pounding, she finally put the two thoughts together. *My God, what happened? Farah ... where is Farah?* She slowly pushed to her feet and scanned the area for her baby. To her horror, she spotted a tiny bundle on the floor against what was left of the counter. "Oh no, Farah, no God, please no."

Sara rushed over and picked up her baby girl. Her piercing scream rang out amidst the chaos and commotion around her. "Noooooooooooooooo!"

Sara held her lifeless baby close to her chest, stumbling out of the building and back toward Amani's apartment. Sirens wailed, people screamed, and the dust and smoke hung thick in the air. Sara stumbled over something and then gasped at the sight of a dead body. She held on tighter to her baby and pushed forward. *If I just get out of here, maybe I will wake up and all of this will have been just a dream. Please, let this be a dream.*

As Sara neared her destination, Amani came running out of her apartment building. When she reached Sara, their eyes met;

then Amani saw the bundle held tightly to Sara's chest and tears began pouring down her cheeks.

"Amani, please tell me this is a dream. Please tell me my baby isn't dead. This is a dream, right? Please!" Sara felt her legs give out from under her, but Amani caught her underneath her arms. They slumped down to the ground and Amani wrapped her arms tightly around Sara and Farah as they sobbed together.

How can I ever go on? What hope is there without my Farah?

Another pair of familiar arms instantly wrapped around Sara. Shacker had heard the blast from his downtown clinic and immediately came running. He glanced at Farah's body in Sara's arms and knew his child was gone. Through sobs, he whispered into Sara's ear, "We will get through this together."

Shacker and Sara held their lifeless child between them as they touched foreheads. After a few minutes, Shacker turned to his sister and said, "Let's take them to your apartment and call Mom."

Chapter 23

Through her living room window, Sara watched the rain splatter off the backyard porch. It was only 2:00 pm but the sky was dark with angry clouds. Farah's memorial service had ended about an hour before, and now everyone was gathered in her home to grieve and remember. "All I feel is hate," Sara mumbled to herself as she continued watching the rain pelt the porch.

The events of that tragic day had surfaced: a young Palestinian suicide bomber had caused the explosion that killed Farah and ten other Israelis.

Sara's mind had tortured her day and night ever since. *I want to kill every Palestinian on the face of the Earth. I want revenge. Maybe with revenge, this pain will stop.* Sara shook her head as if trying to erase the thoughts from her mind. She felt Shacker nearby. He placed a hand on her shoulder and then he headed to the food table. *He is just as lost as I am. How can two drowning people save each other?*

The house was full of low whispers and sounds of sniffling. Suddenly, the quietness was broken as Shacker's father stood up. Sara looked over at him as he puffed out his chest and spoke loudly for everyone to hear. "I need to say something. This family needs to come to grips with the fact that Farah's death was God's way of telling us that Shacker's and Sara's union is evil. Evil begets evil. Palestinians and Israelis should not marry. They should not have children. It's time for this travesty to end."

The complete silence that followed was what broke Sara's heart. She looked over at her husband, but all Shacker did was stare at the carpet. Then she looked over at Amani. She considered her a sister in the truest sense, but she too just sat still staring out the window. Sara's fury and pain reached new heights. She stormed out of the room, went into her bedroom, and slammed the door. The house remained silent, as though everyone was frozen in shock, until Sara came out again carrying a backpack.

She looked at the faces of the people who were supposedly her family. She put on her bravest face. "Thank you, everyone, for coming to honor our beloved daughter. I'm leaving now to try to find my way through this pain. My heart is broken. Maybe being alone will bring me some peace. As far as what Dr. Rahim said, I personally don't agree. But everyone's silence, especially the silence from my own husband, seems to indicate something different."

Sara walked over to her mom and kissed her. Then she turned to the door, but Shacker grabbed her arm and looked into her eyes, pleading. "Please, don't go."

"I have to go. You have broken my heart." She broke loose from Shacker's hold and walked out the door.

Sara's mom got up and grabbed her coat. Then her anger got the better of her and she looked directly at Dr. Rahim. "You did this, you bully. There is nothing like kicking someone when they're down. You are a thoughtless pig. I can't be here anymore either. I have thought of all of you Palestinians as friends and family, but where was your loyalty to my daughter and me when this pig spoke? Shacker, are you a man? Sometimes it's important to fight for what you love. Does Sara's love and honor mean nothing to you? I cannot be around such hate. Your silence has spoken volumes."

Ms. Salinger walked out the door and left. Shacker sat on the sofa with his face buried in his hands. Finally, he got up and went into his bedroom. He pulled out his phone and called his wife, but it went straight to her voicemail, so he left a message.

"Sara, I'm sorry. I was as stunned as you by my father's words. I don't know what to say. I was wrong for not immediately coming to your defense and telling him to leave. Please call me. I don't want to lose you too."

Chapter 24

The next morning, Shacker woke early. His heart sank as he again realized what had become of his family. He turned over and stared at the empty space that Sara's warm body usually occupied.

He got up quickly and called Sara's mom. Feeling desperate but determined, he quickly spoke. "Salam, Ms. Salinger. Please don't hate me. I was wrong for not immediately reacting to what my father said yesterday. Please, I don't want to lose Sara, too. I love her. I called her multiple times last night but she never picked up. Please just tell me if you have heard from her."

"Shacker, she made it clear that she wanted some time alone."

"I know. But I need to know she is okay, and I need to know that we will be okay. I know I really blew it."

"You sure did. It is going to take a lot for Sara to trust you again. Her heart was completely broken by what you did." Ms. Salinger's voice was firm.

"I know. Would you please call me if she calls you?"

"I will. I know you are worried, but remember that Sara is strong, and she will get through this."

"Thank you, Ms. Salinger. I feel better. I really am sorry about yesterday." Shacker hung up and sighed heavily. The weight of the world was on him, but he was determined to do whatever it took to get his wife back.

As he walked back to the living room, he looked out the front window and noticed a man standing outside across the road. He had been there since Farah's death. He was old and dirty and definitely Palestinian. He just stood leaning against the wall smoking. Shacker, determined not to keep ignoring the man, opened the door and yelled, "Hey, you over there! What are you doing? Go away; we don't want you standing there!"

The old man, looking a bit frightened, put his cigarette out and moved on like he was walking away. But later, Shacker realized that he had returned. *I don't know what that guy wants, but he's not hurting anyone. I guess I will just ignore him. I have bigger things to worry about.*

~~~

Sara walked into her small motel room on the outskirts of Tel Aviv. The bed had a bright and cheery quilt on it and the adjoining bathroom had a tub she could soak in. She set her bag down on the chair and put her keys on the desk.

After her few settling-in tasks were complete, she didn't know what to do. Reliving how her daughter was taken from her life so senselessly brought on a flood of emotions. *For the first time in my life, no one can help me. No one can help make the pain go away.* Sara lay on the bed and cried deeply. She battled with thoughts of retribution and revenge. *If I can just make someone else hurt the way I hurt, I will get even and my pain will go away.*

An image of Sara's father suddenly filled her thoughts. She saw her red wagon and the flowers they used to admire in their old neighborhood. *You always believed that I was like a flower, able to push through the dirt to bloom. But right now the dirt feels so heavy and deep over me; I don't think I can ever break through. I'm sorry, Father.* Sara's body shook uncontrollably with another wave of emotion and tears.

Later that night, Sara got up and washed her face. She peeked out the motel window and saw that the moon was big and full, lighting up the streets with its glow. She decided to take a walk outside.

As she strolled along the streets surrounding the motel, she thought about her wedding. She remembered the beautiful vineyard. There were so many flowers everywhere; her mom had spent a fortune on them. She could see Amani in her light blue dress, and then she could picture Shacker. *The love of my life.* Sara remembered how they became one, even though he was a Palestinian and she an Israeli.

Our life together was blessed. Dr. Rahim was the only problem. Our baby was a beautiful blending of both Shacker and me. She was a delight. At parties, my family passed her around, delighting in her cuteness and sweet spirit. She loved the attention and rarely cried. So then, what did I do wrong? Why was she taken from me?

Suddenly, Sara felt exhausted. She went back to her motel room. Soon she was lying on the bed, her clothes still on. *Why couldn't Farah and I have stayed at Amani's ten more minutes? We would have missed the bomb and Farah would still be here.* Out loud, Sara pleaded. "Why, God? Why have you done this to me? Why did you finally give me a beautiful daughter and then take her away? I do not understand. I'm not leaving this room until you tell me why."

She lay her head back down on the pillow and fell into a deep sleep.

Suddenly, she was standing in a beautiful meadow in the woods. There were enormous trees all around. The air was fresh, and Sara felt a light breeze on her face. She heard a sound and noticed there was a narrow, clear creek flowing by her feet. There were yellow, blue, and white wildflowers blooming everywhere. A butterfly flew by joyfully. The sun was warm and full, and Sara started to walk along a path that wound through the meadow. She stopped suddenly as she discovered in the distance a woman in a white, flowing gown walking towards her. The gown was iridescent and shimmered as the woman walked. She had black curly hair and there was a smile on her face. Sara's heart filled with love when she looked at the woman. As she neared, Sara realized the woman looked familiar; she looked like Amani. The woman stopped and looked lovingly into Sara's eyes.

Realization suddenly dawned on Sara. "You're Farah. I'm right, aren't I?"

The woman smiled a mischievous smile, just like Shacker. She nodded yes and then gave Sara a big hug. Sara started to cry, so Farah held her even tighter and said, "Mama, I'm okay. I have come because I want to talk to you. I don't want you to give up on your life."

Farah pulled out of the hug to look into her mother's eyes. "Let's go sit over there." She pointed to a nearby log at the edge of the meadow. The two women sat and held hands.

"Mama, I really am fine. I love you and I'm still with you."

Sara weakly responded, "It sure doesn't feel that way. It feels like one minute I was a mom and now I'm not. And it hurts so badly, Farah."

"Look and see. Can you feel me in your heart at this moment?"

Sara quickly responded, "I feel love."

Farah nodded. "Yes, that is where you will always find me. Mama, I want you to know that I came to you for a very specific reason. Over the next two nights, I will be coming to you to tell you why I left and to tell you what is next. For now, I just want to be with you so that you know that I am okay and that I still love you and Papa and Aunt Amani."

Farah held her mother as she sobbed in her arms. Sara felt healing in her heart as she was embraced by Farah's love. Then Farah looked directly into Sara's eyes and said, "Mama, I must leave now, but I will come again tomorrow and the day after. Let my love heal your broken heart. I love you completely."

"Farah, wait; don't go. I want to go with you!"

"Mama, you have a mission. You must stay. Trust me, everything will be okay."

Sara woke with a start. She sat up and looked around her motel room. Moonlight shone in through the window. She rubbed her head and questioned herself aloud. "Did that just happen? Am I going crazy? Did I just see and talk to Farah?" She got up to go to the bathroom, trying to wake up more fully and clear her head.

Chapter 25

Shacker looked at the phone in his hand. His body fidgeted with worry. It had been two days and he still hadn't heard from Sara. Nobody had.

He called his mom. "Mom, I just don't understand her. Why did she need to leave and be alone?"

Mrs. Rahim sighed heavily through the phone. "Sweetheart, she didn't do this because she doesn't love you. She just needs some space. I can't imagine the depth of her pain after losing Farah."

Shacker shook his head in frustration. He ran his free hand through his hair. "I told her that we would get through this together."

"Sometimes when I get emotionally overwhelmed, I need to be alone and be quiet. I would bet that is what is going on with Sara. Shacker, when you carry a baby for nine months, your connection becomes very deep. I can't imagine what she is going through. I would give her a few days. Please remember that she is not doing this because she doesn't love you. She is taking care of herself emotionally, and you need to support her."

Shacker swallowed hard. "So you don't think she wants to get away from me because she doesn't love me anymore?"

Mrs. Rahim's voice was certain. "Heavens no; she loves you, Shacker. She just needs some space."

"Ok, I will give her one more day to communicate with me. If I don't hear anything by tomorrow, I'm going to go looking for her. I'm worried."

"That sounds like a good plan. I know you are also hurting. Please take care of yourself."

"Thanks, Mom." After the call ended, Shacker tossed the phone on the bed and lay down, still in his clothes.

That night, Sara fell asleep quickly again—almost as soon as her head hit the pillow. She was exhausted. All day she had walked the beautiful vineyards surrounding her motel. As she walked, she realized that she felt much better than the day before. She felt hopeful. And this feeling made her believe the encounter with her daughter was in fact real—or at least the dream was real. She cried and then laughed, and then she would cry again, and yet each time she felt a presence that made her feel held and loved. On the one hand, she had never felt more alone in her life, but on the other hand she was aware of not really being alone at all. It was a strange and wonderful experience. As she walked around, she thought of Farah. She laughed, she cried, and she rejoiced in the feeling that she was indeed still a mother, even though her baby was gone physically.

Soon, in her dream, she was back in the meadow. Farah walked toward her and they hugged.

"How was your day, Mama?"

"Oh Farah, I walked and walked and just let your love in. I cried and laughed. I feel much better."

"Mama, I'm so happy. I don't want you to give up. I want you to use this experience to help others and to stop the pain. I came to you and left again so you could show the world a different way to respond to pain."

"What do you mean?" Sara asked.

"Most people believe that there is only one way to respond to pain, so it will go away—with retribution. But pain is only buried with retribution. It will still color your life. When you are willing to see things differently, and to see with compassion, then love has a chance to be experienced and it has the power to heal even a broken heart."

Sara was quiet, considering what her daughter had told her. "I don't understand."

"Well, Mama, tell me this: Have you expressed hate for the person who did this to you? Have you felt like a victim? Have you wanted retribution?"

"Of course. Isn't that normal?"

Farah smiled warmly. Her whole demeanor was very peaceful. "Yes, it is the normal way to respond, but it isn't the best way. Getting even doesn't solve anything. You think it heals the hurt, when in fact it just makes things worse. The pain goes underground and it begins to color your world in a very bad way."

Sara pondered this for a moment. "So what you are asking me to do is to show the world that I can respond with understanding instead of with hate. But, Farah, how can I do that?"

Farah took a moment to respond, looking deep into her mother's eyes. "It all begins with your willingness to do something different. Hate begets hate. If one person hates another, that person will hate them in return, and on and on—it never stops until someone does something different."

Farah stooped down to pluck a flower from the meadow. She twirled it between her fingers and continued. "Imagine a train moving down a track. As it progresses, it builds up momentum. It goes faster and faster. Maybe it even seems out of control, unstoppable. One way to slow it down is to introduce a hill. Once the train's momentum slows, it can be diverted to another track going in a completely different direction. Responding to pain with anger, hatred, revenge, fear, or depression is what gives this train its current momentum. This momentum fills people's lives with more fear, hatred, and sadness, and it keeps the train moving faster and faster. The only way to slow this train down is to do something different.

"The 'something different' is the hill. That is where you come in. If you respond to your pain with understanding instead of revenge and with hope instead of hopelessness, a new vision will emerge. This vision will help the train to begin to move in a new direction, making it possible for it to switch to a completely new track, going in a better direction. You may think you don't have the power to do this, but I want you to know that change always happens when one person has the courage to say 'No More.'"

Sara's shoulders slumped and she sighed. "But I feel so hopeless. I miss you so much, Farah, and I feel such hate."

"Yes, it takes courage to change the train's momentum. Do you want to remember me with revenge or with love? You can't bring me back and you can't change what happened, but you can change how you feel about it. I was killed because of hatred. The person with the bomb was a kid who was taught by his father to hate all Israelis. It's time for someone to say, *'No More!* It stops here.' You have the courage to do this, Mama. Your love for me will help you."

As Sara and Farah sat together on a log, they could hear the trickle of a nearby stream. Sara took a deep breath. "How do I do this?"

Farah answered lovingly, "Tomorrow we will talk about that. But for now, I want you to ask yourself whether you are willing to be the person who says 'No More.' Are you willing to stop the hatred? Are you willing to move the train into a new direction? To change it to a Peace Train? You have the ability to do this. The question is, do you have the will to do it? Let my love guide you, Mama. We will meet again tomorrow."

They hugged and Sara woke. Her motel room was awash in moonlight. She hadn't pulled the blinds closed before falling asleep. She took out her phone and saw the messages from Shacker, Amani, and her mother. She quickly typed a message to her mother:

I'm okay. Just needed this time alone. Can I stay at your house for a while?

She ignored the messages from Shacker and Amani. She knew her husband was probably still awake, but she wasn't ready to engage in dialogue with him just yet. She put her phone on the bedside table, slipped into her pajamas, and easily fell back to sleep.

The next day was like the previous one. Sara walked and walked, thinking all the while about Farah. She grieved, rejoiced, and tried to be present in each moment. She wondered aloud, "Do I have the will to say *No More*?" *I feel such hate. How can I say No More? Am I crazy? How do I get myself to feel differently? What needs to change here? I don't wish this on anyone, and I hate the man who did this to me. I hate him for taking my love. What did Farah say? This hatred just leads to more hatred, and I can stop this so that it doesn't happen again just by saying it ends with me. I don't wish this on anyone. I really don't.*

Suddenly a black hooded figure appeared in front of her. She also found herself holding onto a rope. The rope had a sign on it that said HATE. The hooded figure pulled the rope and almost pulled Sara over. Sara pulled back. Her hate rose and as she pulled again, her hate got stronger and more intense. Then the conflict started. *To hate – no, don't hate. To hate – no, don't hate.* Again and again until her mind was so confused she couldn't think. Then in total and complete confusion, she let go of the rope and dropped down into a pile of tears. She felt a hand on her back and knew it was Farah. The masked man and the rope vanished. She sat in the shade of an olive tree for hours, just being with what had happened.

When she got back to her room that night, she was unusually tired. She had difficulty falling asleep. Finally, she picked up Farah's favorite toy, which she had stuck in her bag. She held it close to her heart and soon sleep found her.

She was in the meadow with Farah again. Farah took her hand. "Yesterday, you asked how to respond differently to acts of violence and hate. My answer is this: One step at a time."

Farah paused to let her words sink into Sara's mind, and then she continued.

"When you went to camp many years ago, you learned about friendship and its power. That experience was everything. It allowed you and Aunt Amani and Papa to become close and to discover your love for one another.

"Now is the time to bring the camp experience to the people. If you do this, the train's momentum will slow down, and the direction will change one person at a time—from the inside out."

Sara's heart raced. *Bring the camp to people?* "How?"

"That is for the three of you to figure out. How did camp change you? How did you become friends? If you answer these questions, you will discover how to bring the camp to other people. Let your love for me guide you. Let the words *No More* be your anthem. Trust yourselves. You can do this."

Sara's chest tightened. "Farah, I'm sad and scared again. I know that you will be leaving soon. I'm not sure I can do what you ask."

Farah responded abruptly, "The question really is, are you willing? Are you willing to honor the loss of me with love instead of with hate? Are you willing?"

Sara paused to thoughtfully consider this. "Of course, I'm willing. I don't want to remember my dear daughter with thoughts of hate. I want to remember and hold you with love forever."

Farah smiled. "Then go home and talk with Papa and Aunt Amani. First, tell them that I love them and will always love them and that I have a mission for them. Then tell them about your dreams. The three of you can do this. If you are willing, you can do this."

Tears streamed down Sara's face, but she felt a peace and a strength rise up within her. "We will try, in memory of you, my daughter."

"I must go, Mama. I will be with you forever. I mean this. I love you." Farah reached over and hugged her mother.

Sara woke with a start and sat up in bed. Her eyes were full of tears. As she blinked, the pools in her eyes spilled over, running down her cheeks. The clock read 3:00 am. The moon lit up the room once again. She stood up and walked over to the window to look out at the night sky. Her body felt light and full of hope. She thought of Shacker and Amani and wondered aloud, "How are we going to do this?"

Chapter 26

Sara walked into her mom's house looking tired but determined. She and her mom sat down on the same familiar sofa Sara had sat on as a kid.

"Mom, I need to tell you something, and it may be a bit difficult for you to believe."

Ms. Salinger's eyes were full of relief and love. "Honey, I'm just so glad to see you. Have you talked to Shacker yet?"

Sara looked down at her hands and shook her head. "No, I'm not ready to see him or speak with him." She took a deep breath and began to share the experiences from the past few days. "I went to Tel Aviv and stayed at a motel. You won't believe it, Mom, but Farah came to me in my dreams."

Sara's mom moved closer and took her hand. "Farah came to you in a dream?"

Sara continued. "Yes, and it was so real, Mom. She came to me for three nights. I know this sounds crazy, but I think she came to me for a very specific reason."

"Well, it does sound crazy, but go ahead and tell me everything."

Sara sat up straighter and tried to focus her thoughts. "This is what she said: She was born so that we would all fall madly in love with her and, when she left, our hearts would be completely broken. She said that in our brokenness, she would ask me to respond to my pain in a new way."

Ms. Salinger looked confused and said, "So she was talking to you in your dream? Then she wasn't a baby?"

"Mom, Farah was all grown up. She was beautiful, and she looked a lot like Amani with beautiful thick hair. She was comforting me, Mom. I just cried and cried."

"Oh, honey." She leaned over and put her arm around her daughter.

Sara's eyes filled with tears. Her mother's touch brought her emotions back to the surface. "Mom, Farah asked me to respond to my pain by saying *No More* to hatred and revenge. The anger needs to stop here with me." Sara thought about Dr. Rahim. "At Farah's memorial, it is like Shacker's father dropped a bomb with his hatred and it blew our family to the far winds."

Ms. Salinger nodded with regret. "Oh, Sara, you are so right."

Sara continued, "As long as I respond to this pain with revenge or hatred, the pain will repeat itself again and again."

"But Sara, isn't hatred a normal response? I hate the people who killed Farah and there is no other way for me to feel."

Sara quickly said, "But that's what she was talking about, Mom. That thought is what perpetuates the pain and hatred. And most people think it's normal and okay. I don't want to remember my daughter that way. By saying *No More*, everything can change."

Ms. Salinger shook her head in disagreement. "Everything? Sara, I don't think so."

"It all begins with a willingness, Mom. Are you willing to say, 'I don't want another person to feel this way'? Tell the truth, Mom—do you really want another person's baby or child to die in this senseless way? Isn't it time to say enough?"

"Well, Sara, when you put it that way, yes." Ms. Salinger let out a big sigh.

Sara took hold of her mother's hands again. "According to Farah, the first step is to be willing. I spent three nights talking to her, and I have never been more willing. I feel it in every cell of my body—a desire to stop this pain. I never felt such pain and such hopelessness as I did when Farah was taken from me. Never. I don't wish that on any other mother. I don't care about nationality. It doesn't matter anymore. I don't wish this pain on anyone, and if I can stop this cycle, then I will."

"But how, Sara?"

"I'm not sure. I need to find a way back to Shacker and Amani. Farah talked to me about camp. The answer will be found in our memories of camp."

~~~

Shacker's mind was on Sara as he walked home from work. It had been five days since she had left. He kicked at a pebble on the path and watched as it skipped ahead across the cobblestones. He kept looking down at the ground as he walked without even noticing how the sun shone in the cloudless sky.

He reached into his pocket to grab his house keys, ignoring the old Palestinian standing against the wall across the way. Shacker wondered again what he was doing. But, in truth, he really didn't care. He glanced up toward the door before ascending the steps and saw that it was ajar. He tentatively peeked inside and heard a familiar sound. It was Sara talking to herself in the baby's room! His heart leapt. He quietly entered the house and moved without breathing, to Farah's bedroom. There he saw with such relief his love, his wife, sitting and holding one of Farah's toys.

She looked up and stopped talking.

Shacker's voice was quiet as he spoke. "I have been sitting in here every day after work. I am lost, Sara. It is so good to see you." Shacker walked into the room and moved toward Sara. "I don't want to lose you too."

Sara got up and put the toy she had been holding into the crib. Shacker came over and put his hand on her back. She turned and said, "Shacker, we are not okay."

Shacker moved away to give her space and began walking around the room. "Shacker," Sara's anger welled up as she spoke. "I am so angry. When you didn't say anything to your father and looked at the floor, and Amani didn't say anything and just looked out the window, it felt like the greatest slap in the face that I have ever experienced! I needed you. We were supposed to be friends and lovers and you both just let him spew his lies. You have always let him spew his lies!"

Shacker kept walking and said nothing. *What can I say? She is right.*

By now Sara was so angry, she was yelling. "Shacker, for God's sake, say something!"

Shacker continued pacing and said nothing. *I just don't know what to say. If I say anything I will lose her.*

Completely frustrated, Sara grabbed her purse. "I am leaving!"

Shacker reached out and touched her arm. Quietly, he began to speak. "I froze. I—uh—froze." They gazed at each other as he continued. "I knew it was a Palestinian that killed Farah. I felt guilty. I thought maybe you would be better off without me. I am so sorry."

Sara backed away, "I loved you and you said you loved me. You said we would get through this together. And then you froze?"

"Yes. I froze. I made a mistake—a huge mistake. What can I do to fix this? I love you."

"I don't know. I just don't know. Is it possible that down deep you really do hate Israelis?"

Shacker, unwilling to believe what he had just heard, asked in an incredulous voice, "What?"

Sara quickly responded, "The way your father treats me, and you never stand up for me!"

Shacker, now a little defensive, felt his own anger beginning to rise. "I do stand up for you. We always leave." He walked over to the rocking chair near him and sat down dejectedly.

"Yes, that's the way you solve everything, you just leave!" Sara was beside herself. She had never felt so frustrated. *I can't believe how this feels. How can the love that was so real for me days ago, just be gone? I have never felt so lost and alone.* She picked up Farah's stuffed toy and silently asked Farah for help.

Shacker got up out of the rocker and began walking around the room again. Suddenly he stopped and looked directly at Sara. "I'm going to talk to my father and find out why he pushes you away. I'm going to demand that he treat you with respect, or I won't be around him anymore."

Sara softened, feeling her heart once again. "Are you sure you want to do that?"

Shacker again looked into Sara's eyes. "Yes. You mean everything to me. I love you."

Sara gave Shacker a grateful look. "Thank you." *I feel hope for the first time in days regarding Shacker. I wonder if Farah is with us in the room right now.* Sara noticed the picture of Amani and Farah hanging on the wall and smiled. She remembered all the pretty dresses that she bought for Farah. All the darling shoes and outfits. It warmed her heart.

"What is going on with Amani? I called her, and she doesn't call back."

"She's mad because you didn't call her back while you were away."

Sara was immediately engulfed in feelings of dismay. *How will I ever do what Farah has asked me to do?*

"Shacker, I had three dreams and Farah was in each of them."

Shacker moved closer, surprised. "What did she say? I am desperate to know anything. Please tell me."

"Not now, Shacker. I just wanted you to know that the dreams have changed everything for me. I feel so much better."

Shacker, desperate to know that his marriage is still intact, moved closer to Sara. Feeling love in every cell, he asked, "Will you please spend the night?"

Sara looked at him lovingly. "I can't. Not yet."

Shacker felt his heart breaking, along with new determination. *Sara is my love and I have already lost too much to lose her, too.*

Chapter 27

Dr. Rahim's office was cold; the plastered walls were covered with medical diplomas. When Shacker entered, his father stood up from behind his desk and greeted Shacker with a hug. He pulled out a chair for his son and told him to sit. "So Shacker, you said this was important. Does it have to do with you and Sara? Are you breaking up for good?"

"No Father, we're not and we never will. I'm here because I want to understand why you hate Israelis so much. More specifically, I want to know why you hate my wife. What happened to you as a kid?"

Dr. Rahim sat at his desk and strummed his fingers in agitation. "You know the story, Shacker. My younger brother was killed by a stray Israeli bullet. My parents were never the same. They just gave up on life. It made me so mad. My father told us to never touch an Israeli again. Son, they moved into our country and took over. It completely infuriates me. They treat us terribly."

"But Father, what does that have to do with Sara?"

"I hold her responsible—it's her people that have done this to us. You give them an inch, and they will take a mile."

"Sara has done nothing to you. She is a person just like you and me. Her label means nothing."

Dr. Rahim stood in anger. "Shacker, how can you say that? They are scum. They want to annihilate us. They disrespect us, and if you can't see this, I need you to leave this office immediately."

Shacker stood to go. "You are the most irritating human being I know. I just can't believe that you are my father."

Pacing the floor back in his apartment, Shacker picked up his phone. When Sara didn't answer, he left her a message. "Salam, Sara. It's Shacker. I spoke with my father and it didn't go well. I don't want to talk to him anymore. But I called because I think I have a way for you and Amani to get back together. Meet me at Amani's place about 9:00 tonight and I will tell you more."

Shacker and Sara entered Amani's apartment before she got home. They sat on the sofa in the dark. They had their flashlights on. Sara whispered, "What time is Amani going to be here?"

"Her shift ends at nine, so she'll be here a little after that."

Sara looked over at Shacker. "So what are we going to do exactly?"

"We're going to capture her, feed her ice cream, and make her talk to you. I brought rope if we need it. I used to do this to her when we were kids when she wouldn't talk to me."

Sara nervously asked, "Are we going to kidnap her?"

"Not really. You'll see."

A few minutes later, they heard the sound of keys in the front door lock. Shacker and Sara quickly turned off their flashlights before the door opened. Amani came in and fumbled for the light. She turned it on and then screamed when she saw Shacker and Sara sitting on the couch.

"Salam, Sis." Shacker got up and grabbed her arm and led her to a chair. "We want to talk to you. We have ice cream."

"I don't want any, and I don't want to talk to her."

"Fine." Shacker loosely tied her into the chair. Sara put a bowl of ice cream on the table in front of her. Shacker dipped the spoon into the ice cream. "Now, Amani, you can do this the easy way or the hard way, and you know I always win."

Amani opened her mouth and Shacker put the ice cream in.

"Good. Now, doesn't that taste good? Doesn't it make you feel warm and fuzzy all over? Okay, Amani, what do you have to say to your good friend Sara?"

"Nothing."

"That's a good start. Sara, maybe you should say something."

"Amani, I'm sorry I didn't call you back. I was really hurt by what your father said. I just wanted to be alone. Your silence at the memorial hurt me deeply too. I know now we were both terribly sad. Can't we start over? Farah wants us to work together on a project. I love you, Amani."

Shacker force fed Amani another spoonful. She took a moment to eat it.

"Sara, I thought we were friends forever. Period. But you're not my friend. I called you to apologize, and you wouldn't call me back. I haven't heard from you in days! Don't you realize I have been grieving the loss of Farah, too? It would have been so much easier if we could have gone through this together, but you just took off. So I'm done."

"Please don't say that. I wasn't myself. I was hurting. Your father was so hateful and I couldn't think straight. I had to leave. I would've died if I hadn't left. Amani, I needed to be alone."

Amani turned her head away from Shacker and his spoon. "You could have called, Sara." She glared at her brother. "Will you please untie me? This is ridiculous. We aren't kids anymore. I want you two to leave. Please go."

"I couldn't call. I called no one. I had to find my way back alone. Farah came to me in a dream and she wants the three of us to do something. It's important and I can't do it without you both. I need my best friend back. Please."

"What do you mean? What did Farah say?"

"She said she loves us. She said she will always love us. She wants us to bring the camp experience to people."

"What does that mean?"

"I don't know exactly, but I need you and Shacker to help me figure this out. I will do anything to get you back. What do I need to do? What can I do?"

"I don't know. Right now, I'm too exhausted. I just did a twelve-hour shift and want to go to sleep."

"Okay. But can we talk again?"

"Maybe. For now, please leave."

Chapter 28

Sara sat in her mother's kitchen. She slammed her phone down and let out an exasperated sigh.

Ms. Salinger walked in at that moment. "What is it, Sara?"

Sara put her head in her hands. "I don't know what to do, Mom. If one more person gets mad at me, I think I'll scream."

Ms. Salinger came over and put her arm around Sara. "What happened? Who was on the phone?"

"That was Shacker's mom. She's all upset because I didn't call her when I got back into town. Mom, what am I going to do? I can't get anything right anymore." Sara looked up at her mom. "Farah made it clear that she wanted Shacker, Amani, and me to create something, but we can't even be friends. Now I'm at odds with Shacker's mom. This whole thing is a mess. What am I going to do?"

"I wish I could help. She opened her magazine and then stopped. Sara, do you remember when you told me about that circle thing you did at camp that helped with problems?"

"The campfire circle?"

"What if we did that with our families? It might help us reconnect or at least stop fighting."

Sara brightened. "Mom, that's brilliant! But how would we get Amani and her mom to do a family meeting?"

Ms. Salinger shrugged. "Maybe Shacker could pick them up for a visit and not tell them."

"We would have to hold it at our place. It might be good to meet several days in a row, like at camp. I'll call Shacker."

"How are you two doing?"

"Better. Much better."

~~~

Ms. Salinger sat on the couch across from Sara and Shacker. Sara noticed that the apartment she shared with Shacker was a little more cluttered than usual. She had been gone a week or so and she could tell their home needed some deep cleaning.

Ms. Salinger looked at her watch. "What time are they supposed to be here?"

Shacker paced in frustration. "They're late."

Sara fidgeted with the hem of her skirt. "Did they say they would definitely come?"

Shacker looked over at his wife and softened his tone. He could tell she was nervous. "Yes, they did."

Soon there was a knock at the door. Shacker got up and welcomed his mom and Amani into the room. They were surprised to see Sara and Sara's mom there. The recognition stopped them. Sara felt panicky. *Oh, please stay.*

Amani immediately said, "I don't think I want to be here."

Shacker gently replied, "We would appreciate it if you would stay."

Shacker's mom stated angrily, "I don't have anything to say to these two."

Shacker decided to appeal to everyone's heart. "We decided it was time for us to stop hating one another and start telling the truth about how much we care for each other in memory of our daughter, Farah. What do you say?"

There was a long pause where no one said anything. Everyone looked down, avoiding eye contact. Finally, Amani spoke reluctantly.

"Okay. I'll do it."

"Good. I would like everyone to move so that we are all sitting in a circle." Everyone picked up their chairs and moved into a circle. Then Shacker began again. "We are going to do what we did at camp. Everyone gets to say what they want to say. And everyone else gets to listen. No crosstalking. We need to hear each other. Who would like to begin?"

Sara raised her hand and began. "I'm sorry for my behavior over the last few weeks. I was totally annihilated by the loss of my daughter. I've never felt such pain. I left the memorial because I couldn't stay. I had to find myself. I was lost in my grief and didn't know how to climb out. Dr. Rahim's words were like a knife in my heart, but I was more hurt by everyone's silence afterwards. The bomb killed my daughter, but it also blew us apart. I want what we had back. I want to let everything go and start over. I miss everyone. I love you guys. There's a huge hole in my heart."

Shacker replied, "Sara, I understand how and why you did what you did. I felt the same pain. Remaining silent after my father said those words is something I will always regret. I ache for you to be back in my life fully. Mom, I can't stand for you to be mad at me. And Amani, you know how much I love you. I miss you. I'm sorry, and I will do anything to get everyone here back in my life. Anything."

Shacker's mom spoke next. "I don't know what to say. Everyone has disappointed me—everyone."

Shacker had a box on the floor by his chair. Amani, always curious, noticed it and asked, "What's in the box, Shacker?"

"Don't worry about that now. It's for later. Do you want to continue, Mom?"

"Yes. As I was saying, I'm disappointed. We were supposed to be a family and everyone just left. I have not heard from anyone for weeks. Don't you think I've been hurting too? I don't know if I can let go of this. I want to, but I don't know if I can."

Amani, in a depressed voice, said "I feel empty. I don't want to be here and am pissed that you got us here on false pretenses. I hate this. How did this happen? How did we let this happen?"

Sara's mom raised her hand. Her heart pounded, and her mouth was dry, but her resolve was rock solid. "Sara and I have been talking a great deal since she got back. I realized that what we had was pretty wonderful. I don't think Farah would like us acting this way. We have all done stupid things. I have said things I regret. They were said at a time when we were all hurting, and I would like a chance to start over in memory of my granddaughter."

Shacker picked up the box and smiled. "I was wondering if you would like to guess what is in this box now?"

Amani huffed and crossed her arms in front of her chest. "Shacker, I'm in no mood for games."

"Amani, trust me. You'll love what's in this box. I'll give you a hint. You can't eat it. Oh, I guess you could if you wanted to."

Sara caught some of Shacker's light-heartedness. She happily asked, "What color is it?"

Shacker, in his usual fun loving way, responded, "All colors. Bright colors. Fun colors."

Shacker's mom chimed in, "Is it a small planter?"

"Nope"

Amani lightened a little and ventured a guess. "Is it a flower?"

"Nope."

Sara's mom guessed, "Is it a colored pen?"

"Nope. Sara what's your guess?"

"Is it a colored rock?"

"No again."

Amani and Sara both giggled. Shacker smiled and asked, "Do you give up?"

Everyone nodded their heads. Shacker opened the box and pulled out a stack of pictures from their summer at camp.

He passed the pictures to Sara and Amani. Amani burst out laughing.

Shacker's mom smiled and moved closer to get a better look. "How come I have never seen these?"

Shacker said, "They're Aharon's. He took them. Aharon showed them to me yesterday, and I thought it would be fun for all of us to look at them."

Sara picked up a photo and nudged Amani. "Remember this? It was the pie-eating contest. Becca thought she would try to shove the whole piece in her mouth at once!"

Amani threw her head back and laughed. "Oh, wow. What memories. These are great. Shacker, you have whipped cream all over your face in this one."

"Let me see." Shacker got up and walked over to stand behind the girls. He leaned down to get a closer look over their shoulders. He pointed at another picture. "Who is this with her face in a pie? Is that you, Sara?"

Sara grabbed the picture and looked. "Oh my ... yes, I think it is. I got so sick after that. Remember, Amani?"

"I do," she laughed.

The two moms watched as their grown kids relived that special summer at camp. Something melted in their hearts as they saw their kids enjoying each other once again. Mrs. Rahim and Ms. Salinger looked at each other and smiled.

Suddenly, there was a lull in the conversation, as often happens when people are together. But this one felt different. The three friends were back at camp for a moment in the place that had changed their lives forever.

Amani broke the silence. "I'd forgotten how good it all felt there. I've missed this."

Shacker gave his sister a kiss on the cheek. "Sara and I thought that maybe it might be good for all of us to meet two more nights like this. What do you say?"

Mrs. Rahim questioned, "Honey, why?"

Sara, finding her strength, said, "We have been hurting, and we have hurt each other. We need time to reconnect like we did at camp."

Amani nodded her head and said with conviction, "I'll be here. Mom, what do you say?"

"Sure honey, I'll be here. But this doesn't fix everything, or really, anything."

Carefully, Sara's mom answered, "We know. But it's a step in the right direction and that feels really good."

Chapter 29

The day after the family 'campfire circle,' Ms. Salinger answered the door to find Shacker on her doorstep. "What a nice surprise. Come on in."

Shacker's heart pounded but he tried to act cool. "That's okay. I'll just wait out here. Can you ask Sara to meet me? I have a surprise for her."

"You bet." Sara's mom could sense Shacker's adrenaline, and she knew he was up to something. This made her heart swell with hope for their reconciliation. She called up the stairs for Sara. Soon she came down.

Sara rounded the corner and saw Shacker standing outside the door. Her heart leaped as she walked towards him. Trying to seem somewhat aloof, she said, "Shalom, Shacker. What's up?"

Shacker looked at her with his devilish grin. "I want to ask you something. I know it might sound a little strange, but here goes. I have always wondered what it would feel like to kiss an Israeli."

Sara smiled coyly and played along. "Well, young man, I've been wondering what it would feel like to kiss a Palestinian."

Shacker's heart pounded even harder. "Really? You want to experiment?"

Sara paused for a moment, remembering all that had passed between them—all the love that they had shared and all the hurt that had filled their hearts. "I'd love to."

Shacker gently pulled his bride to him. Sara leaned in and they kissed. To Sara, the kiss felt magical—like she was home once again. They touched foreheads and laughed and hugged.

~~~

Sara and Shacker were shooting hoops at the local high school when Amani joined them. Sara welcomed her with a hug. "Want to play?"

"Sure, I would love to. Shacker, have you heard from Father lately?"

At the mention of Dr. Rahim, Sara grew edgy. "Can we not talk about him right now? I am ready to tell you about Farah and the dreams I had. She wants us to do something together."

Amani dribbled the ball a bit and then held it steady on her hip. "What exactly did Farah say to you?"

Sara sat on the ground and began to reminisce about those amazing nights. The others watched her and were completely still. They knew what was about to be said was important. "When I left here, I didn't want to live. I was devastated. That first night as I dreamed, I found myself in a meadow. I saw a beautiful figure walking toward me, and I knew in a moment that it was Farah. She looked just like you, Amani. I fell into her arms and just cried."

Shacker and Amani came over and sat with Sara and put their hands on her.

Shacker carefully asked, "Did it feel real?"

"Shacker, when I woke, I wasn't sure, but I felt so much better. She said love can heal anything. On the second night after I fell asleep, I was back in the meadow. She was very loving. It was love like I have never experienced. She asked me if I was willing to respond differently to her tragic death. To give up revenge. To show the world that there is a better way. That next day, I struggled with that question.

"She talked about a runaway train always moving in the same direction. If the train was to go in a different direction, creating a Peace Train, it had to slow down. Slowing down means doing things differently. She asked me if I wanted to remember her with hate or with love."

"Wow," exclaimed Amani, obviously moved by Sara's story.

"I told her hate wasn't an option. I know that may sound crazy to the two of you, but it is how I feel as her mother."

"On the third night, she came just like before. I was a little sad because I knew I would not be seeing her again. She asked if I was willing to say, *No More*—the pain ends with me. And she asked me if I would join with you two and create a camp-like experience for the people."

Thinking aloud Shacker quietly says, "That seems like a huge request."

"It does, Shacker, but she told me that change begins when one person is willing to say, *No More*, and I am that one. I would love for you two to join me."

"Sara, what is the camp experience? Adults would never come to camp."

"Farah has left that for us to figure out. I have no idea."

"I just remember we made friends easily."

Shacker added, "Count me in. I want to remember her with love too."

Amani then quickly added her support. They sat in silence for what seemed a very long time. The three had been touched by Farah's message and challenge. They wondered what could be created. Sara felt that same presence she had felt while she was away. She had a feeling that Farah or some angel was with them encouraging them. Just for the three to sit quietly brought a healing to each of them. They would feel better somehow. Something was being healed.

Shacker broke the silence. "Sara, I know this isn't going to feel very nice, but I really need to do something with Father first."

"I know, Shacker. I also know that I wouldn't walk across the street for that man. He is mean and thoughtless. And your delay with this project just frustrates me. Farah is waiting."

"I know Sara. I hear you. I do."

Amani asked, "Shacker do you have a plan for what you want to do with Father?

"Not really, but I think he would come to one of our family meetings."

Sara responded with a half-smile, "Remind me not to attend."

Amani bristled, "You might be able to get him there, Shacker, but he might not stay. He'll hate the format. He never listens to anyone."

Shacker's voice took an encouraging tone. "I'll speak with him. You never know."

Sara is off. I understand your anger about the Israelis and how some of them treat Palestinians, but Sara isn't a part of all that. She's different. Yes, she's an Israeli but not all Israelis

Chapter 30

The family gathered again at Sara's and Shacker's home. This time the house looked bright and clean with fresh flowers—Sara had moved back in. The family all sat in the living room. Dr. Rahim was there, obviously uncomfortable. He entered with his usual flair, commenting on the man standing outside.

"Father, we're really glad you are here," said Shacker. "We've felt like you've been on the outside of our family since Farah's death and we want to see if we can fix that. The way we have been conducting these meetings is that everyone gets a chance to speak and say their piece without being interrupted. Can you do that, Father? Can you listen when someone else is talking?"

Dr. Rahim rolled his eyes. "I think so, Son. I'm not that insensitive."

"Good. I'd like to go first. Father, I believe your thinking is mistaken when it comes to Sara."

Dr. Rahim interrupted, "Shacker—"

Shacker put up his hand. "Father, stop. Remember, you need to listen and let me finish; then you can have a turn to speak. As I was saying, I think your thinking about are the same. Treating Sara disrespectfully isn't going to change anything; it's just going to create more anger. I don't want to be around you if you can't find a different way to treat my wife." Shacker let out a sigh and rubbed his sweaty palms together. It felt good to finally say what he had needed to say to his father for a long time. He looked at Dr. Rahim. "Father, do you want to go next?"

Dr. Rahim's face turned red. "This arrangement stinks. Who came up with it? You want to know the truth? Okay, I'll tell you the truth. Yes, you all know my story. I've always hated Israelis. They've always treated me poorly, especially at work. I don't like them. I don't want to be around them. I loved my granddaughter because she was Palestinian." He paused for a moment realizing what he had just said. He stood. "I think I need to leave."

Dr. Rahim walked towards the door. Shacker grabbed his hand. "Father, you don't need to leave. What you said is perfectly fine because it is how you feel."

He ignored Shacker and walked out. The rest of the group looked around at each other uncomfortably.

Sara said, "Well this is an interesting development."

"Let's just continue. There's a chance he'll come back," replied Mrs. Rahim.

"You think so, Mom?" asked Shacker.

"Absolutely."

Shacker looked around the room. "Okay then, who's next?"

Mrs. Rahim raised her hand. "I'll go. I love these meetings. They've helped me so much. I get a great deal of pressure from my friends at work to hate Israelis because we are treated poorly by many of them, but I want to celebrate our family."

Suddenly, the door opened, and Dr. Rahim walked in. Mrs. Rahim smiled sweetly and calmly as though she expected the interruption. As he entered, he apologized, "Sorry. I'm back."

Shacker got up and welcomed him back to the circle. "Mom is talking right now, so please sit quietly."

"But I wasn't finished."

"You'll have to wait your turn. Mom, continue, please."

Ms. Rahim nodded and sat up a little straighter. "Where was I? I love these meetings. They remind me of what we have. We're all mixed up, and I like it that way. Sara and her mom are wonderful to be around, and they make me forget that I have enemies. Actually, I wonder if I really do." She sat back against the couch thoughtfully and then said, "That's it."

Still standing, Dr. Rahim impatiently said, "Can I go now?"

Shacker nodded his head.

"I've been disrespectful to Sara because I've believed she was the enemy. She has never treated me badly. She loves my son. I don't know why, but I need to hate her for all that has happened to me. I just do. I hate this format. It's stupid. I need to leave again." He turned and walked out the door.

"Mom ... what's going on with him?"

Ms. Rahim calmly replied, "Shacker, honey, he's embarrassed. He's never been very honest. He's just self-righteously angry. He's said some things here today that I've never heard him say before. He might be back."

Sara raised her hand. "I think it's time that I speak. I completely trust what is happening here. This is essentially what we did at camp when there was a problem. When honesty is shared and received, change happens. It doesn't matter that Dr. Rahim left. His honesty was received. Something is going to happen to him. I just know it. I'm going to make a prediction. I am going to bet that he and I will be good friends within two months."

Sara's mom shook her head. "I'm glad you have faith, because I don't have any respect for that man. What nerve he has to call Farah a Palestinian. She was Israeli *and* Palestinian. We all know that. That's why she was so special. You want me to be honest here, so here is the truth: I can't stand Dr. Rahim. I hate the way he treats Sara."

Amani was seated next to Ms. Salinger. She put one arm around her shoulder and then looked towards her brother and raised her hand. "May I go next? I wish my father was still here. I never talk to him. My father is my enemy too. I don't know how this distance between us happened. It makes me sick." Amani quickly wiped at the tear that ran down her cheek.

The door opened again, and Dr. Rahim walked in holding a sack. There was a lighter energy about him. Sara noted that he no longer seemed stormy, and she was curious about what was in the sack.

"I'm back," he said as he held up the sack. "And I have ice cream. In our family, we solve problems by eating ice cream, not by talking and not by sharing our feelings. We simply eat ice cream."

Everyone looked at each other, not knowing what to do. Finally, Sara said, "Okay. I'll get the bowls. We have chocolate sauce too."

As Dr. Rahim served the ice cream, everyone started chatting. For the first time in a long time, they were having a good time.

Peace Train

Chapter 31

Shacker's phone rang. He looked and saw that it was his father calling. The ice cream experience had definitely been a step in the right direction, but Dr. Rahim had still remained obstinate towards Sara. After suppressing a groan, Shacker answered the call.

"Salam, Son. I wondered if I could stop by to see you after work this evening. Something strange is happening to me."

Huh, father rarely asks to see me. He usually just barges in without consideration. Could he possibly be changing? What is he talking about feeling strange? Without trying to sound too shocked by his politeness, Shacker replied, "Sure, Father. That sounds nice. Sara will be here, but she will most likely be working on her radio show in the office."

Dr. Rahim gently, almost sheepishly, said, "That is fine. I don't mind if she is there."

After hanging up, Shacker sat back in his seat. He couldn't suppress the hope inside of him. He quietly said aloud, "I hope he really is changing. It would all be for you, Farah. The one thing about your grandpa is that he certainly loved you with all his heart." Shacker smiled, feeling the presence of his daughter as love radiated through his body.

~~~

When the doorbell rang, Sara closed herself in the office to let Shacker and his father talk in private—well, in semi-private. If Sara kept quiet, she could actually hear their conversation through the wall.

Shacker gestured for his father to have a seat on the couch. After several minutes of small talk, Dr. Rahim said, "Shacker, something has happened to me."

Shacker raised his eyebrows. "What do you mean?"

Well, I hated that family meeting thing the other night. I mean, it's not what I like to do. I really made a fool of myself."

"Father, that's not true."

Dr. Rahim put up his hand and let out a sigh. "Wait, let me finish, please. I want to talk to you because something has happened to me. At work, I noticed that something was different. I wasn't sure what it was, but then my friend said something to me. He actually laughed and wanted to take my temperature because he thought I was sick. He kept questioning, "Where is your fire? I miss it." With that I realized that I'm not as angry as I was before, but I'm not sure why."

"Father, what do you mean, you are not as angry?"

Dr. Rahim stood up and paced. "Well, I'm aware that I've been angry for most of my adult life. But now, I'm not angry most of the time. It's strange; it feels like an old friend has left me. What happened?"

"Maybe it happened because you were willing to share honestly how you feel."

Dr. Rahim's eyes looked different. Instead of being filled with fury and fire, they were calm, but there was uncertainty there, too. "What do you mean by that?" He sat back down on the couch and took a sip of his water.

"Well, I know that at camp, when we did this activity where we spoke honestly, it changed things for us. We weren't as afraid or angry. I think it's powerful to be heard and accepted."

"I don't understand. Give me an example."

"Okay. Sara used to forget to lock the front door when she came home. It frustrated me because I felt like she was being irresponsible. When I complained to her, she got very defensive. So I decided to use this technique that I learned from a relationship book. I told her that I wanted to understand her perspective on the situation. The minute I said those words to her, her defensiveness evaporated. She told me that she suddenly realized she was distracted when she came in through the door, and she was always thinking about the next thing she had to do. So, the door was rarely locked; sometimes she even left it wide open.

"When I heard this, I could completely relate. I do so many things while distracted every day. With that realization, I was no longer mad, and then I could share my perspective from a place of understanding rather than condemnation. I simply told her why I thought it was important for us to keep the front door closed and locked. She completely understood and something shifted in her. Every day since that conversation, she has come in, closed the door, and locked it. Everything is energy, you know that, Father? There is good energy and bad energy. There is power in listening to each other—it heals."

"So you're telling me that just because I told the truth about how I felt and people heard it, it made the anger go away?"

"I think so, Father. Perhaps the process let you release some belief that was making you angry. I don't really know. I also want to say that you did not make a fool of yourself the other night. Yes, you may have said more than you wanted to say, but that was perfect."

"I don't understand this, and I should; I mean, I'm a doctor, for heaven's sake."

"Father, stop trying to figure this thing out. Just enjoy the benefits."

Dr. Rahim shook his head. "I don't know if I can do that. I don't know if I can treat Sara differently. I want to because I know that if I don't, you won't be in my life, and I couldn't live like that."

"Father, all I ask is that you try." Shacker put his hand on his father's shoulder. "You might just like her. She's really a wonderful person. We're going to continue our family meetings. I hope you will come again. It was nice having you there."

He stood quickly, ready to leave, "Call me. I might come, but I can't guarantee it."

Sara had her ear up against the office door. When she heard Dr. Rahim say *might*, her heart leapt within her. *Maybe he is changing, Farah!*

~~~

Shacker sat himself down beside Sara on the couch. He gave her a quick peck on her cheek. "What are you reading, Babe?"

Sara sighed. "It's a book I got from the library about peaceful communication. I don't know, Shacker—you think we will ever be able to make a difference?"

Before Shacker could reply, he heard a knock at the door. He got up to answer it and saw his father standing at the door with a big smile on his face and a bouquet of flowers in his hand. He walked pass Shacker and directly to Sara, handing her the flowers. "Peace."

Peace—the word enveloped her heart in warmth.

Sara shook her head to make sure she wasn't dreaming. She smelled the flowers and then smiled widely at her father-in-law. "Thank you!"

Shacker asked, "Can you stay for a bit, Father?"

Dr. Rahim smiled at Sara and then shook his head. "I have to go, but I will see you soon. By the way, that man is standing outside your door again. Why haven't you done something about him?"

Shacker responded, "I have. I yelled at him and I then realized he's not hurting anyone so I just decided to leave him alone."

Chapter 32

Shacker, Sara, and Amani sat around the kitchen table strategizing. They were trying to fulfill the task Farah gave Sara, but they were having trouble coming up with a plan.

Shacker ran his fingers through his hair and then took a sip of his water, trying to revive his energy. "So what did Farah say to you in the dreams again, Sara? I think I need to be reminded. It feels like we just keep going around and round without figuring out a strategy."

Sara cleared her throat. "Well, she said that she came to us for a very specific reason. She said that she came so that we could respond to her death in a brand-new way."

"What do you think she meant by that?" asked Amani.

"I'm not sure, but she kept saying that she wanted us to bring the camp experience to the people."

Shacker suddenly stood up. "Hold on! I know what she's talking about. We have been doing this over the last few weeks. The camp experience is the family meeting. That's why Father had the reaction he had. We did the camp experience on him."

Sara's face brightened as she slapped her hand on the table in realization. "Shacker, you're right. How did I not realize this before?"

"And it's been working perfectly, too," Amani added.

"So, the elements to the camp experience are this: we meet, no cross-talk, we do something fun, and then we eat. Is that it?" asked Sara.

"Yes, that's it. I wonder why it works so well," Amani mused, pulling her hair back into a ponytail.

Sara waved her hand like a school girl. "I know the answer! When a person is allowed to say what they feel honestly, and if it is received by another, then things change. I believe that love is what does the changing."

Shacker shrugged. "I don't know if that is exactly what happens, but I will say that things have been changing in our family. The camp experience got all of us talking again and Father is not the same person he was, that's for sure."

"Amen," added Sara.

Amani furrowed her brow. "My question is, would this make a difference? Would this help to accomplish what Farah wants us to do?"

"I think so," said Sara, nodding. "She wants us to say, *No More*, which means that the pain of her death ends with her. She asked us to not respond with revenge or with depression, but in a new way that connects those who we could easily hate. It's about discovering whether friendship is possible, which seems almost impossible until you think about the family meetings. Look at what has occurred with your father. It's a miracle. And yet it isn't. It works. Farah said the first step is always a willingness to say, *No*

More. You may still feel the anger but are you willing to feel something different and find understanding."

"Wow ... So if I understand it correctly," Amani said, standing up, "Farah wants us to bring this experience to the people. We could do that with the radio show. Since we have personal experience, we could talk about it with some authority. But what would we call it? We couldn't call it a family meeting."

"No, it's not a family meeting. It's a meeting with people of differing backgrounds and opinions," answered Shacker.

Amani snapped her fingers as an idea came to her. "We could call these meetings Friendship Meetings, or Friendship Trains, or Friendship Groups. No, no, I have it—Friendship Pods!"

Sara smiled and nodded. "Friendship Pods?" She paused to consider it. "I think this could work. We will want the friendship pods to be small."

"I kind of like it," said Shacker. "It's different and strange, which seems just right. You girls could announce it on your radio show."

Sara jumped up. "That's a great idea, Shacker! I'll talk to my boss tomorrow. We can probably start this week. What do you say, Amani?"

Amani nodded, grabbing her phone. "Guys, you have got to see what was on my phone this morning. It took my breath away. I'm warning you."

She showed a picture to Sara and Shacker. They both gasped and then looked at each other. Sara cried quietly and Shacker put his arm around her. It was a picture of Sara and Farah after the blast as Sara walked down the street. The caption over the picture read: "Friendship would never let this happen again."

Peace Train

Sara soon found strength to speak again. "Wait a minute. This is perfect. This is our anthem. We must have posters of this made and we can sell them on our website. This is what Farah was talking about. This violence will never stop until we begin to understand one another. The Friendship Pods will do this. The people who were with us at camp will make up our first pods. We can train them if necessary, but it won't be that difficult. We can put the rules on our website. I have a feeling that this is really going to make a difference. It may even go viral."

Shacker was excited too. "So, we are going to call them Friendship Pods. I like it."

"I do too," exclaimed Sara and Amani together.

~~~

Over the next few days, the girls shared the Pod idea with their moms. Both were very excited. They felt in their heart that it would work. Sara and Amani decided that they should plan a weekly meeting with the family and call it a Friendship Pod. Shacker invited his father to be part of these meetings, too.

Sara finally felt well enough to return to work. It had been almost three months since she had been on the radio. Thankfully, her boss was more than understanding, allowing her time to grieve and heal.

When she walked through the doors of the studio, she breathed in deeply. *Oh boy, it feels good to be back here.* She saw her boss across the way. His tall, lean frame moved slowly through the studio as he tried to read the script in his hand without bumping into any of the equipment or other workers as they went back and forth. The place bustled with its usual chaos.

Sara called out, "Hey, Jimmy! You got a minute?"

Jimmy looked over his dark glasses and brushed his messy hair from his eyes. "Sara, welcome back!" He smiled warmly and walked over to give her a hug. "How are you feeling?"

"Much better! That's why I want to talk to you."

"What's up?" Jimmy folded his arms across his chest and gave her his undivided attention.

"Jimmy, I really don't want others to lose their babies like I have."

"Okay ... "

"Shacker, Amani and I have developed something that I think has the potential to bring more friendship between our countries. Let me show you a picture that was taken."

Sara pulled out the picture of Farah and herself after the bomb. Jimmy looked at it and blew out a heavy sigh. "Geez, Sara. That is powerful."

Sara nodded in agreement, taking back the photo to keep it safe in her purse. "I know, Jimmy. And someone has to say *No More* to all the anger so another situation like this doesn't happen again. I think that someone is me, Jimmy. To that end, the three of us have come up with something we're calling Friendship Pods. We did these pods at camp long ago when we were teenagers, and we've been doing them with our family over the last few weeks. The bomb and Farah's death really tore my family apart, but the pods have brought us back together. It's powerful, Jimmy. After we began the Pod meetings, things really shifted. What we want to do is bring these pods to other people and into their homes."

Jimmy nodded, encouraging Sara to continue.

"The reason I'm telling you this is because we would like to use the radio show to launch this project. We want to talk about it on the show and encourage people to participate. We can even do video trainings on our website, and we'd like the station to be our headquarters. Everyone working on the project will work from their homes with their computers, but we need a homebase. I would like to put up a poster of the picture I showed you. What do you say, Jimmy?" Sara's heart pounded. *Please understand the importance of this. Please jump on board with this project.*

After a moment of consideration, Jimmy repositioned his glasses and said, "If I don't have to do anything, you can use this station any way you want. I think this is a great idea, but if I'm being honest, I really wonder if it will make a difference. I don't want to discourage you, Sara; I'm just trying to be realistic, but let's wait and see how the ratings go."

Sara's shoulders slumped a bit, but then an image of Farah flitted across her mind. She stood tall, with a renewed determination. "Thanks Jimmy. I appreciate the chance to try this out. I hope the show will surprise you by being a success." She gave Jimmy a hug and they went to their offices.

Sara contacted a couple of her friends from camp that afternoon and asked them if they would help with the Friendship Pod project. Both persons were excited and happy to help in any way possible.

Once she had made her last phone call for the day, Sara sat back in her chair and closed her eyes. *We are on our way, Farah. We're in the flow of the river. Everything is falling into place. I wonder if you are helping us in some way?*

Chapter 33

The next evening, the family gathered at Shacker's and Sara's apartment. After they were all seated, Shacker stood up. "Sara, Amani and I have decided that Farah's death is not going to turn into more hatred. The three of us have made a commitment to bring our camp experience to homes all over our two countries."

Dr. Rahim drummed his fingers on the arm of his chair and asked, "Just how are you going to do that?"

Shacker held up both hands. "Just hold on, Father. I'll let Sara explain."

Sara's voice shook slightly as she began to retell the dreams she had experienced. She told of Farah and how real it all felt. "It changed my emotional state almost instantly. I suddenly felt hopeful and directed." She then went on to explain the idea behind the Friendship Pods. "They provide a way to bring the camp experience of friendship to everyone. In fact, these family meetings we've been having are actually Friendship Pods."

Though Dr. Rahim had come a long way in his acceptance of Sara, he still had far to go. "Humph, Friendship Pods? That sounds ridiculous. I have no interest in a camp experience."

Ms. Salinger and Mrs. Rahim eyed each other knowingly. Then they looked sweetly at Sara, encouraging her to continue.

Sara cleared her throat. "We want our family to kind of be the guinea pigs of these pods. And we hope each of you will participate."

"Sara, that sounds great, but what about our extended family? It would be great to bring more of our relatives into this," Ms. Salinger suggested.

Sara beamed at her mother. *She has really bought into this idea!* "We will definitely include them, but later. It would be nice to first have this small pod established and working well before expanding it."

Ms. Salinger nodded as Sara continued. "First, we want to show you a picture that someone posted on Facebook the other day. We don't want you to say a word; we just want you to look at the picture. Then you can comment on it. Deal?"

Everyone in the room nodded yes. When Sara showed the picture to everyone, there was a collective gasp.

Shacker honored the silence that followed. After a pause, he asked, "Can we all sit now in a circle and begin?"

Everyone moved into a circle. Shacker, sitting next to his mother, began. "We want to hear what you have to say, and we want to understand your perspective. We want to know what is important to you. There is to be no cross talking."

Sara cleared her throat and said, "I will begin, if that is okay with everyone. I'm energized and excited about what we are doing. I know it will make a difference. When I saw that picture for the first time, it took my breath away. Then, when I read the caption, I felt inspired. Amani and I used to talk about how we would feel if we ever lost one of our children in the warring between our countries. We both wondered if we could survive such a tragedy. Well, I've survived and am fully committed to the prevention of future tragedies. Someone has to say *No More*, and I am that someone. For me, these pods are my action to make sure that what happened to all of us doesn't happen again." Sara quickly wiped away a tear that ran down her cheek. "Dr. Rahim, thank you for the flowers. In the interest of being honest, I also want you to know how much the way you have treated me in the past has hurt me. It broke my heart to see your willingness to accept my daughter, yet turn your back on me just because I was Israeli. I know my culture has hurt you, but I have not. And I want you to know that your words at her memorial almost destroyed me. I pray that this dance between us is over." Then she turned to Ms. Salinger. "Mom, do you want to go next?"

Ms. Salinger grabbed Sara's hand, then gave her a quick kiss on the cheek. "Sure, honey. The family meetings have helped me. My heart has been so heavy, both for you and for Shacker. I've not known what to do to help you. I really don't know if this plan of yours will work, but for Farah's sake, I think it's worth a try. All my issues with the Palestinians are old—*very* old. I really want to let them go and start over. I've enjoyed having our blended family. It's nice to have different people loving different people, and it keeps life interesting. Thank you for this. By the way, I think the poster is perfect."

Shacker reached over and gave Ms. Salinger's arm a tender squeeze. Then he looked at his sister and raised his eyebrows. "Amani, would you like to go next?"

Amani began to speak, but her words got caught in her throat. After a few moments, she mastered her emotions enough to say what she was feeling. "I've felt such guilt. I had a feeling, Sara, that you and Farah weren't supposed to go to the café that day, but I said nothing to stop you. When I heard the blast from my apartment, I knew something awful had happened. I've felt like Farah's death was my fault. I hope you all can forgive me, and I hope I can forgive myself for not listening to my intuition. I want to do this project with all my heart. Because we lost Farah, we can speak from truth and people might be more willing to hear us. I have a feeling that this is the answer we have been looking for." Amani wiped her tears and looked at everyone in the room. "I want to thank each of you for being here. We can't do this alone."

Mrs. Rahim walked over and gave her daughter a hug. Then she went back to her chair and shared what was on her heart. "I was stunned to see the picture of you and Farah. It's a powerful image, and I think it says a lot. I want to handle my granddaughter's death differently. I really do, and I'm willing to try this pod thing. It actually feels good to express my feelings, so thank you for allowing me this opportunity."

Shacker cleared his throat and said, "Thank you for sharing, Mom." He sniffed back tears. "The pain that I have felt over the last weeks makes me think about all the other people connected to the café bombing who have been feeling this same kind of pain. And then I think about all the people who, for the last fifty years or so, have endured this same kind of pain because of similar senseless tragedies. I know there are many who will join us in wanting this madness to stop. I will do anything to promote peace. I am here for all of you one hundred percent, and I want to thank everyone here for supporting me and Sara. It means more than you know. I love you all."

Dr. Rahim stood up and went over to his son and put his arm on his shoulder. Then he raised his hand to speak as he sat back down. "I will try to stay today. I still don't prefer this format, but I have to admit that it is working. I'm not sure why, but I can honestly say that I've experienced a shift in my emotions over the last few days. I'm not as mad as I've been over the past years. I talked to Shacker and he tried to explain it to me, but I still don't understand. Getting Palestinians and Israelis together seems crazy to me, but perhaps I need to learn something in this regard. I will just have to see, but for now, I'm here and I don't feel the need to leave. Sara, I had no idea that what I did and said to you hurt so much. I was just doing what Palestinians and Israelis do to one another all the time. It's just what we do. I didn't know it hurt so much."

After Dr. Rahim had finished sharing, there was a collective pause as everyone looked quizzically at each other Then Ms. Salinger said, "So, what do we do now?"

Amani, Shacker, and Sara looked at each other and shrugged. Amani said, "We're not really sure. Why don't we talk about our plans for the Friendship Pod?"

Sara spoke up. "I think it would be fun to play a game before we have refreshments. I have a balloon in the other room; why don't we see how many times we can hit the balloon back and forth without it falling on the floor? How does that sound?"

The moms were hesitant, but surprisingly Dr. Rahim appeared excited by the idea. He helped Shacker push the furniture back to create an open space for the game.

Sara went to get the balloon. *Nobody seems very excited about this idea except for Shacker's father. Fingers crossed—I hope this works ...*

As soon as the balloon was in play, the shouts and laughter began. Ms. Salinger lunged after the balloon and hit it towards Amani, who squealed and managed to keep it in the air with a fantastic save. Ms. Rahim exclaimed, "I feel like a kid again!"

Finally, the group decided it was time for refreshments. They all wiped the sweat from their brows and Sara took the balloon back to her bedroom. As she did, she realized something. *The*

Friendship Pod sharing time opens the door for connection to happen, and then the connection actually occurs when we all work together doing something like playing a game. This could really affect change in a huge way—I think we are onto something, Farah!

An hour later, Shacker said goodbye to both mothers and his father and closed the front door. He made his way back to the living room where Amani and Sara sat chatting. He plopped down next to Sara. "That went way better than I imagined it would. I felt some relief when I spoke. Just saying how I felt really lessened the hold my emotions have had on me. I feel less sad and more hopeful."

Amani leaned forward and rested her elbows on her knees. "I felt that, too. How about you, Sara?"

"Yes, I definitely felt relief, and when we played the balloon game, I noticed that something important happened: true connection began. When we were trying to hit the balloon, we didn't think about race or status or position; we just reacted. We laughed and had fun. I even had fun with your father!" Sara smiled at the memory. "I think participating in a game is key and should be part of every Friendship Pod."

Shacker's enthusiasm was visible. "I agree. At camp, that's what happened! We forgot ourselves, started having fun, and discovered we could be friends."

"Maybe tomorrow we should come up with a bunch of games, ones that are similar to the balloon-hitting game, and then we can list them on our website as a resource," added Amani.

Sara nodded her head. "Great idea. What else did we learn tonight?"

Amani raised her hand. "I think the opening is important. Shacker, when you said that you wanted to hear what everyone had to say and that you wanted to understand their perspective, those words seemed to create a space where everyone felt comfortable and willing to say how they really felt. Will you please type the gist of what you said tonight so we can put that on our website, also? It would be great to have an example for people to follow."

"Absolutely."

Sara felt inspired. "We did it, guys. I think this is what Farah wants us to do." She wiped away the tears that were starting to fall.

The threesome talked for a few more minutes and then Amani yawned and stretched. "Hey guys, I'm beat. I need to go home. This has been great, and I really think what we are doing is a catalyst for major change. It could even become a movement!"

Amani grabbed her purse and hugged Shacker and Sara. Shacker walked her to the door and said a final goodnight. As Shacker opened the door, he noticed the man standing across the way. *Why is he there?*

When the door closed, he turned to Sara and embraced her tightly.

She hugged him just as tightly and said, "Shacker, I feel whole again."

"Me too, Babe; me too."

They turned out the lights and walked hand-in-hand back to their bedroom.

PART THREE

Chapter 34

The day after the pod meeting, Sara sauntered down a cobblestone street in Jerusalem towards her radio studio. The sky was a bit overcast, and there was a slight chill in the air. She pulled her cardigan more tightly around her body. She caught herself looking down at her feet again—a bad habit her mother always tried to discourage when Sara was a child—and reminded herself to glance back up. A bright light, brighter even than the sun, suddenly appeared before her but then vanished just as quickly. Sara's heart pounded.

What was that?

She shook her head and figured her fatigue was finally catching up with her. The last few nights had been restless.

~~~

After kissing Shacker goodnight, Sara fell quickly asleep and found herself in her radio station. With her headset on, she was about to switch to the next caller when she caught sight of Farah through the doorway standing just outside her office. Farah smiled, blew Sara a kiss, then disappeared. Suddenly a blinding light filled the radio station.

Her heart pounding, Sara awoke and sat up in bed. Her forehead beaded with sweat. She looked over and saw Shacker sleeping. She gently nudged him awake.

"Wha … what is it, Babe? Is everything okay?"

Sara's eyes were wide open with a mixture of anxiety and surprise, but then her face relaxed into a smile as her mind put the pieces together. "Shacker, Farah has been with us this whole time. She is helping us with the pods, directing our steps the entire way. I know it sounds crazy, but she has shown herself to me, like she did just now in my dream. I know it is her, Honey." Sara's eyes welled up with tears, and she could feel her daughter's love in her heart. It was so strong that Sara could almost picture Farah in the room with her.

~~~

Everyone gathered once again for another pod meeting in Sara's tidy living room. The room smelled fresh, like pine. Shacker stood up in front of his family to set the ground rules for the evening. "We want to hear from each individual and we want to understand your perspective. We want to know what is important to you." Shacker rubbed his hands together. He felt a burning in his heart and decided he needed to share first. "I want to say that I'm committed to this Friendship Pod program." He turned toward Dr. Rahim. "Father, I know that you are trying to be kinder to Sara. I appreciate that. I know that Sara does too, and I hope that you and I can have a better understanding of each other through these pods. I've always disagreed with you, but I think I'm now open to understanding why you feel the way that you do. I'm very happy that you are here."

Dr. Rahim nodded to acknowledge his son's comment.

Ms. Rahim shifted in her seat and raised her hand. "I must say that the Friendship Pod experience last week made a big difference for me. I've been grieving just like the rest of you. After the pod meeting, I felt much better. I haven't been as sad, and I've even found some happiness again." Ms. Rahim looked over at her son and smiled. "To answer your question, Shacker, what is important to me is that we find a way for all Palestinians and Israelis to get along and to like one another."

Amani raised her hand and said, "I'd like to share next." She turned to Dr. Rahim and said, "Father, I've always been afraid of you and have never been able to understand your anger over my friendship with Sara. I would like to understand; I feel distant from you and I would like that to change. After the last pod meeting, I felt better. I was less sad, less tired, and less angry. And the thing that is important to me is that the kind of pain I have felt from Farah's death does not repeat itself in the future, for me or for anyone. I want that kind of senseless pain to stop."

Ms. Salinger nodded in agreement and understanding. Then she raised her hand. "Like the girls, I've felt different this week. I've been grieving the death of my granddaughter for months, but now I feel better. I felt safe talking last week. It must be the structure of this circle, because tonight I feel very safe too. I just want all of us to get along. That's what is important to me."

Sara leaned over and squeezed her mom's hand. Then she raised her hand to speak. She turned to Shacker's father. "It helped me to understand you better last week when you shared that what you did to me was just what Palestinians and Israelis do to one another. It made me realize that we hurt each other without knowing it, and this puts walls between us. That is how we can so easily kill one another."

Dr. Rahim cleared his throat and shifted uncomfortably in his seat. "Well, I guess I'm next then. To tell you the truth, I'm a bit uneasy with this format again. Talking about my feelings doesn't come naturally to me, but I will tell you this: Palestinians and Israelis should not be together like this because we are just too different. Nothing good ever happens when we're together. I know you all judge me for the way I treat Sara, but I've only been trying to do what is right for my son. When Shacker told me he was thinking of marrying an Israeli, I couldn't believe my ears. Shacker is good-looking and could have had any woman, but he came back from this camp and all he could talk about was this Sara girl. I was sick. I hoped that he would grow out of it, but then Amani told me that this same girl was her best friend. It made me crazy. What was happening to my children? I wondered what my father would have thought if he were still alive."

Dr. Rahim paused for a minute, almost as though he had forgotten where he was. Then he continued. As he did, the other family members tried to listen and not judge, but it was very difficult, especially for Sara. "I could just imagine my father turning over in his grave," Dr. Rahim said as his face went a shade redder. "When I was a kid, my three-year-old brother was killed by a stray Israeli bullet. My parents were never the same after that. I remember my father being angry all the time. He used to sit my other brother and me down and tell us awful things about the Israelis. He told us to never touch them. I loved my father, and I believed everything he told me. Some of you probably think I didn't love Farah since she was half Israeli. I loved that child, but to tell you the truth, sometimes I wanted to throw her across the room because of her Israeli blood, but I never did."

Ms. Rahim and Ms. Salinger both gasped at this confession. Dr. Rahim paused for a moment, realizing what he had just said. Then he shook his head and said, "Why am I telling you all of this? Maybe it's because I don't want to lose my son. I'm willing to find a new way to feel about Sara. I don't know what's happening here, but I feel different. Maybe Sara and I will someday be good friends." He looked over at Sara and laughed as though what he had just said was the most ridiculous idea ever.

He thinks it's all a joke, Sara thought. *He really doesn't believe we will ever be friends, but I do. Only time will tell.*

After the game, which involved a lot of laughter, just like the previous time, the family members went to get some refreshments. Amani was having a nice discussion with Ms. Salinger when Dr. Rahim walked up and interrupted them. Everyone noticed and stopped their conversations to see what he would do next.

r. Rahim placed his hand on Amani's shoulder. "Daughter, excuse me for interrupting, but I wanted to thank you for what you shared earlier. I don't want there to be anything between us." What he did next, shocked everyone, but no one was more surprised than Amani. Her father wrapped his arms around her and gave her a warm hug. Tears instantly pooled in her eyes.

Sara's eyes welled up with tears, too, as she knew Dr. Rahim hadn't gotten that close to his daughter in years. Suddenly, Sara saw that he now stood in front of her. Through her tears, she saw him smiling and looking at her.

"Sara, I meant it when I said that maybe we could be friends someday. I don't know how to start, but maybe a handshake will work." Dr. Rahim extended his arm and Sara grabbed his hand in hers.

It's a start! Sara thought as her thoughts filled with images of her daughter.

Chapter 35

Amani and Sara sat on their stools at the radio station. They put on their headphones, like they always did, but today they had extra butterflies in their stomachs. They were going to announce their Friendship Pod idea to the listeners of their show, and Sara planned to talk about her experience of losing Farah also.

Three, two, one...

Sara adjusted her headset and began. "Shalom, everyone, and welcome to the Sara & Amani Show. We're so glad that you're with us. We have something very special to share with you today. Most of you know that my daughter Farah was killed in a suicide bombing a few months ago. When that happened, I thought my life was over. I had never been so devastated, but something else happened that changed everything. After Farah was killed, I ran away to Tel Aviv. While I was there, I had three dreams over three nights. These weren't normal dreams because I still can remember every little detail of them. I don't know how to explain what happened. All I can say is that these dreams were as real to me as anything I've ever experienced." Sara took a deep breath and looked over at Amani for strength. Her best friend gave her the thumbs up sign, and she continued.

"My beautiful daughter came to me in these dreams, but she was all grown up. She came to me to ask me to respond differently to pain. What do we normally do with pain? Sometimes we fall into a depression and then we try to get out of it by turning to hate and revenge. That's what I had done. It's a normal response, and maybe even reasonable. However, my daughter is asking us to stop this behavior because it's the only way to stop this pain from happening again. I don't want another mother to lose her child like I did that day. My anthem is, '*No More*.'" Sara paused to take a sip of her water. Then she sighed deeply and silently prayed, *Farah, give me strength to continue.*

Sara opened her eyes again and spoke into her headset. "In these dreams, my daughter encouraged Amani, Shacker and myself to create an experience for people, similar to what I had experienced at Peace Camp when I was a teenager. The goal of this experience would be to help support a new way of responding to pain.

"As many of you know, Amani, Shacker and I met at a camp in the United States when I was just sixteen years old. We became friends almost immediately. Actually, almost everyone did. It felt easy. After my dreams, the three of us began meeting to figure out how to bring a camp-like experience to others. This experience would give people of differing heritages and beliefs an opportunity to meet and interact in a safe and accepting environment. Fear is taken out of the equation, creating a place to discover whether tolerance, respect, and understanding are possible."

Sara glanced out through the doorway and spied Jimmy giving her the thumbs up. *His gesture must mean that a lot of people are tuning in to the show. Okay, Farah, we've got to keep going. I need more of your strength now.*

"We fear each other mostly because we don't know each other, and we don't understand each other's position. Many of us think we have nothing in common with people from other cultures or with other beliefs. Actually, before camp, I believed that I had nothing in common with Palestinians. But when Amani and I met, we could not believe how alike we were."

Amani laughed and piped up. "It's true! Sara and I could talk for hours, or we could just be in each other's presence and not say anything at all. We have always been completely comfortable with each other. That is, until Farah died. The hatred and pain we felt against those who had been involved with the bombing almost tore us apart."

Sara nodded. "That is true, Amani. I don't think I have ever felt more alone. I had no one. I had never realized how much I had depended on you until you were gone. I pray that never happens again."

So Shacker, Amani and I have created something quite exciting. The purpose of what we have created is to heal the generations of mistrust and hatred that results in so much misery and loss. It's called the Friendship Pod."

"Friendship Pods are made up of six to eight people of differing heritages and beliefs. Each pod is started by two people from different backgrounds who have already discovered friendship and connection, like Amani and me. The next step is to invite more people into the pod who are open to meeting and interacting in a safe environment with someone different from themselves. The purpose of the pod is to listen to one another and discover whether tolerance and respect are possible. Most people with differing heritages never have the opportunity to meet in a safe environment and understand one another."

"The meeting is run in a very specific way so that respect is maintained. The pod meets weekly. Videos and written instructions on how to run a pod meeting are available on our website.

"The three parts to the pod meeting are as follows: First, there is sharing with no crosstalk. It is important for each member to share their story while everyone else listens. This is a very powerful and respectful process. Next, the group plays a simple game for a few minutes. Finally, they enjoy refreshments together. What is shared in the circle can't be discussed during the refreshment time. Anybody can do this. It's all very simple."

Sara looked over at Amani. "Amani, how about you tell the listeners about the benefits of Friendship Pods."

Amani beamed. "I'd be happy to, Sara. Well, we've been experimenting with these pods for the last few weeks. We invited our mothers and my father to our first two meetings. After the first meeting, both our mothers reported that their grief over the loss of their granddaughter had lessened considerably. They also reported that they were feeling a deeper connection to the others in the group. My father came to one meeting and said that he was no longer angry. If you knew my father, you would know that this was a huge victory. I appreciated his openness and vulnerability. It helped me to understand him better. We've never been very close, but those two meetings brought us far closer than ever before."

"Thanks Amani," Sara chimed in. "We're going to take a quick break now. Please go to our website and look at the poster that is printed on our first page. We'll be back shortly to talk more about the pods and about this poster."

The girls took off their headsets and breathed a sigh of relief. "Amani, I think it is really going well." Amani nodded in agreement. Sara continued, "You know, I think we should talk a little about how the pod is a way to bring camp home. When we get back on the air, why don't you talk about the poster and the *No More* slogan."

Sara peeked at the time and realized they were going to be on the air in *3, 2, 1* ...

"Shalom, everyone, and thank you for tuning back into the Sara & Amani Show. We're going to continue our discussion of peace. Before the break, Amani and I spoke of the camp we attended when we were teenagers. I have spoken with many campers over the years who attended similar camps in the United States. Most of us shared a similar feeling of frustration for not being able to bring the camp experience to our lives and to the lives of others when we returned home. I know that I was frustrated, and I know that Amani and Shacker were too. We believe the Friendship Pod is a way to bring the ease of friendship to people who don't believe friendship is possible. We have the power to make a difference. Amani and I remember how easy it was to make friends at camp, and now we have a tool that will allow us to do that here. I would like Amani to talk further about the pods and the picture that I hope you had a chance to look at."

Amani smiled widely and spoke into her headset. "Salam, everyone. I hope you all had a chance to look at the poster on our website during the break. The day we began putting the pod idea together, a friend posted this picture on my Facebook page. It shocked us at first and then it became the inspiration for what we are doing—it essentially became our battle cry. Farah asked us to say, *No More*. So the pain stops with us."

Sara glanced around the studio and noticed that the usual hustle and bustle wasn't present. In fact, every other studio engineer was silently watching and listening to Amani as she talked. Even Jimmy, who rarely stopped, sat in a chair with his eyes fixed on what Amani was saying.

She continued. "The Friendship Pods, I believe, will support all of us in saying *No More*. I don't wish the pain I experienced from the senseless death of my niece to be transferred to anyone else. We have to stop doing hateful things to one another in the name of revenge or in the name of being right and justified. The only way that's going to happen is with understanding and respect.

We fear each other because we don't know each other. I want to hear and understand your story. The Friendship Pod gives each of us a place to share our story so that it has the potential to be understood and appreciated and released."

"Please remember that, in order for the pods to work, they have to be run in a very specific way. It is not difficult, but please read the directions and view the videos on our website. We are here if you get stuck and need us. Remember that each pod begins with two people of differing heritages who are already friends."

Amani glanced down at her notes. "I want to say again that we are calling out to all the graduate campers who were frustrated with their inability to bring camp home. This is your chance to change everything. Find a friend who is not like you. Visit our website and learn how to run the pod meeting. Invite two new people who are different from the two of you and discover the magic of the pod. It's easy, and we're here to help you. We would like to hear how things are going, so please contact us via email or phone. We have volunteers manning the phones from 5:00 to 7:00 pm each day. If you do set up a Friendship Pod, we'd like to know about it so that we can keep track of our numbers. Once your Friendship Pod is working, we would like you to help start another Friendship Pod. We will talk more about that next week."

Sara pulled the microphone piece back down by her mouth. "It looks like we're about out of time for today. Thanks for listening, and we will share more next week. Until then, let's end the momentum of hatred and fear by saying *No More*. Until next week."

Amani and Sara slipped off their headsets and sat back in their chairs. Jimmy walked through the door soon after. "Awesome job, ladies. I think my initial reaction to your idea was wrong. In fact, I would like to set up a Friendship Pod with some people I know."

Sara was about to comment, but before she could, the social media manager rushed into the room. "Guys, our Facebook page is going crazy. There are already so many comments and posts about the show that it will probably take a week for us to respond to all of them!"

I guess people really do listen to our show. Farah, you were right ... this is working!

Within a month, there were over a hundred pods in the city and beyond. The poster was put up for sale on the website, and over two thousand posters sold within the first few weeks.

Chapter 36

The next week, on pod night, the family showed up on time to Shacker's and Sara's home. The members quickly got seated in a circle and Shacker said his usual introduction.

Dr. Rahim raised his hand. "I would like to begin, if that is okay with everyone."

The group nodded.

"I want to tell you all about the last two weeks. Last time I was here, I said some things that I really didn't want to say. I was truthful but I'm sorry if I hurt anyone's feelings. I'm here because something amazing has happened to me. I haven't told many people the story about my family. Anyway, what I want to share is that, during the past few weeks, I haven't been as angry. Usually at work I'm always mad because of the way Palestinians are treated. For the last two weeks, for some reason, I haven't been as angry about this.

"I went into the supply office to see if they could order a new piece of equipment that I need for inhalation therapy. The lady in the supply office is an Israeli and we've always hated each other. She is always giving me the runaround, never accommodating my requests. It drives me crazy. This last week I went into her office with an intentionally calm demeanor. She seemed a lot more peaceful too. She told me that she would check into the availability of the part I needed. She asked me to check back in two days because, by then, she would have an answer for me. Well, I did that, and she told me that the part would be in on Friday. I almost choked. This has never happened, ever! So, I looked at her and jokingly asked, 'You aren't by any chance in a Friendship Pod, are you?' You won't believe this, but she said yes. She then told me that her daughter had gone to one of the peace camps in the United States a few years ago.

"Last week this same daughter invited her to a Friendship Pod. She didn't know anything about it, but she went anyway and loved it. I told her about all of you. We laughed and talked about our experience. A lady in the same office came over and wanted to know what we were talking about, so we explained to her about the Friendship Pod. I let the first lady explain. Then I went back to my office, laughing. I'm at a loss for why I feel so different, but I do. I've let go of something, and letting go is changing my life for the better."

There was a moment of silence before Amani chuckled. "Shoot ... if this can work on my father, it can work on anyone!" The group laughed, but no one laughed quite as heartily as Dr. Rahim.

Sara looked over at him. *Wow, he really has changed. This is amazing!* She then raised her hand. "When we announced the Friendship Pod to the world on the radio station, it felt wonderful. I felt empowered. It feels like I'm doing exactly what Farah wants me to do. I feel hopeful that my cry of *No More* will be heard by many people. It won't just be a saying, but it will effect change. It will be a movement."

After the rest of the group shared, they played a game. Afterwards, Dr. Rahim walked over to Sara and looked into her eyes. "Sara, I have to apologize to you again. Please forgive me for the things I said during our last meeting."

Sara smiled and held out her hand to shake his. "Apology accepted."

After the parents left, Amani, Shacker and Sara sat down in the living room together. Sara blew out a big sigh and said, "Wow, that sure went well. Did you see your father come over and apologize to me during the refreshment time?"

Amani, who always noticed things, announced, "It's the camp experience, Sara. It's working like magic, even on my father."

"Why do you think it is working so well?" Sara asked.

Shacker smiled and replied. "The Friendship Pod is all about energy. Maybe when there is a safe space and we are honest with one another; a field of love is created. A book I read talks about how love can transform and heal anything. Sometimes when you see what you don't like about yourself, if you *really* see it, it will go away. Maybe that is what happened with Father."

~~~

A week later, everyone was gathered in Sara's and Shacker's house once again. During the social time, Sara stood by the food table and munched on a carrot. She noticed Dr. Rahim coming towards her.

In a somewhat loud voice, so all in the room could hear, Dr. Rahim said, "Sara, I think we need to stop the war between us. What do you say? Since I'm the one who started it. I guess I should be the one to stop it. So come over here. I'd like to give you a hug."

The memory of Shacker first asking her to experiment with a kiss at camp flashed through Sara's mind. The memory made her smile. She walked into the open arms of her father-in-law. He kindly and gently wrapped his long arms around her in acceptance. For the first time, Sara realized her father-in-law smelled faintly of peppermint. Her eyes filled with happy tears.

A quote she had once read came to Sara's mind. *The holiest of spots on Earth is where an ancient hatred has become a present love.*

Chapter 37

The Friendships Pods gained momentum quickly throughout the city and beyond. Each week callers went on the air to tell Amani and Sara of their miracles. By the second month, there were more than 2,500 pods countrywide. People traveled to different towns just so they could be in a pod. Sara had rallied ten volunteers who worked non-stop finding pods for new participants. Unfortunately, this growth and movement wasn't all good news.

During the middle of the night, the phone rang, waking Shacker and Sara from a deep sleep.

Shacker answered the call and then handed the phone to Sara.

"Shalom," she said sleepily. It was Jimmy. Sara sat up.

"Sara ... the station was bombed. Fortunately, it is still standing and the equipment is mostly okay, but there is a five-foot hole in the wall. The note said it was because of the Friendship Pods. I hate to do this, Sara, but I hold you responsible for this. You know the station is on a tight budget, and I simply do not have the means to fix the damage."

The adrenaline coursing through Sara's body made her now fully awake. "Was anyone hurt?"

"No, and like I said, there isn't much damage to the inside. The hole needs to be fixed, though, and insurance won't cover it. We have some boards in place to block the hole, but come over in the morning so you can see what it looks like. We will have to figure out how you're going to pay for this."

Sara let out a deep sigh. "I'm glad you are okay. See you in the morning." She hung up the phone and looked over at her husband and explained what Jimmy had said. "What are we going to do, Shacker? We have to cover the cost of fixing the hole. Plus, what if more of these acts of violence happen? Fortunately, no one was hurt this time, but we may not be so lucky next time."

Shacker reached over and took her hand. "Sara, we will figure out how to pay for it, so you don't have to worry about that part. As for future acts like this one—well, no one can predict the future and we can't live in fear. We just have to keep doing what we think is best."

Sara lay back in bed and tried to sleep, but her mind wouldn't rest.

~~~

The next morning, Amani and Sara met at the station to assess the damage. The gaping hole on the side of the building was hard to miss. Amani groaned and then stepped closer to get a better look. Finally, both women went inside to talk to Jimmy.

Sara sat down in his office and folded her arms across her chest as her brow furrowed. "How much do you think this will cost to fix?"

Jimmy thought for a moment as though doing calculations in his head. "Maybe 4,000 shekels. But who knows, maybe you can get some of the work donated."

After talking with Jimmy about the logistics, Amani and Sara headed over to their office to chat. Amani threw up her hands. "How are we going to pay for this, Sara?"

Sara's shoulders slumped, but then she had an idea. "What if we put a call out to all our listeners? Maybe someone will have an idea on how we can get this fixed."

Amani's eyes lit up. "That just might work, Sara. Heck, it doesn't hurt to try. What have we got to lose?"

That afternoon, the two friends put their headsets on and got ready to tell their listeners about the situation. Sara opened the show, saying, "Shalom, everyone. This is the Sara & Amani Show. We have a situation that has developed that I would like to address in today's show.

"When my daughter was killed, she wasn't killed by a bad person. She was killed by fifty years of unresolved anger. For years in our region, things have been happening that have hurt a lot of people. We can carry that hurt and anger forward with us like a ball and chain or we can let it go by putting a new voice to our pain. The Friendship Pods are not about winning or losing. They have to do with friendship and finding that new voice."

"Here is our situation," added Amani. "Someone blew a hole in our radio station wall because of the Friendship Pods. Insurance won't cover the needed repairs, so we are asking anyone with the proper skills to come and help us repair the wall. We don't have the funds to fix it by ourselves. If anyone can help, we would really appreciate it."

Sara continued. "We've talked briefly on the show about having the pods do monthly projects together. I know this is asking a lot, but perhaps one or two pods with construction experience could come together and help us repair the wall. Amani and I will pay for the materials. We just need someone to donate their time and experience. If you can help, please call in to the station. "

The rest of the show was filled with callers sharing their pod success stories. Many callers shared how they felt the hole in the wall was actually a symbol of success showing that the radio show and the pods were communicating an important message. By the end of the show, members of several pods had called in to donate their time.

Amani smiled. "Apparently there are a lot of people with construction skills willing to help!" She giggled in delight as she took off her headset. "I can't believe that one guy even said he would donate the materials. Sara, that means this repair project won't cost us a shekel!"

Sara swiveled around in her chair to face her friend. "I know, Amani. This just proves that we are doing something right with these pods."

~~~

The following Saturday, all of the volunteer construction workers arrived at the radio station to help. Members of other pods in the area came and brought food. One pod had a DJ who came with his music to make the atmosphere more festive. Unfortunately, some protesters had arrived before the work crews. They positioned themselves with clubs and blocked the entrance to the station.

Shacker looked at his wife and confidently said, "Don't worry, Sara. They will be gone in no time." After a quick phone call, law enforcement officials arrived and their presence sent the protesters scampering. With that problem solved, the crews got right to work.

All of Sara's questions about whether the pods were working were erased that day as she watched Palestinians and Israelis working together, sharing tools and building materials. She even saw two men shake hands. It was poetry in motion, and they were doing a beautiful job.

By 3:30 pm the wall was fixed. Jimmy was pleased and went around to shake everyone's hand. Then the party began.

A couple of bands set up to play and soon people were dancing, eating, and talking with one another. Sara roamed through the crowd chatting with people.

A Palestinian woman in her mid-forties came up to Sara. The woman had a drink in her hand and her eyes sparkled with joy. "Sara, I want to thank you for everything you and Amani have done with the pods. I've been attending one for a couple of weeks now, and already I notice such a difference in my life. There is so much joy and acceptance within the group."

Sara heard more stories that day about people living fuller lives and becoming more peaceful. Later in the afternoon, Amani found Sara amidst all the people, and the two friends hugged. Then Amani said, "It's crazy to say, but the hole in the radio station wall was really a blessing. It has shown the power of the pods. I think we need to get a list of community projects together for each month and let the pods sign up for different volunteer work. This is all too amazing, Sara. We've got to keep up with the momentum and foster more experiences like this one today."

Sara's mind started rolling with that idea. "We could have a list on our website of different needs. This would do two things: it would strengthen the friendships in the pod and it would strengthen the communities where the work is being done."

By 10:00 pm that night, the festivities had come to an end. People helped pack up and clean up, leaving the property spotless.

As Sara grabbed her belongings, Jimmy came over to her. "These Friendship Pods may be your best idea yet, Sara. And hey, I'm sorry for putting this all on you to figure out. But I gotta say, you sure did a bang-up job. I'm amazed at the results." Jimmy patted her on the back and walked off.

He's right, Farah. It really is working.

When Sara got home that night, she was so filled with joy that she felt compelled to report about the event on the radio show's blog and Facebook page. She thanked everyone and posted pictures she had taken throughout the day.

There was a huge surge of new pods right after the wall repair event. By the end of the next six months, there were 50,000 pods between both countries involving more than 350,000 people.

Chapter 38

Amani and Sara met for an early morning walk. The streets were quiet, as the shops weren't yet open and there wasn't much traffic so early in the day. Both women were silent, too, lost in their own thoughts. The sounds of their footsteps on the cobblestone street created a peaceful rhythm as they walked. Soon, they heard another pair of footsteps behind them.

Amani turned and saw a stout man coming upon them. His face was red with anger and he yelled out, "Hey, are you the pod girls?!" Though far smaller than Sara in stature, Amani put her arm out in front of Sara in protection. She assumed a powerful stance and said, "Yes. Do you need something?"

The man stopped a few feet from the women and didn't seem to have any intention of coming closer. He pointed his finger at them. "You girls must stop what you're doing. My wife won't talk to me."

Sara felt a little afraid and then she saw the little man from outside her house standing next to this man and he began pushing him away. The little man said, "Back." The angry man said, "NO!" and he pushed the little man back. The little man was thrown backwards and almost fell before catching himself, and he just kept coming. Every time he was pushed away, he just kept coming harder. Amani and Sara just stood there watching this with amazement, not knowing what to do. Finally, the angry man turned to them and asked, "Who is this?"

Sara answered, "I don't know." Sara and Amani turned and walked away. The angry man again blocked their path and said, "You must stop doing the pods or I will stop them for you."

The little man came back and Amani put her hand out while saying, "Please stop. We are fine."

Sara then looked the angry man in the eye. "Why won't your wife speak to you?"

"Because I won't join her friendship pod," he said with a huff.

"Why won't you join her pod?" asked Amani.

The man rolled his eyes. "What a stupid question. I don't do things like that. I don't do girly things."

"Well, have you gone to a meeting?"

"No," he said with a look of total disgust. "Why would I do that?"

Sara wondered if she could reason with this angry man. She decided to give it a try. "Listen. My father-in-law, who is a doctor and very professional and serious, came to our friendship pod. He really likes it. He is even going to bring his good friend."

The man seemed to calm a little.

"Look, just go once. Then if you don't like it, I'm sure she will understand, and she will start talking to you again."

Amani agreed. "My father wasn't thrilled with the format. He walked out a few times, but he really likes it now."

The man crossed his arms over his chest. "I don't do that kind of thing."

Amani shrugged. "What kind of thing?"

"Share my feelings and play games. It sounds too embarrassing. I'm a man. I work. I don't talk about how I feel."

Sara tried to reason with him a bit more. "Well, you are sharing your feelings right now with us. It was apparent when you approached us that you were angry. Consider going to a pod meeting one time. You certainly don't have anything to lose and it may be a positive experience. Remember, at the meeting, you don't have to say anything you don't want to say."

The man walked off in a huff.

"Did that just happen?"

Amani shook her head. "We need to talk about this on the show. I even wonder if we should have Father on the show."

Sara's eyes grew wide. "Whoa, do you think he would do it?"

Amani nodded slowly and thoughtfully. "I do. Whenever he gets excited about something, he tells everyone about it. Just like that lady he hated but was having a good time with. He is very courageous, and he doesn't care about what people think of him. That is why he is known at the hospital as a bull dog."

~~~

The next morning, the two friends talked to Dr. Rahim and asked if he would be on their show. To their surprise, he happily agreed. The next day they all met at the radio station to record the show.

The engineer took the three of them into his room to fit Dr. Rahim with headphones, and then he did a sound check. As they waited, Sara's mind spun, and her stomach tightened. *What have Amani and I gotten ourselves into? Who knows what Dr. Rahim will say on the show? I sure hope I can keep him under control. I wish Shacker were here to help. He is always so good with his father.*

They walked over to their usual recording room and Jimmy brought in an extra stool for Amani's father. Dr. Rahim sat between the two women. For some reason, this configuration made Sara feel even more vulnerable. She took a deep breath, the countdown began, and the show went live.

Sara straightened up in her seat. "Shalom and Salam, everyone. Welcome to the Sara & Amani Show. We are very glad you're with us again. We have a special guest today. It is Amani's father and my father-in-law, Dr. Rahim. Amani and I were walking the streets the other morning and a man came up to us and started yelling. He was angry because his wife wouldn't talk to him over his refusal to join her Friendship Pod. We suggested that he go just once and see if he liked it. He was concerned that attending the pod would not be viewed as a manly thing to do. So, we've brought Dr. Rahim to our show to discuss this issue. Dr. Rahim is a well-known physician in this city. He has been coming to our pod meetings for quite a while." Sara turned to face Dr. Rahim. "Welcome to the show, Dr. Rahim. We're so happy to have you on the air today."

Dr. Rahim adjusted his mic. "I'm glad to be here too."

"Dr. Rahim, tell us how you felt when you first heard about the Friendship Pods."

"Honestly, I thought they were a little too woo-woo for me. It seemed like something only women would do. I really didn't want to participate at all. But I decided to try it one time. I figured if I didn't like it, I wouldn't go back. As it turned out, I was intrigued enough to attend the second meeting. Then I really began to enjoy myself. It was especially nice to be in a pod with my family."

"Were you uncomfortable at first with the format?" asked Sara.

Amani suppressed a giggle as she watched her father nod vigorously. She sat quietly beside Dr. Rahim, remembering how slowly and ungracefully her father had warmed up to the idea of the pods.

Dr. Rahim continued. "Yes I was, but there was no pressure to say anything I didn't want to say. I got a little angry and said some things that surprised me and I left the meeting early. I wasn't going to come back, but what changed my mind were the benefits. Simply put, I'm not nearly as angry as I used to be."

Amani jumped in. "Please explain that."

"I didn't realize this, but I've always been very angry. I'm sure my children have always known, but it wasn't obvious to me that I had so much anger hanging over me for so many years. I simply wasn't aware of it. It felt normal, like an old friend. I noticed the day after my first Friendship Pod meeting that something was missing. I felt more peaceful and the anger had lessened."

"How did that make you feel?"

"I was less stressed. Things didn't bother me as much. My good friend asked me what was up. I wasn't sure at first, and then I thought that maybe the pod was having an effect on me."

Amani said, "Father, why don't you share the story about the lady at work."

A warm smile, the kind Sara had never seen on Dr. Rahim before, flitted across his face. "Oh yes, this is good. There is an Israeli lady at work who has been a thorn in my side for years. She is never helpful to me and interactions with her have always been miserable. Well, the day after the first pod meeting, I had to talk to her about getting a piece of equipment. In the past, she had been totally unaccommodating, but on that day, something was different. She was nice to me and I just happened to ask, as a joke, if she was a member of a Friendship Pod. And she said 'yes!'"

"That must have been such a surprise," Amani said, chuckling.

"Absolutely."

Sara added, "We would like to know what you would say to men who are unwilling to try the Friendship Pod."

"I would say don't be so chicken. Go one time and see what it is really like. It might make your life better, like it has made mine. I have something else to say. Ladies, if your guys won't go to the pod meeting, go on strike. Tell them no dinner and no sex until they try."

Amani and Sara leaned back in their stools to look behind Dr. Rahim at each other. They both covered their mouths in shock. Amani quickly recovered and said into the mic, "Nice advice, Father. I remember hearing that, in some part of Africa, the women wanted their men to stop their violence and put their guns down. The women joined together and gave the men an ultimatum. They asked them to put their guns down or else there would be no sex. I guess at first the men laughed but when they discovered that the women were serious, the guns were put down rather quickly."

Dr. Rahim added, "Sometimes you have to speak the language that will best be understood."

Sara, aware of the time, announced the commercial break. Before she could turn off her headset, the engineer's voice was in her ears. "Sara, you got a caller on line two. She sounded really determined to speak to you, so maybe you could take it even though you're on a break."

Sara agreed and pushed the button for the call to come through. "Shalom, this is Sara. How may I help you?"

The voice on the other line was full of energy. "Shalom, my name is Anna. I was listening to your show today and, when that man on your show suggested what he suggested, I just had to call. About three weeks ago I did this exact thing to my husband. It was one of the most courageous things I've ever done but, like your guest says, sometimes you have to speak their language to get your message heard. I would like to share my story."

Sara received a warning message from the engineer, which meant that in less than a minute, they would be back on air live. *This woman's story could be perfect, Farah. If she gets out of hand, I can cut her off.*

Chapter 39

The countdown began. Three, two, one …

"Welcome back," said Sara. "An interesting call came in during our break. A lady by the name of Anna has used the idea that was suggested in our last segment. She wants to share her story with us.

Amani added, "Salam, Anna. Why don't you tell us a little about yourself?"

"Ok. Well, my name is Anna and I am Israeli. I've been going to pod meetings for over six months now. I love them. They're the best thing for me at this point in my life. I'm a homemaker and my husband works for the military. He's really a nice guy, but when he comes home, it is all about him. My job is to keep him happy and to support everything he does. I've always been there for him. When I first went to the pod meeting, he was very much against me going. But I think that's because I always came home in a good mood. He told me that he really didn't mind if I went. Still, he made it clear that he would never go with me. Well, I have been asking him to come, just to try it, for a long time now. I figured it was a reasonable request, since I support him in everything that he does. I keep a nice house. I feed him well, and we generally have a great relationship as long as I do what he asks me to do."

Sara interrupted. "So how did you get the idea of withholding food and sex? What prompted you to do this?"

"Some of my friends in the pod and I were talking about how we could get him to come to the meeting just once. Someone, as a joke, said, 'Why don't you threaten to not feed him if he doesn't come?' That is how it all started. Then I began thinking that, for him, food and sex are very important. So, I hatched a plan."

"So, what was the plan?" asked Amani.

"Well, on the next pod meeting day, I would cook a really nice dinner. Then I would tell him that if he refused to go to the meeting with me, I would go on strike, which would mean No More food or cleaning or sex. Period."

Sara's eyes grew wide. *This woman's got guts!* "Were you afraid?"

Anna laughed loudly. "Afraid? I was terrified! I always try to do what he wants me to do, but I felt rebellious. Like I said, my husband works for the military and he is very set in his ways. He wants his drink and his dinner soon after he gets home from work."

Amani leaned into to the mic. "So, set the stage for us. What happened?"

"Well, as I said, I cooked his favorite dinner. When he got home, he went immediately to the refrigerator and grabbed a soda. I asked him if we could have a talk before dinner and he rolled his eyes and said yes, as long as it was short. So I sat down and told him that I really wanted him to go to the pod meeting that night. He told me, 'Never!' Then I asked him why. I told him it was only fair that he supported me in something that is important to me. I also added that I thought the pod could contribute to our relationship. This was not a good thing to say. He flew off the handle and began going on and on about how hard he works for me and that I wouldn't have the life that I have if it weren't for him. This made me mad. I told him that I was not asking for the moon; I was simply asking him to accompany me to one meeting. He then said, "I don't do women things." My anger gave me courage to say, 'Okay, I'm going on strike until you agree to go to one pod meeting. That means I do not cook, I do not clean, and there will be no sex."

Amani whistled low into the mic. "How did he react?"

"I thought he was going to drop his soda. I wish you could have seen his face. It was priceless, actually. I think it was the first time he ever really heard me."

"Amani chuckled then asked, "Can you describe it?"

"He looked stunned, like I had thrown a bucket of water on him. I think he was completely shocked that I had the guts to talk to him that way."

"So what happened next?" asked Sara.

"I had made Malawach, his favorite, and I knew he knew that. He saw it when he went in the kitchen for his soda. I got up and told him that he had five minutes to decide and if he didn't decide to go to the meeting, this would be his last supper. I then told him that his five minutes started now."

"How did he react?"

"Well, he got all flustered. He wanted me to wait a minute, and he followed me into the kitchen as I repeated that he had five minutes to decide. Then he began to beg. He said, 'Please don't make me do this.'"

Amani shifted her weight on the stool. "I bet you felt really powerful."

"I did! I just stuck to my guns. Finally, he came over and said, 'Okay, you win. I will go just this once.' I assured him that one meeting was all I was asking for."

"So, what happened when he went to the pod meeting?"

"I'm so glad I get to share this. When he got there, he recognized someone he used to work with. During the first part of the meeting, I thought he might leave, but when his friend spoke, he listened intently. His friend shared about something that had happened to him as a child. When it was my husband's turn, he said, 'I would like to add to the story that my friend told.' He then talked about when he was a little kid; he was always really scared. The kids around his block use to beat him up because he was Israeli. His mom was always afraid, and he didn't feel like he could protect her. That is why he went into the military. He wanted to feel safe and to protect people.

"I had heard this story from my husband before, but I was glad he shared it with the others in the room. When we left the meeting, his first words were, 'Are you no longer on strike?' I assured him I wasn't. He said he wouldn't be going again."

Sara's voice was filled with compassion. "What did you do when he said that?"

"I didn't react. I just said that was fine. I didn't mention it again. One week later, when I was about to leave for the pod meeting, he announced that he wanted to go too. I tried not to react, but I had to know why he had changed his mind. He said he just felt better after going to the meeting, and he wanted to go one more time. He now goes every week and is even more enthusiastic about it than I am."

Amani clapped her hands in joy. "What a wonderful story! I'm so glad you shared it with us. I hope that the men who are listening tonight will realize that pod meetings aren't just for women. They are for everyone. Trying it one time to see if it is right for you won't hurt. You may even like it."

Sara ended the show by saying, "Thank you, Anna, for sharing with us. Our time is up. Until next week! Happy podding!"

Sara had an immense feeling of satisfaction. Currently, there were over 100,000 Friendship Pods between Israel and Palestine. Some were even popping up in the United States and other countries. The movement was rolling like a Peace Train running downhill at top speed.

Dr. Rahim had stuck around the station until the end of the show. As Sara and Amani packed up, he came back into their room and said, "By the way, girls, I didn't tell you, but I have a date with the Israeli lady at work!"

After the initial shock, Amani managed to say, "Great. What is her name?"

"Rebecca."

"A good Israeli name. Is she Jewish or Christian?"

"I don't know. We are just friends, really."

Amani and Sara looked at each other in amazement. They said goodbye to Dr. Rahim and watched as he walked out the door with an extra bounce in his step.

Sara looked at her best friend with wide eyes and a mischievous smile. "A date? Amani, do you realize how much he has changed over these past few months? He went from being a do-not-touch-Israelis kind of guy to a man who now dates them. Ha!"

Amani brushed her hair back as she put her purse on her shoulder. "I know. I can't wait to tell Shacker. He will never believe this."

Chapter 40

When the Peace Camp people in the United States began to work with the Friendship Pods, they truly made a difference. They understood what Sara and her group were doing. They spread the word to other peace organizations, who also got on board to spread the pod idea. It seemed to Sara the pods supported something that was aching to be expressed: true friendship.

~~~

Over time, Sara became aware of a growing curiosity about the man who had been standing 'watch' outside her and Shacker's apartment since the bombing. She decided to find him and ask him directly. Shacker asked her not to do this. When she insisted, he asked that she at least take her cell phone so she could call for help if needed. Sara assured him that she would be careful, explaining that she didn't think the man was dangerous.

Early one morning, Sara left the house and began to walk, hoping the small man would find her. She walked through the old city streets.

It was her favorite time of day. The merchants had not yet opened their shops, and the sun was cresting over the hills. Sara soon noticed a small man walking behind her. She turned slightly just to make sure it was him. Yes, it was. To her, he almost seemed like a presence of protection. She didn't sense any fear of threat; the man seemed peaceful, but she was curious about his presence. She stopped and turned around and slowly stepped toward him. He immediately turned to walk away, so Sara shouted, "Excuse me, sir. Wait! Please wait!"

The man stopped in his tracks. When Sara caught up to him, he was staring down at the ground. She carefully moved so that she was facing him. "Salam. Please tell me who you are."

He continued to look downward. She could tell he was an older Palestinian who hadn't bathed in days. His clothes were dirty and his hair unkempt. Sara repeated, "Please, sir, I've had this feeling that you have been protecting me. Am I right?"

He answered without looking up. "Angel told me to."

Sara stood motionless for a few minutes. Then she pressed. "What angel?"

He shook his head no but he lifted his face a bit. Sara saw that he had no front teeth. Still, his eyes were clear and bright.

"Please tell me about this angel."

"Dream ... "

"You met the angel in a dream?"

He nodded.

"What did the angel look like?"

"White," he said as he ran his hands down his side indicating a dress, and then he touched his hair and said, "Dark. I ashamed; I not talk to you."

Sara's heart pounded in her chest. "Wait, I'm desperate to know more. Please tell me about this angel. She had on a white dress and her hair was dark? Was it also curly?"

He nodded yes. *His angel must be Farah. I'm sure of it.* She waited a moment then said, "I had a dream too." He cocked his head. "It was my daughter who came to me. She too had on a white dress and her hair was dark and curly. She was all grown up in my dream, but in life, she died as a baby. She was one of the victims of the café bombing last year."

"I ... I go."

"No, I must know who you are. Please. I need to know."

"I ashamed."

"What did the angel ask you to do?"

"Protect you."

Sara's heart filled with love for her daughter. "Why? Why did she come to you? Why you?"

He shrugged.

"Do you know why?" Sara pressed.

He quietly answered, "My son die with baby."

"What?" Sara's head spun and she felt faint. She asked for clarification. "Your son died in the blast with my baby?"

He nodded.

Sara's mind reeled. *Farah picked this guy to protect me because his son died too.*

"I feel better protecting. I filled with shame. Angel tell me protect. I feel better."

Sara's heart shattered for this broken man. *Farah came to him to make him feel better, as she came to me. All this time this man has been standing outside my door to protect me because my dear Farah sent him.* Sara looked into the man's eyes. *Why do I feel like this is not the whole story? Why does he feel shame? What is he not telling me?*

"Sir, thank you for sharing this. I feel much better knowing who you are. But what are you not telling me? Why do you feel shame?"

He shook his head and put his hands up in front of him. "Must go—not say more."

"Please, this is important to me. Please."

He looked down. "Much shame. My son die. He have bomb."

Her mind screamed inside her head. *His son killed my baby!* The rage inside coiled around her like a snake. She wanted to take this man by the neck and throw him to the ground and stomp and kick him. The hatred in her heart felt suffocating. *Farah, what do I do?* She then saw an image of her daughter in her head. Farah smiled and reached out to her. Sara heard the words, *No More.*

Suddenly, the anger was gone.

Sara bent over, her hands resting on her knees. She took a deep breath and then looked up. Instantly, she was surprised to see the pain in *his* eyes. *I know that pain. That is my pain I see in his eyes. This is where we must begin*

Finally, Sara found her voice. "I see your pain. It's like mine. This is a new day, and I will not hate you. I want to understand. Your pain is my pain."

He said nothing. Sara then realized they stood on the corner where the bombing happened. There was a new café. She said, "Please, let's have coffee and celebrate the love of our children. Please."

"I no money."

Sara brightened. "I have money. I would like to call my husband and have him meet you too."

He stared at her. "I shame. Why not mad?"

"I want to do things differently, and my husband does too. It will be okay. I promise."

Chapter 41

Sara and the man walked over to the café and ordered a coffee. They found a table, then Sara called Shacker. While they waited for him to arrive, Sara asked the man about his son.

"He a carpenter—an artist. He not marry. He good to his mother. He good boy."

They quietly sipped their coffee and then the man added, "You know my son. He go camp with you. He name Tarif."

Sara almost dropped her mug. She could no longer breathe, and the world seemed to stand still. When Shacker arrived and saw Sara's face as white as a sheet, he wrapped his arms around her and whispered in her ear, "Are you alright?"

Sara shook her head no, but then she nodded yes. She pulled out of the hug, wiped her tears, and introduced her husband to the old man. "Shacker, this is … I'm sorry, I never got your name."

"Bahir. Call me Bahir."

"Bahir, this is my husband Shacker and I am Sara."

Sara's mind screamed, *This is the man whose son killed your baby. This is Tarif's father. Tarif killed your baby! How can you have coffee with him?*

Somehow, Sara silenced the voice of pain inside her mind and found enough courage to speak. "Shacker, Bahir's son was killed with Farah; Farah came to Bahir in a dream and told him to protect me."

Shacker pulled out a chair and sat down. "Wow. So that is why you have been outside our house. You were told to protect us?"

Bahir nodded. "There more."

Shacker looked at Sara. After a long pause, Sara let Bahir tell Shacker the whole story as she prayed. *Shacker, please don't kill him.*

Bahir began. "I fill son with hate. I hate."

Shacker scrunched up his face. "What?"

"My son tie bomb to body."

Shacker understood and looked down. His breathing was hard and strained. Then in a very rational and controlled voice, he asked, "So it was your son who killed our daughter?"

Bahir; nodded slowly and began to cry. "I so ashamed." He wept and wept, his body heaving with each sob.

Shacker and Sara looked at each other as they grabbed hands. Silence gripped them; they didn't know what to do.

Sara finally spoke. "There is more, Shacker. Bahir's son was Tarif, our friend from camp."

Shacker sat stunned as he squeezed Sara's hand tighter.

Bahir looked him in the eye. "When Tarif come home from camp, I tease him. He tell me he make friends with Israelis. I sick. How could that be? I call him names. I call him Israeli lover. I wake him at night and call him Israeli lover. I so afraid. I afraid I lose son. He stop being happy. He mad all time. I keep calling him names. My wife mad at me. We fight over son. Son move out and we not see son much. He look sad and mad when he left. When son die, wife blame me. I know my fault. I undo if could."

Minutes felt like hours to the young couple. *I don't know what to say to him, Farah.* Then, inspiration. "I have a great idea." Bahir looked up. "Bahir, you must come to our Friendship Pod meeting this week."

He furrowed his brow and Sara realized he didn't understand her.

She spoke slowly. "Let me explain. Our daughter came to me like she came to you. And she asked me to respond to her death in a new way. She was fine, and all grown up in the dream. So Shacker and his sister Amani and I decided to create something that would heal the hurt between people. We have hurt here." She pointed to her heart. "The purpose of the Friendship Pod is to heal hurt and to help people become friends. This may sound crazy, but I want to understand why this horrible thing happened."

Bahir's mouth dropped open.

Sara leaned closer. "Your son didn't do this because he was evil. I knew him. He was not evil. He did this in response to hurt—your old hurt. We need to let this old hurt go. I want to respond to my daughter's death with love instead of hate. Like I said, I know that sounds crazy, but it is the only way to stop the killing. It is the only way to stop the pain. Someone has to say *No More*, and that someone is me. So please, will you come to our meeting this week?"

Sara felt Shacker suck in a deep breath.

After a few moments, Bahir agreed that he would come. Finally, he stood, and the three said their Shaloms and Salam. Then the young couple followed Bahir; as he left the café and walked slowly down the street.

As they walked back to their apartment, neither spoke. They were lost in their own thoughts and Shacker was trying to contain his anger.

When they entered the house, Shacker blew up. He threw his hat across the room and turned to Sara, "Sara what were you thinking? This man turned Tarif back to hatred and he then killed our daughter. I want to kill that guy. I don't want to see him again!"

Sara took a deep breath. Her response sounded almost upbeat. "I know. It's perfect."

Shacker had been pacing the room like a caged lion. He froze, responding with disbelief. "What are you talking about? Did you hear me? I want to kill that guy. He took something very precious from me. He deserves to die!"

Sara turned to Shacker. "Yes."

"He killed our daughter. I never want to see him again!"

Sara remained calm. "Shacker, do you believe what has happened to us tonight? The man standing outside our home for months is there because Farah asked him to be. He is also the father of the bomber that killed our daughter, and we know the bomber: his name is Tarif. We went to camp with him. Someone is trying to tell us something."

Shacker fired back. "Yah, kill the bastard."

"Shacker!" Sara stared at her husband, unable to believe what had come out of his mouth.

Shacker "Let's call Amani."

"You're right. But let's sleep on it first. I will call her in the morning. I am totally beat. I'm going to bed."

~~~

Sara walked into the living room the next morning to find Shacker sitting on the sofa drinking coffee. Sara continued to the kitchen to pour herself a cup. She was worried about Shacker. He was up all night. As she reentered the living to join him, Shacker began to talk. "It's a crazy thing, revenge. It's so satisfying. I mean, the thought of it is so satisfying."

Sara sat down next to Shacker on the sofa, listening and agreeing.

Shacker continued. "Truth. I would like to kill the bastard. I can't seem to feel anything else. I know that Farah wants something different from me. But it just isn't there."

Sara looked at Shacker lovingly. "Don't worry, Shacker."

Shacker's voice reflected his confusion. "How can you say that? I hate the man. How can I just say *No More*?"

Sara took a deep breath. "Sweetheart, *No More* is not said because you are no longer hurting. *No More* is said because you do hurt, and you don't wish that hurt on anyone else including your enemy." Sara paused for a moment and then continued. "Shacker, to tell the truth this morning, I am a little concerned about Bahir coming to the pod meeting."

"Finally." Shacker's voice expressed relief.

"Yes, I am scared. But this meeting is important. Being willing to say *No More* when you want to kill the guy is step one. Step two involves giving an olive branch of understanding to your enemy. Until that happens, *No More* is just words on a page. I believe the pods help to achieve peace as they did at camp and with our own family. Shacker, we don't even know Bahir's story."

After a long pause, Shacker got up and walked around the room several times. Finally, he walked over and sat again next to Sara. "I still want to kill that bastard. I'm terrified at what my father might do. I just hope the Friendship Pod works on me so that I can feel better."

Sara's voice resonated with understanding. "Shacker, being willing is everything. I talked to Amani and she said to come over any time."

Chapter 42

Once they were settled in Amani's living room, Sara began. "Amani, yesterday I decided to find out about that man who has been protecting us all these weeks. You know—the one who is always standing outside our apartment and who tried to protect us from the man whose wife wouldn't go to the pod meeting."

Amani knew right away who Sara was talking about. "Oh good. So who is he?"

Sara glanced at Shacker, then continued tentatively. "Well, he told me that Farah came to him in a dream and asked him to protect us."

Amani's eyes grew wide. "Really? Why?"

Shacker looked up. "Put your seatbelt on, dear sister, because you're not going to believe this."

Sara took a deep breath then slowly let it out. "The man first told me that his son was also killed in the bombing. Then later he said that it was his son who did the bombing."

Amani covered her mouth. "Oh my God!"

"Wait, Sis, there's more," added Shacker.

Sara looked into Amani's eyes. "His son went to camp with us, Amani. It was Tarif."

Amani's mouth dropped, and her eyes welled up with tears.

Shacker then pointed to Sara. "And do you want to hear what she did? She invited him to our pod meeting this week!"

Amani digested this news for a few moments, then calmly asked, "And why did you do that?"

Sara shook her head. "It was an impulse. It just came to me. Isn't this what the pods are all about? Farah came to him in a dream. Doesn't that mean anything to you?"

Amani crossed her arms over her chest. "I know, but he poisoned his son to kill. I don't think I want to be around someone like that."

Shacker sat back in his chair. "Exactly how I feel."

Sara leaned forward. "Wait, he didn't ask Tarif to kill. Yes, he did teach him to hate. But what is his story? Why does he hate the way that he does? What do we need to understand so that this doesn't ever happen again? This is exactly what the pods were created to do: to build a bridge between enemies. It's going to take courage and willingness. You don't need to not hate him. You just need to know that you are committed to the idea of *No More*. Let the Friendship Pod do its magic. You don't know what might happen."

"Humph," said Shacker, "All I feel right now is hate."

Sara turned to her husband. "Are you also committed to the idea of *No More*?"

"I am. But I'm consumed with hate right now."

"I am too," replied Amani. "Let's take the day to be with this. We have a whole other day to consider this before the meeting. I want to think over what we've talked about. Let's continue this discussion tomorrow after work."

"I think that's a great idea," said Sara. "And I think it's wise not to tell our parents about this just yet."

Amani and Shacker nodded in agreement.

~~~

After arriving home from work the next day, Shacker seemed less angry and more open. He asked Sara if they could talk. "I want to do what Farah wants us to do. I want her death to mean something," he said, as they sat on the living room couch.

"What do you think that would take?" she asked.

Shacker considered her question. "I don't know because right now all I can think about is getting back at Bahir."

"Shacker, I know you are hurting. But getting back is the old way—an eye for an eye. It will not fix your hurt. Farah wants us to show the world a new, better way of responding to anger and pain."

"But Sara, I'm so filled with anger and hate right now that the only thing that feels right is to strike back."

"I know. Farah said that the first step is always a willingness to *not* take revenge and to do something different. So, I guess the question is, can you find the willingness to respond differently?"

Shacker looked down at his hands and sighed. "Yes, there is willingness, but I still feel hurt and angry. I just don't feel as motivated to do something about it."

Peace Train

"I think the Friendship Pod can help with this. I want to understand Bahir's story. He doesn't seem like a bad person. I would like to know him better and maybe, with that knowledge, we can all exchange our hurt for understanding."

"That sounds great, but what do I do with these feelings?"

Sara put her hand underneath Shacker's chin and lifted his face up. "Don't try to change those feelings, but hold on to your willingness to say *No More*. This willingness is the most important thing. I believe that my willingness to say *No More* caused Farah to come to me when I was ready to strangle Bahir. Her face and words reminded me about my pledge. This reminder led to me to seeing Bahir's pain instead of my hatred. Seeing Bahir's pain changed my anger into understanding. I recognized his pain as my own."

Shacker raised his eyebrows and let out a deep breath. "When you put it that way, I must say that my commitment to *No More* is pretty strong."

"Great. The pod is not about being friends necessarily. It's more about receiving another person's story so that understanding can be experienced. It's about discovering if friendship is possible. It's being willing to open to something new. It is about possibility. All you have to do is be willing to be honest about how you feel and be committed to *No More*."

"So, you are asking me to trust this process?"

Sara nodded and smiled. "Yes. It may not work this time, but if it does, we have something to share with the world. If it works in this tough situation, it can work anywhere."

"Don't you think we should tell our parents?"

"I don't think so. I think we have to have faith that what has worked in the past will work again. I do have a little concern. Does he want to feel differently? *No More* means you are willing to feel differently. I think he does. He is really sad about losing his son. That pain changes everything."

Shacker grabbed onto his wife's hands. "Sara, I could never do this without you."

She ran her fingers through his hair, and then touched his cheek. "I could never do this without you either."

Chapter 43

The next day after work, Amani arrived at Sara's and Shacker's apartment for dinner and to discuss what they were going to do about Bahir and the pods. They sat down at the kitchen table and Amani started right in.

"I've come to the conclusion that we need to trust what has worked before." Sara and Shacker looked at each other as Amani continued. "I think that Bahir is no different from us. It will be hard to be around him, but if the pod is going to work, it will work in this situation and we need to trust it.

Shacker concurred. "That is exactly the conclusion I came to today. It scares me, and I'm a bit afraid of what I will say because I have some pretty strong feelings."

Amani then asked, "Do we tell our parents before they come?"

"No. Let's see if this pod works first," replied Sara.

Shacker nodded. "I can't believe I'm saying this, but I agree."

Sara headed into the kitchen to finish preparing dinner. As she took the plates down from the cupboard, she said, "Honey, you have got to be very clear with the directions. Being honest without name-calling is essential."

As they ate dinner, their conversation wasn't as lively as normal. Their minds were on Farah, Bahir, and the pods.

When Amani left around 9 pm, she gave Sara a big hug. "I love you and I'm so glad we're doing this together."

~~~

After Bahir had left the coffee shop and said goodbye to Shacker and Sara the day before, he caught the bus home as usual. He arrived at the refugee camp and walked between the narrow passageways to his apartment. When he opened his front door, his wife greeted him.

"You don't look so well, Bahir," she said in Palestinian Arabic. "Here, have a seat." She led him to his old worn-out rocker. He slumped down in the soft brown fabric. His eyes were tired as he looked around at the bare walls of the sparsely furnished room. He stared at the old rusty key that hung on the wall above the stove. It reminded him of his grandfather and how he left his land and home, thinking he would be back in a few days, but here Bahir was—an old man still living in the house his family had moved to years ago.

Bahir's wife hovered her small frame near his rocker as she fussed over him, trying to cover him with a blanket.

He looked up at her and realized for the first time just how much Tarif had looked like her. He grabbed onto her hand weakly.

She stopped and looked into his eyes. "What is it, Dear? What happened today?"

He quietly replied, "I met the lady I have been guarding."

She covered her mouth. "I told you *not* do that. Did she attack you?"

"No, she was very kind."

"What? How can that be?"

"She looked me in the eye and, after I told her, she said we have the same pain. We have both lost a child."

She gasped. "What? I don't understand."

Bahir cleared his throat and continued. "I'll tell you everything. She took me to a coffee shop for coffee. Her husband came. They both knew Tarif. They both liked him and said what a nice young man he was. I thought the husband would be angry at me, but he held his peace. They told me their daughter came to them in dream and asked them to be different with their pain. They said *No More*. We sat quietly and then the lady asked me to come to a friendship meeting at their house. I did not understand, but they are not mad and I think it's okay to go."

His wife sat befuddled on the ottoman in front of Bahir's chair. "I still don't understand. Why didn't she attack you? I would if she had killed my daughter."

Bahir shrugged his shoulders as his eyes welled up with tears. "I have such shame; I treated Tarif so bad. I just don't understand their reactions."

Chapter 44

The morning of the pod, Bahir was waiting outside of Sara's apartment. When she left her home to go to work, he walked up to her.

Sara smiled at him. Then she saw the expression on his face.

"I not coming tonight."

"What? But why?"

"I not feel safe."

Sara's heart filled with compassion. "Bahir, there will be more Palestinians at the meeting than Israelis."

He took a step back and put up his hands in defense. "I think trap."

"All these weeks when you were guarding our house, I knew you were Palestinian, and I didn't throw rocks at you. Did we yell at you or call you names? Did we ask you to leave?"

"No."

Sara threw up her hands. "Well, does that sound like someone that wants to trap and hurt you?"

"No."

Sara's tone softened. "When I was at camp, I was surprised to learn that, if I felt safe, I could connect to the Palestinians easily and I really liked them. When Farah was killed, I began to hate Palestinians because I knew the bomber was of that heritage. It put me into a very bad place emotionally and I carried around so much hatred. Then I had the dreams with Farah and she told me to do something different. She asked Shacker, Amani, and me not to hate and to bring the camp experience to the people. The camp experience changes fear into understanding and friendship. This meeting we have invited you to is a safe place. We ask everyone to leave their fear outside the door. We truly want to understand why Tarif did what he did. He was not a bad person. I knew him as a friend. So why did he kill himself and a whole bunch of other people? I want to have understanding about what really happened—not to hate but to find understanding."

"How you do that?"

Sara motioned for him to join her on her walk to work. "Well, we sit in a circle and Shacker tells us what we can and cannot do. We share what is in our hearts and what is important to us, and no one can interrupt us or ask questions. Everyone has a turn. Then we play a fun game. Finally, we have refreshments. There are no expectations here. You may not want to come again. That is fine. We would just like to understand why Tarif did what he did."

Bahir hung his head. "I so sad. I not know he kill self. I hate Israelis all life. I teach my son this hate."

"I understand. I really do. And I know how much you loved Tarif. Maybe telling the group about Tarif and how much you loved him will help you to not feel so much shame. Maybe if you tell us the truth about your hate, it will not be so strong. We really do want to understand."

Bahir looked up. "What I need to bring?"

Sara smiled. *He's going to come after all!* "Nothing, just yourself. I know everyone will be kind to you. I was personally affected by the fact that you have been protecting me. I'm also affected by the fact that my daughter came to you and asked you to do this. I know it was not easy for you. I'm sure you were afraid most of the time."

He shook his head. "I not afraid. I so sad about Tarif, I not care if I die."

"I understand. So you will come tonight, then?"

There was a long pause. Sara finally heard him quietly say 'yes.'

Sara felt a joyful softening in her heart towards Bahir. *I like him. I hope he will have the courage to share more about Tarif. I think that just knowing what happened will help me to let go of any of my remaining grief. How could it be that opening to the bomber actually heals the pain? It really doesn't make sense. But it is true.*

Chapter 45

That night, after the usual members had arrived for the pod meeting, Sara told them that a visitor was going to join them that evening. Then she heard a light knock on the door. She went over to the front door and opened it. Bahir was standing there.

"Salam, Bahir. Come on in."

Sara noticed that his clothes and brown shoes were worn. He was wearing a bright Kufiya on his head. After he took a seat, Shacker reviewed the rules of the meeting.

Shacker then looked over at his wife, inviting her to tell the group a little more about Bahir.

Sara shifted in her chair. "The other day I decided to find out who the man was that has been standing outside our house for weeks. I learned that his name is Bahir. He had a dream about Farah, too. He didn't know who she was, and he thought she was an angel. She told him to guard us. His son died in the blast with Farah." Ms. Salinger and Ms. Rahim both gasped and put their hands over their mouths. Sara then took a deep breath and exhaled slowly, then said, "His son was the bomber." A bigger gasp rippled through the gathering. "His son, Tarif, went to Peace Camp with us. We knew him and came to like him that summer. When Bahir told me about his son, I wanted to strangle him. In that moment, I was completely consumed with rage.

Then I saw Farah's face and heard her saying, *No More*! The next thing I saw was the pain in Bahir's face; I realized it was my pain as well. We were parents who had lost our children. I realized in that moment that he and I were not that different. The truth is that we are both grieving over the loss of our dearly loved children. The story of how it happened is secondary. His pain is mine. I knew in that moment that this pain was our connection and our beginning. That is why I invited him to this meeting. I want to understand why we both lost our children so that it doesn't happen again. I want to understand his story so that I can let go of my remaining grief and anger. I want to put new words to my feelings so this never happens again, at least not in our country "

Sara then held up a piece of the olive branch that Tarif had given her at camp and showed it to Bahir. "Your son gave this to me when we were at camp. I have kept it all these years and I want you to have it."

Bahir looked at the small piece of olive branch and then at Sara with tears in his eyes. He took the branch from her and gently closed his hand around it. Silence enveloped the group, each person lost in their own thoughts. Then Bahir said, "Thank you, Sara. It my turn?"

Sara nodded.

"Sorry I not speak well. I not understand your kindness, Sara. I tell story. Great grandfather own a big ranch. I born there. Very wealthy. One day all gone. Taken. We not know where to go. We think we be back in few days. We have key on kitchen wall to remind. No money. Everybody angry and scared. We hate Israelis. My grandfather good man but very angry. He get sick and we have no money. He die. I fill with hate for Israelis. I teach hate to my boy. There more. Sara say son good person. When he come home from camp, I tease him for Israeli friends. I make him miserable. I wake up at night and call him Israeli lover. I hide behind doors. Tell him he not my son any more. He become very angry. He move out; not talk to me. I sad I lose son. He everything to me. I know, he kill for me so I proud. I have shame. I have sadness. My son gone because of me. Angel come to me. Tell me protect Sara. I protect and feel better. I not worthy be here. I sad Tarif gone. My fault. I sorry."

"Everyone is welcome here, Bahir," said Shacker.

Ms. Salinger raised her hand and quietly said, "I am stunned. I don't think I can be here. Is this condoning what was done? I can't do that. Sara, please help me!"

Sara looked at Shacker. "Should I take her into the other room for a moment?"

He nodded. Sara walked her mom into the office and closed the door.

When they were alone, Ms. Salinger said, "Honey, how could you bring him into your house? Do you realize what you have done? Your daughter is worth more respect than this."

Sara took her mom's hand. "When he told me who he was on the street the other day, at first I thought I could kill him. I was so angry and filled with hate. Then I saw Farah in my mind and she smiled at me. I heard the words in my head, *No More*. When I looked up, I saw the pain in Bahir's eyes and I realized that his pain was mine. We must not remember our lovely little girl with hate. We just can't do it, Mom."

Ms. Salinger sat down in the office chair. Sara knelt beside her. "But I feel such hate, Sara. I don't know how to do this."

"Can you go back to the circle and be honest about how you feel, Mom? I think it will help you move to a new place emotionally. The pod is about being honest without pointing fingers and being verbally hurtful. Can you do this and trust the pod?"

"I don't know. But I'm willing for Farah's memory to be about love instead of hate. I'm willing, but right now I'm not there."

Sara stood up and rested her hand on her mom's shoulder. "Talk about how you feel about Farah. Talk about where you want to be and where you are now. It's okay to be honest."

"All right, I think I can do that."

The two women reentered the room and took their seats.

"Thank you for being patient," Ms. Salinger said. "I loved my granddaughter Farah almost as much as I loved my own children. She brought such joy to my world. When she died, a part of me died too. When I heard it was a Palestinian bomber, I wanted revenge. I know why hatred continues. The hurt is so overwhelming. I know that Farah has asked us to respond differently and to say *No More*. I want to be able to do this. Right now, I can't see how to do this but I'm willing to try." She turned towards Bahir. "I was touched by your story. I know you have experienced tremendous hurt too. I want to feel differently. Maybe I will in time."

There was a long pause. Then Mrs. Rahim began. She looked at Bahir. "I could hate you so easily, but a long time ago I made a promise to myself that I would not do what my parents did. They spent their whole lives hating. When I sent Amani to camp, I had hopes that she would find an Israeli friend, and she did. I was also overjoyed that Shacker had found Sara. I didn't want to hate like my parents. It destroyed them. I wanted something new. I'm so thankful to finally hear Bahir's story. Thanks for sharing your pain. I believe that it is mine, too."

Amani spoke next. "I must admit that, at first, I really didn't want Bahir to be in our pod. Then after thinking about it overnight, I remembered that Farah asked us to do things differently. After hearing your story, my feelings have very much softened. I want to see you differently."

It was Shacker's turn to respond. "I heard some of this story for the first time the other day. To be honest, I've had some pretty strong feelings come up over the last two days. Bahir, it helps me to hear your story more fully. It must have been so difficult to lose your land and have nothing. I truly wish I could make this up to you. I understand why my daughter died. I am glad we are doing this, even though I'm struggling with my feelings. It is the other side of the coin. If I respond to my daughter's death with love and understanding instead of hate, that is one side; then if I respond to my daughter's killer with love instead of revenge, that is the other side. Both sides are healed. The coin is whole again. The momentum of the past hatred is stopped. Period. It's *No More*."

Silence settled over the group for a couple of minutes. Then Shacker's father raised his hand. "Son, may I speak?"

"Sure, Father, but I want to remind you of the ground rules."

"Don't worry; I remember them. If Bahir had come to this group a few weeks ago I would've surely done something that would have put me in prison. What feels really good is that I don't need to hate him tonight. I feel a very strong need to understand his pain. His pain is my pain. We are both Palestinians. What happened to my granddaughter did not happen out of hatred; it happened because of our pain. I think he can help me let go of mine, and maybe I can help him let go of his. The good news is that I want this for both of us. This Friendship Pod is really something special. I have never felt so safe."

The group was quiet for a moment. Then Dr. Rahim stood up, walked over to Bahir, and shook his hand. Ms. Salinger then did the same thing, with everyone else following suit. The atmosphere in the room was almost surreal. A year ago, when Farah died, each person would have killed Bahir.

Finally, Bahir pointed to Sara. "Please, outside. Have something." Sara followed him out the door.

Bahir walked down the front steps. Sara watched as he picked up a brown paper sack from the ground. He walked back up the steps and handed it to Sara. "I not want to hate anymore."

Sara carefully opened the bag. Inside was a baby olive tree that was ready to be planted. Her heart swelled, and tears pooled in her eyes. *How I wish I could hug him, but for now I will hug him with my eyes.* She felt emotion surge through her. "All I can think is that my baby's life has not been wasted."

Sara heard movement behind her. She looked back and saw the others standing in the doorway. She noticed Amani and Mrs. Rahim wiping their eyes. Shacker wrapped her in a warm hug.

~~~

One hour later, Sara, Shacker, and Amani sat in the living room trying to grasp what had just transpired. Finally, Shacker broke the silence with a question. "So how do you think it went?"

Sara lovingly responded. "You tell me."

Shacker was surprised by her response. "Well, I don't want to kill him anymore, which is amazing." Sara then turned to Amani, who also seemed surprised. "I don't know how I missed this. He lost someone too. He must be grieving just like we are."

"Yes, we sat in a room with our enemy." Sara begins thoughtfully, "We listened to his story and he listened to ours. No one was disrespected. There is nothing more loving than listening and receiving another. This may seem like a fairytale. But it isn't. Shacker, even in your anger you allowed love because you were willing to say *No More* and you were willing to feel differently. When love is allowed into the equation, anything is possible. And the three of us are the living proof. I sit before you not angry, not filled with hate, not depressed, but hopeful. My daughter was killed senselessly a year ago, and I feel hopeful. Why? Because we have a new way to respond. This is what Farah came to give us and I think the world is receiving this gift through us."

Chapter 46

Sara climbed into bed. The past few days had felt different. Ever since the Friendship Pod with Bahir, the pain she felt from Farah's death had relented further.

"Good night, Shacker." She kissed him and lay her head on her pillow. Within moments she was in a deep sleep.

Sara was in the meadow again. It was just as beautiful as before. Huge trees surrounded an open area of grass and flowers. A path wound its way through the meadow. Sara followed its course with her eyes and saw a beautiful woman walking towards her. *Farah!*

Sara's heart filled with joy. Then she realized that Farah was not alone. Walking beside her was a young man. As they came closer, Sara saw that they were holding hands and smiling.

Tarif! He looks so handsome ...

Tarif was dressed in a golden caftan. It shimmered as he walked. As she watched them, Sara's eyes filled with tears. They stopped a few feet in front of her, put their hands together and bowed. Then Sara did the same. They looked at each other and smiled with the deepest love Sara had ever known.

EPILOGUE

One year later.

Sara walked through Amani's apartment, then peeked her head into Amani's bedroom. She smiled as she saw a framed picture on the dresser of her sweet Farah. Sara rubbed her growing belly and gently spoke to the little being inside. "That's your big sister, Baby." Then Sara saw Amani in the adjacent bathroom. "You about ready? The show isn't going to wait for us."

Amani finished putting her earrings on and then quickly slipped on her green flats. "I'm coming; I'm coming ... I'm a bit nervous too. It isn't every day that a person gets asked to be on the Gold News Hour. Can you believe we are going to spend the afternoon with Shara Gold? Her show broadcasts worldwide! It's just a good thing I figured out what I was going to wear last night or else we'd be *really* late."

"I know, I know, Amani, so let's get going," Sara teased.

Soon, the girls were out on the streets of Jerusalem, walking toward the Gold Radio Station. The studio was nothing like where Sara and Amani worked; it was a first-class operation, with clean, sleek décor and high-end equipment.

The technicians greeted Sara and Amani and helped them get set in their chairs with their headsets.

A charismatic woman came in wearing a flowing outfit. Her long, dark hair was piled stylishly on the top of her head and her makeup was impeccably done—heavy but tasteful. "Welcome to my studio, ladies! Soon we will be on the air. I think this is going to be a fabulous show," Shara exclaimed with a wide smile that revealed perfect white teeth. Shara walked up to Sara and beamed. "You look like you are just about ready to have this child! When are you due?"

Sara smiled as she leaned in to hug Shara. "I'm about a week overdue, so it should happen any time."

Shara threw her head back and laughed. "Well, if it happens while you are here, maybe I can help catch the baby!" Shara gave Amani a hug and then said, "Shall we get started?"

As they got situated, Shara reminded her guests that the show would be recorded for later airing.

After a classy musical intro, Shara spoke into her mic. "Shalom and Salam. Welcome everyone, wherever you are. This is The Gold News Hour and we are very lucky to have two celebrities with us today. I like to refer to them as the Pod Sisters. We have Sara and Amani from the Sara & Amani Show, headquartered here in Jerusalem." Shara turned toward her guests. "So ladies, bring us up-to-date on what is happening with the pods."

Amani began. "Well, first, thank you for having us, Shara. As for the pods, truthfully, we have lost count on how many there are. People used to let us know when they created one, but today, they are everywhere. We estimate 80 percent of the people in both the Israeli and Palestinian areas are pod members, and many people in other countries around the world have formed their own pods. It truly has become an international phenomenon and movement. In addition, the poster of us after the bombing has sold all over the world. In fact, we've sold over 1,000,000 copies so far.

"We are so grateful to be here, Shara," added Sara. "Our radio show is now reaching more than 500,000 people weekly, worldwide."

Shara asked, "What have you heard about the impact? Are the pods really changing things?"

Sara nodded. "People call in and tell us stories all the time. For example, we heard a story about the guards at the borders.

Usually, those guys are unduly negative and give people a hard time. But change is happening. People have been reporting that the guards have been kinder and even polite. Apparently, crossing the border is much more pleasant. Sometimes they even have music playing."

Amani continued. "You've probably heard about the holes in the West Bank Wall. There are at least five of them and people use these holes to travel to and from pod meetings. We have no idea who is creating them, but the people are happy. The wall was put up to stop bombing activities and there have been none reported since the holes first appeared."

"I have not read of any thoughtless actions on the part of anyone," added Sara. "People just seem to be more pleasant. There is also talk about uniting our countries. The name would be the United States of Israel and Palestine. I'm not sure of all the details but it looks hopeful."

"Why do you think the pods have had such an impact?" asked Shara.

"Long ago," said Sara, "Albert Einstein, the scientist, wrote a letter to his young daughter and asked her not to share it with the world because the world was not ready to hear what it said. I have just recently read this letter and it talks about sending love bombs into the world. I think that is what the pods do. People think they know those around them, but really, we have a lot to learn about each other. Not knowing leads to misunderstanding. The Friendship Pods are about listening and wanting to understand. As the pods continue to undo the hate, they tip the scale towards love. They are becoming an example to the world. The bombs of love will change everything."

Shara smiled at her guests. "That is beautiful, Sara, and I hope what you say is true. So, what is happening with your family and Bahir?"

Sara rested her hand on her belly. "Well, my mother is working with him, and the two of them are building a *No More* fountain that will be on the grounds of the university. *No More* has been our driving force. They're also going to put the names on the fountain of all the people who died in the blast, including Bahir's son. It's going to be beautiful."

"Wow, that's a switch," Shara admired. "I bet it was difficult for your mom to become friends with Bahir."

"It wasn't as hard as you might expect. The purpose of the pods is to do just that. Being honest with your feelings in a loving environment creates miracles. It didn't take long for Mom and Bahir to become very close."

Shara shifted in her seat. "What other news is there?"

"Well, Amani, why don't you mention your news?"

"Oh, yes. One of the campers from our camp experience years ago—Aharon, an Israeli—well, he and I have always been good friends. We dated years ago, but then my father's unacceptance of him kind of put a damper on our relationship and we went our separate ways for a while. I'm happy to say that we're getting married this summer."

Shara grinned and clapped her hands together. "Congratulations, Amani."

Sara smiled too, but then she felt a strange sensation in her body. She grabbed hold of her belly and instinctively stood up. *Bam!* Her water broke, and the fluids gushed to the floor. With her headset still on, she said, "Oh my! Shara, I told you this baby might come at any minute. Amani, I think we need to go. Your new little nephew or niece is about to make an entrance."

Shara chimed in, "Girls, don't worry, we have plenty recorded for a show. Just take off your mics and get to the hospital. Fortunately, we're already downtown, so you don't have far to go. In fact, walking will be quicker than a cab. Now go!"

Sara grabbed onto Amani for support and they made their way out onto the street. Sara pulled out her phone and called Shacker. "Honey, my water just broke. I'll meet you at the hospital."

"Sara, who is with you?"

"Amani is; we just did that radio show with Shara downtown. Can you pick up my bag at home?"

"No problem. I'll be there in a flash. Just relax. I love you!"

"I love you too."

Amani and Sara walked to the hospital with only one big contraction along the way. At the hospital, the medical staff quickly moved Sara into the delivery room. Amani disappeared and, a minute later, Shacker walked in. He kissed her on the forehead as she sat up on the bed. "How are you doing, Sweetie? Why are you all alone?"

Sara smiled weakly. "Amani went to find the bathroom."

Shacker pulled a chair up next to the bed and grabbed Sara's hand and kissed it. "I've been thinking of Farah all day. I wonder if she knows what is going on." He then smiled at Sara. "Thank you for taking this journey with me. I could never have done this alone."

Sara rubbed her belly, her heart filled. "I think Farah knows, Shacker."

A huge contraction kicked causing Sara to grab the sides of the bed. Shacker reminded her to relax and breathe.

Amani stuck her head in the room just as the contraction eased up. "You two doing okay?"

"Hey Sis, we're just fine."

"Okay. Well, hang on, Sara. We're with you." Amani left to greet the other family members who had arrived and were in the waiting room. She found her father by the water cooler. "Hi, Father."

Dr. Rahim gave her a peck on her cheek. "Everything okay in there?"

"Perfect."

Amani gestured to the seat nearby. She and Dr. Rahim sat down. "Father, how do you feel about this baby?"

"Oh honey, I'm excited. Most of my pain is gone and I'm thrilled about this baby. I'm also happy about you and Aharon."

"Thanks. I feel your support."

Dr. Rahim patted her knee. "Well, Shacker mixed our family all up first, so there is no reason why you shouldn't do the same." He chuckled and then grew somber. "I really do like him, Amani. I think you have chosen well."

~~~

"Push, Babe. Push!" Shacker cheered as he watched a head of hair emerge. Soon, his little boy was in his arms, cleaned and wrapped in a blanket. Tears flowed as Shacker handed the little bundle to Sara.

"Shalom and Salam, little baby." Sara glanced up at her husband. "I think he looks like an Asher." She looked back down at her son and kissed his forehead. Turning back to Shacker, she said, "Aren't we lucky?"

"Sweetheart, we are very lucky."

The nurses finished cleaning up. One of them asked, "Would you like your family to come in and see your new baby now?"

The parents nodded. In a few moments, the whole group was in the small hospital room gushing over Asher. Ms. Salinger kissed Sara and then admired the baby in her arms. "He is so tiny," she marveled. "Sara, I love you."

Shacker's father came over, asking if he could hold the baby. Sara gently placed the sleeping baby in his arms. "Everyone, this is my Palestinian Israeli grandson named Asher Rahim. Isn't he handsome? He is our future."

Everyone clapped.

Sara took Shacker's and Amani's hands and looked at each of them deeply. "What a journey we have taken together." She then looked up and said aloud, "Thank you, Farah! Bless you, my love."

~~~

Out beyond ideas of wrongdoing and rightdoing there is a field. I'll meet you there.

~Rumi

www.ingramcontent.com/pod-product-compliance
Lightning Source LLC
LaVergne TN
LVHW011929070526
838202LV00054B/4556